CHRISTMAS WITH THE PRINCES

HANNAH LANGDON

Ebook ISBN: 978-1-80508-710-6
Paperback ISBN: 978-1-80508-712-0

Cover design: Rose Cooper
Cover images: Shutterstock

Published by Storm Publishing.
For further information, visit:
www.stormpublishing.co

The Feywood Sisters

Escape to the Country Kitchen

Escape to the Country Garden

A Manor House Christmas

Christmas with the Lords

Christmas with the Knights

For Sarah,
who generously gives both moral and practical support.

ONE

'Turn right, then you will reach your destination.'

The droning voice of the satnav cut into my thoughts, and I slowed my car down as I looked for the entrance. Ah, there it was, a painted sign on a low wall saying 'Lyonscroft'. I turned into the driveway and was greeted by a glorious view. Huge lawns, iced with frost, flanked the narrow road and at the far side of one I saw a figure on a trotting horse, the breath of both clouding the cold morning air. The house that stood before the lawns was simply magnificent: a Georgian villa of immaculate proportions and symmetry, built of beautiful, honeyed local stone and boasting three storeys, with two wings of two storeys each. A lichened path edged with rose bushes, bare now, led to the front door, and either side of the columned porch were huge bow windows. I had only ever paid to visit houses like this; it was odd, but also exciting, to think that I would be living here. I followed the drive around to the side of the house, where I could see a couple of other cars, and got out. I went to get my things out of the back of the car and a wave of well-being washed over me as the cold air hit my face and I drank in the perfect silence.

'Hey, you!'

The silence was broken by a loud, slightly panicky, male voice. Was he yelling at *me*? I looked around but couldn't see anyone, so I carried on; it was probably someone calling their dog or something.

'Hey, you, over by the car!'

Not their dog; definitely me. I put my bags on the gravel and closed the door of the car, looking around again. Now, I spotted a man in a thicket of trees about fifty yards away, waving both arms above his head. Waving back, I jogged over and, as I got closer, the man disappeared back into the trees. I hesitated as it occurred to me that running into the woods after strange men might come with its hazards, then ploughed on. Notwithstanding my reluctance to get involved with my sister Steph's upcoming wedding, I am generally a helpful person who goes towards people in need, and the flitting images of what might happen next were swept away by my desire – maybe even my need – to be of assistance.

'Hello?'

I had reached the trees.

'Over here!'

The voice sounded muffled now, but was loud enough to locate, so I swung a left. I'm not sure what I had expected to find – someone who had fallen and hurt an ankle, perhaps, or a wounded rabbit in need of care. I would have liked that. What I had *not* expected to be confronted with was the – admittedly rather nice – view of a long pair of legs and a bottom clad in black jeans poking out of some thick shrubbery. The man's voice spoke again.

'For goodness' sake, Steve, let me get a proper hold of you.'

The mystery grew deeper. Maybe Steve was the rabbit? I cleared my throat artificially loudly, not wanting to make Black Jeans jump, or for him to say something he might regret me hearing.

'Er, you needed some help?'

The legs and bottom started backing out of the bush towards me, and I stood aside as they were followed by a slim torso in a waxed jacket and a handsome, if dishevelled, head. The man had thick, chestnut brown hair with matching eyes and stubble, and looked worried. He frowned at me.

'It's my bloody dog; he's got himself stuck in the middle of this bush – *again* – and he can't get out. Go in, would you, and grab him? You're smaller than me; I couldn't get close enough. Why I ever thought a red setter was a good idea, I don't know.'

I stared at him as a scuffling noise and small yelp came from the depths of the bush.

'Sorry, you want *me* to go in there and get your dog?'

'Yes.' He suddenly smiled, and his face transformed. Still handsome, yes, that hadn't changed, but now I saw humour and laughter and my knees threatened to give way. If he wasn't careful, he'd have two of us to rescue. 'I can lend you my coat,' he went on, unzipping and shrugging it off. 'It's pretty tough, you shouldn't get scratched.'

'Er, okay,' I said, taking it and putting it on over my own down jacket. It smelt of fresh air and woodsmoke and was warm from his body. I was still slightly confused by the turn of events, but now that a clear way to help had materialised, I geared up to spring into action. 'Steve, was it?'

'That's right,' said the man. 'He won't bite, but he might get a lick in. Just grab his collar, would you, and make sure his legs aren't stuck.'

'I'll do my best...'

I bent down and peered into the gloomy interior of the bush, then knelt and started working my way in. Ah, there was Steve, or his head at least, smooth and shiny and the same shade of rich chestnut as his owner's. I could have sworn a smile came over his doggy face when he saw me, and he emitted a little whine.

'Okay, Steve, it's all right, I've come to help you,' I said in my best nurse's voice, and I reached out to pat him. I was rewarded with a very wet lick. 'Eurgh.'

'Are you all right in there?' said the man, his voice anxious. I wasn't entirely sure if his concern was for me or the dog.

'Yes, fine,' I replied with more conviction than I felt. 'Just getting him now.'

Wriggling a little closer and glad of the coat that was protecting much of me, as the twigs snatched at my hair, I fumbled down Steve's neck until I could grasp his collar. Now that I was nearer, he took the opportunity to plant another wet lick, all the way up my cheek this time.

'Yuck,' I said, wiping my gritty hand across my face. 'I know you're pleased to see me, but could you tone it down a little?'

Securing my position on my knees, I ran the hand that wasn't holding his collar down his front legs.

'All right, those aren't stuck,' I said, and gave a little tug on the collar. 'Can you come this way a bit so I can check the back ones?'

'Do you want me to come in?' said the man. 'I don't think we'll both fit, but I can try... Poor Steve, is he all right? If I just shift you over a bit...'

I felt him grasp my feet and gave a little squeal. I peered back to see his worried face somewhere near my ankles.

'No, no, it's all right! I was talking to the dog, to, er, Steve. No need to come in!'

Handsome he may have been, but the three of us in this bush would have been a little too cosy. I pushed myself forward a little more, reaching to feel for the dog's back legs, one of which was tangled in a long, flexible twig.

'Ah, got you!' I said and, with a thrill of triumph, gently extricated it. My plan, such as it was, was to edge myself slowly out of the bush, with as much dignity as I could muster, the dog sedately following me. He had other ideas. He lurched towards me and I lost my grip on his collar, falling flat on my face as Steve, no longer stuck or hindered in any way, other than by his own lack of common sense, clambered over my head and back, along my legs and out to his master, barking with happiness. As I pushed myself back onto all fours and reversed out, pausing to free a strand of hair from a twig, I could hear the joyful reunion between man and his best friend behind me and I comforted myself with the supposition that the handsome stranger would be too busy embracing Steve to watch my ungainly exit from the bush. I was right. Even when I was all the way out, and upright, he was still fussing over the dog.

'Silly boy, what were you thinking? Come on, we need to get you back for some breakfast.'

Steve was capering about delightedly and, when he saw me, it appeared that his pleasure was heightened, as he bounded over and leapt up at me, promptly sending me right back down to the freezing, hard ground I had just scrambled up from, licking my face which, again, I scrubbed at with my filthy hands.

'Oh dear, let me help you,' said the man, finally remembering my existence. He put out a hand, which I grabbed, and heaved me to my feet. 'Thank you so much. You've got a friend for life now in Steve, but you're a bit muddy, and your hair...'

He moved closer and started plucking bits of twig out of my hopelessly tangled mane, pulled from its neat bun. This was not the calm, efficient – not to mention hygienic – first impression I usually liked to give when I started a new job. I glanced at my watch. I was due at the house two minutes ago.

'I must go,' I said, stepping back reluctantly. It wasn't unpleasant having this man so close, wafting a light scent of nutmeg and all but running his fingers through my hair. But I hadn't been so close to a man since my late husband, Paulo, and my senses were overwhelmed and confused.

'What are you doing here, anyway?' he asked, then laughed.

'Oh, I'm sorry, I haven't introduced myself.' He flicked away a soggy-looking piece of moss, which was his latest find on my head, and held out his hand. 'I'm Nick, I own Lyonscroft.'

I shook his hand.

'I'm Laura – Nurse Wilde. I've come to work with Marilise.'

'Of course, Angela did say you were coming today. How amazing that she managed to find you at such short notice. My grandmother is a very special woman – I'm sure you'll love her.'

I nodded.

'Yes, but I must get to the house, I don't want to be late – well, any later than I already am – on my first day.'

'Don't worry about that, I'll explain everything.'

We started walking.

'I met a friend of yours yesterday,' I said, remembering the awful craft evening I had suffered at the hands of my bride-to-be sister, Steph. 'Araminta. She wasn't sure if you were in the country at the moment.'

'You met Minty? I've known her for years, terrific fun. I've only been back a couple of days – I must give her a call. Are these yours?'

We were walking past my car, and he indicated the abandoned bags.

'Oh, yes, I'll just...'

I went to retrieve them, but before I could get close, he had collected them up and continued striding towards the house, hefting one onto his hip so that he could fish a key out and unlock the door. As he did, the horse and rider I had seen earlier passed by the end of the garden path.

'Nick!' called a voice. 'Have I missed breakfast?'

He grinned.

'Only by about two hours, although I'm sure Angela will find you something.'

'I lose track of time when I'm riding,' said the girl, smiling back. She looked young – in her mid-teens, maybe – with her dark hair drawn back into a neat bun at the back of her head below her helmet. She looked at me. 'Hello, I'm India.'

Ah, Nick's stepsister, horse crazy; I remembered her being mentioned at my interview.

'Hi there, I'm Laura, I've come to work with Marilise.'

'Oh, great, I see. I thought...'

'What did you think?' asked Nick suspiciously.

'Sorry, I shouldn't have said anything, but Laura's wearing your jacket and you've both got leaves in your hair...'

The grin grew more wicked as the heat rose up my face and I quickly started undoing the coat.

'Don't be cheeky!' replied Nick. 'Laura was very kindly helping me extract Steve from a bush.'

'Not again?'

'Yes, I'm afraid so.'

She shook her head despairingly, then lifted one gloved hand in farewell.

'See you both later!'

We waved back, then stepped inside into a large, elegant hallway. The floors were clad in smooth flagstones with a faded but still beautiful rug lying across them. The walls were painted yellow and there was a marble fireplace that had a wood burner glowing in it. A graceful walnut staircase covered in thick cream carpet rose from the centre of the hall to a galleried landing and a tall grandfather clock stood to one side, tick-tocking in a loud but strangely comforting way. I wondered if Mum and my sister Steph would be more forgiving of me if they could see my new temporary home; these were exactly the surroundings they thought one 'should' live in. I had always been happy with mine and Paulo's small house, but each to their own. Nick put down my luggage, and I shrugged off the coat and handed it to him.

'Sorry about India,' he said, hanging it on a nearby hatstand. 'She's fifteen and a bit sassy at times, but basically a nice kid. Angela!'

The sudden call made me jump, and then I heard a familiar tapping of heels coming along an unseen corridor. A white-painted door opened to the left of the hallway and out came a woman I recognised. Angela, a short, cosy-looking, smiling woman with greying blond hair pulled into a messy ponytail, wearing jeans and a flowery apron, had interviewed me in London and I was happy to see her again, her smile as welcoming and friendly as it had been then.

'Nurse Wilde, how good to see you again. Er, are you all right?'

I touched my hair and could feel little bits of leaf and goodness knows what else still stuck in it, then moved my hand to my slightly sticky, grimy face.

'Yes, I'm fine, I'm sorry I'm late, I was just, er...'

I glanced at Nick, who grinned impishly.

'What Nurse Wilde means to say is that she was helping me rescue Steve from a bush.'

Angela raised an eyebrow.

'Again?'

I was beginning to see a theme emerging here.

'Again. Anyway, that explains why she's a bit late, and, well...'

He broke off, apparently not wanting to seem ungallant.

'Dishevelled,' I put in. 'Is there anywhere I can tidy up before I meet Marilise? Oh, and please do call me Laura.'

Angela tucked her arm through mine and led me down the passageway she had come from.

'Come on, Laura. There's a bathroom down here you can use, then join us for a cuppa in the kitchen. Marilise always has a morning nap around this time, so you won't be able to meet her yet, anyway.'

I allowed myself to be steered down a wood-panelled corridor and into a cavernous bathroom, tiled in a startling shade of mustard yellow, with an avocado suite straight out of the nineteen seventies. I wondered which of the Princes had updated it; it was out of step with the rest of the house but felt more familiar to me than the grandeur I had seen so far. I shut the door with some relief, took a hairbrush out of my handbag and looked in the mirror. It was worse than I had realised. Steve's claws had pulled large strands of hair out of its bun as he had scrambled over my head, and there were several twigs and leaves caught in it, sticking out at odd angles. I had a smear of mud over my right cheek and a long, red scratch on the left one. I looked like a scarecrow. Only my clothing – neat and clean, but not a uniform – had escaped unscathed, thanks to Nick's coat. Quickly, I removed the band and pins from my hair and picked out the debris before running the brush through and tucking and twisting everything back into place. I dampened a tissue to clean off the mud and rooted around in my bag in the hope of finding some make-up I might be able to use to cover the scratch. I drew a blank; everything like that was in my suitcase, as I don't usually have time or need for touch-ups during the day. Oh well, it would have to do. I gave my reflection my best and brightest nurse's smile and headed for the kitchen.

TWO

The kitchen, a few steps away from the bathroom, was also large and, to my eyes, the epitome of the perfect country kitchen, straight out of *Country Living* magazine. A large wooden table with turned legs and dressed in a pretty flower-patterned oilcloth stood centrally. Wooden cupboards lined the walls, which were painted a warm ivory, with a fawn tiled splashback behind the deep butler's sink. A cream-coloured aga stood on one side, emanating a gentle, comforting warmth and Steve lay on his side in front of it, fast asleep, a look of absolute bliss on his face. A bay window with a wide sill, cluttered with books, vases and other bits of life's ephemera, looked out over the gardens and let in the weak November sunshine. Nick was sitting at the table, laughing to himself as he tapped away at his phone, and Angela was placing a fat, brown teapot on the table.

'Come and sit down, love. Now, how do you like your tea?'

'Just milk, no sugar please,' I answered, pulling out a chair and finding an enormous, extremely furry black and white cat lying there. 'Oh, sorry, I didn't mean to disturb you,' I said, and stroked its soft body. It instantly started purring so loudly that it made Nick look up.

'I see you've found Tolly,' he said, smiling. 'Scoop him up and put him on your lap, he'll be perfectly happy.'

I picked up the cat, wincing slightly at the surprise of his weight, and sat down, whereupon he wriggled until he was comfortable and promptly went back to sleep again.

'He's so sweet,' I said. 'And I like his name, Tolly.'

'We adopted him,' explained Nick. 'Some wag had named him Barthole*mew*, but that was too long, so Tolly he became.'

I took my tea from Angela, and a macaroon from the plate she pushed towards me.

'Thank you. Are you sure Marilise won't be waiting for me?'

'Not at all, her routine is as regular as clockwork. Don't worry, I won't let you be late. You found the place all right, then?'

'Yes, my parents aren't far from here. This house is so beautiful – it must look amazing all decked out for Christmas.'

'Actually,' said Nick, 'I don't know what we're going to do this year. We normally all decamp to London.' He glanced at Angela, then continued. 'There aren't any decorations or anything here at Lyonscroft. When I was a child, my father wouldn't have anything up at all – he said it was unbearably tacky – so although we always spent Christmas here, it was pretty bleak.'

'What a shame,' I said, as a stab of disappointment hit me. I may find Christmas difficult, and look to keep myself busy working for others, but the prospect of no celebration at all felt even worse.

Angela reached over the table and patted my hand.

'Maybe we can sort something out.' She turned to Nick. '*You* don't mind the place looking more festive, do you?'

'Not at all,' he replied. 'Anyway, I'll be heading back to LA soon. Now, the Angelinos know how to do tacky decorations! You're sprinkled with fake snow from the moment you step out of your front door and constantly startled by life-sized snowmen and Santas. One year they managed to string a huge sleigh across the street, complete with eight reindeer and a Santa Claus that bellowed 'ho ho ho' every time anyone broke an electric beam.' He put the back of his hand to his forehead and pretended to swoon. 'I ended up taking a two-mile detour every morning to get a coffee... my nerves were shot to pieces.'

Angela and I laughed.

'Well, we won't attempt anything that ambitious,' she said. 'How long are you staying this time?'

The merriment left Nick's face, and he shrugged.

'I haven't decided. Not long enough for anyone to get sick of me.'

Angela tutted as I asked, 'What do you do?'

'I'm an app designer, I work freelance. People hire me with an idea, and I make it work. The best thing about it is that I can work anywhere in the world, as long as there's a decent Wi-Fi connection and I can take Steve. Who knows, maybe I'll be in Timbuktu by February.'

'You don't miss home?'

'Home!' He spat the word out as if I had made an utterly ridiculous suggestion. 'No, I don't miss home. Home never missed me,' he added petulantly.

My eyes darted over to Angela. I was aware that I had made a mistake and wasn't sure what to say next. She gave me the slightest comradely eye roll before speaking.

'We do miss you. Home is where the heart is, Nick, and I don't believe that's twelve feet above a Los Angeles sidewalk with a plastic reindeer. It's about the people.'

He opened his mouth to speak, but she continued.

'Your father's long gone; it's time you laid his ghost to rest. There are people here who love you, and we believe you love us, too. Including Marilise. But you know best, I'm sure.'

She pressed her lips together and stood up to empty the teapot. Nick glared at her back.

'I suppose you mean do I care if Marilise dies while I'm away? Well, of *course* I do, but she's got all of you, she's very well looked after.'

Had I heard him right? He seemed to care more about his dog than his grandmother. Mind you, I meet plenty of callous family members in my line of work, so I didn't feel shock, just disappointment.

Angela turned back to face him.

'Nick, you're her grandson. It's only you, your sister Victoria, and her little Sofia left of Marilise's blood relatives, and that sister of yours hasn't visited for longer than an hour or two in years. And that's always when the family's in London. Marilise loves this house, she loves you and she loves Christmas. Even if it sounds like it, I'm not trying to emotionally blackmail you. But I wish I could make you understand that whatever happened in the past, you are wanted here.'

A look of anguish crossed his face. *Maybe there was more to this than met the eye.* I was beginning to feel very uncomfortable as witness to this conversation, but I had no idea where I should go, other than back to the bathroom. I had made up my mind to excuse myself, when Nick started speaking again, quietly.

'Of *course* I love Marilise, and all of you. But this house...'

'You loved that, too, when you were little,' said Angela.

'I did,' he replied. 'But only until I realised it was a millstone and that the only reason behind my birth was so that someone could inherit it. My father's only love.' He sounded bitter now. 'Well, I can't wait to sell it.'

'Sell it?' gasped Angela.

'Yes,' he said, his mouth settling into a stubborn line. 'Astrid will be moving to Texas soon, when she marries that awful man...' He broke off, frowning theatrically. 'Do you think that my stepmother marrying him makes him my stepfather? More opportunities for happy families?' Angela and I just stared at him, and he continued. 'Anyway, with his oil billions I doubt

Astrid will care about Lyonscroft. Victoria will be glad of half the money. Obviously, I hope that you and Greg stay on, in London.'

He switched on his charming smile again, but the colour drained from Angela's face and she turned back to the sink without speaking. His smile faltered as he looked at me.

'Welcome to Lyonscroft,' he said, irony tinging his voice. 'It always was *such* a happy home, and I clearly have my father's knack for keeping it that way.'

He stood up, whistled to Steve, who scrambled to his feet instantly and glued himself to his master's side, and they went to leave the room. However, as they reached the door, it was flung open and in swept India, the girl we had seen earlier on the horse.

'Don't go anywhere, Nick, I need to talk to you about tonight.'

'Tonight?' said Nick.

'Tonight!' shrieked Angela.

'Tonight,' repeated India. 'Don't tell me you've forgotten?'

Apparently sensing that this one was going to run, Steve collapsed in front of the Aga again, with a blissful sigh. I felt like joining him. There had been more excitement at Lyonscroft in an hour than I usually see in a month on jobs, and I hadn't even met my patient yet.

'Oh, dear me, I had *completely* forgotten,' said Angela, bringing the now clean but empty teapot back to the table and attempting to pour herself a cup. Clicking her tongue in irritation at its inability to produce tea from thin air, she put it down and turned to me. 'Laura, I should have told you at the interview, but it flew out of my head. There's a party tonight at a neighbour's house and we've all been invited. Marilise dearly wants to attend. She's been looking forward to it since the summer, when we were first invited.' She must have seen the look of surprise on my face at a party being arranged so far in advance. 'Oh, it was originally meant to be a Halloween party, but the entire family got Covid, so they had to reschedule. Anyway, the doctor said that Marilise's nurse – you – would have to decide if she's up to it, and would have to go, too, to be with her.'

'That's okay,' I replied in my best soothing voice. I stood up, ushered her to a chair and filled the kettle. 'Late notice isn't a problem for me – I'm here at your disposal and I've got a dress that will be suitable.'

It was true. I always packed an odd selection of clothes when I stayed with patients because while sometimes we barely left the house, which only needed something comfortable, other times it felt more hedonistic as my patient enjoyed their final fling with life. And then, who knew where I'd end up going? Recently, I attended the beautiful wedding of the star of *Mayfair Mews*, Jacqueline Honeywood, to Sir Douglas Knight, up in Yorkshire with my patient Essy, who had been Jacqueline's dresser for many years. Another time I recalled, shuddering, I had gone up in a titchy little plane and been strapped to an instructor to follow my patient in leaping out into the abyss. He was ninety-two and fulfilling a lifelong dream; I was thirty-six and terrified. So, I could easily take a party in my stride. I smiled around at the others, who were darting anxious looks at one another. Eventually, Nick cleared his throat and spoke.

'Uh, the thing is, it's um, it's a...'

Another awkward silence. My stomach began to churn. What horror was about to be unleashed?

'It's a fancy-dress party,' burst out Angela, jumping up to attend to the now-boiling kettle.

'But I don't have any costumes with me,' I said, probably unnecessarily. I doubted they had expected their grandmother's nurse to roll up with a case full of sailors' hats and flamenco dresses.

'Oh, you don't have to worry about that,' said India breezily, with the mischievous grin that was already becoming familiar. 'We've got a family theme, and you'll have no trouble fitting in the costume.'

'What's the theme?' I asked suspiciously. 'Something Christmassy?'

'Not in November!' said India, who clearly hadn't visited London any time after July. 'No, when it was delayed from Halloween, the hosts decided to keep the theme.'

Angela refilled my cup and offered me another macaroon.

'We're going as the Addams Family,' she said, an apologetic look on her face.

A vague image of black and white clothing and pale make-up crossed my mind.

'Well, that's all right, isn't it?' I said. 'What costumes do you have?'

'Astrid, my stepmother, is going as Morticia,' said Nick, looking determinedly away from India, who had started giggling. 'I'm Gomez Addams and India is Wednesday. Marilise – if she's well enough – will be Grandmama, with Greg as the butler, Lurch, and Angela as Morticia's pet lion, Kitty Cat.'

'We had the costumes fitted a while ago,' said Angela. 'And when we rang them to ask them to add something extra for a nurse we hadn't yet hired, they said they had something that didn't need to be fitted, that would be fine for anyone.'

India's giggles were ramping up, and she turned away in an attempt to stifle them.

'So, what's the costume?' I asked, my brain sorting through images of vampires, ghosts and ghouls. How bad could it be?

'I'm afraid it's Cousin Itt,' gasped out India, then leapt up and ran from the room, tears of laughter pouring down her face.

'Cousin Itt?' I asked. 'Who's that?'

'He's the character who is completely covered in long hair, from head to foot,' said Nick, whose lips were also beginning to twitch with amusement. 'And he has a hat and, erm, sunglasses.'

I took my phone out and quickly Googled the character. It was basically a walking wig. My stomach dropped into my shoes. I had an immediate urge to say the word that so often sprang to my lips when my own family made unfair demands of me, but that I found so difficult to actually utter: *no*. But then I thought better of it. I had been in this house for less than an hour, and if this was what was being asked of me to facilitate my patient's happiness... Well, I'd faced worse. I thought of that horrid little plane and tried to be grateful for small mercies, summoning up a sporting smile.

'Well, at least I won't get cold,' I said, rolling my eyes. 'Maybe I should suggest this get-up to my sister for my bridesmaid's dress; it's no worse than that's bound to be and at least there's plenty of room to hide cake if I get hungry.'

Angela smiled at me encouragingly, but Nick frowned, then quickly left the room.

'Have I annoyed him again?' I asked, beginning to feel irritated by this mercurial man. After all, I had just agreed to their stupid costume with a good grace. Did he ever stay in one mood for longer than two minutes?

Angela shrugged.

'Don't worry yourself about him, he's rather...'

She stopped talking quickly, leaving me curious as to what she had been about to say, when the door opened and he returned, India behind him, looking sheepish.

'Tell her,' he said curtly, nodding at me.

'Sorry,' she said. 'They dropped the Halloween theme when they had to postpone the party. I thought it would be funny if we all turned up dressed as the Addams family.'

'Did you know?' I asked Angela and Nick.

She shook her head furiously.

'No, of course not.' Then she tutted. 'Now, I'm going to have to find something else to wear — I was relying on that costume.'

'I didn't know either,' said Nick. 'But I had my suspicions. Sorry, India doesn't always know when a joke's over.'

'It's okay,' I replied, too relieved to feel annoyed. 'Thanks for getting to the bottom of it. Maybe India would like to wear the Cousin Itt costume as a penance?'

'Not likely,' she replied pertly. 'I've got a dress ready in case I was rumbled. Laters!'

She darted out of the room before anyone else could tell her off and Nick, whistling to Steve, followed her. I had to smile: it was nice having someone young around, even if I might have to watch out so I wasn't pranked by her again.

'I'm so sorry about that,' said Angela. 'You've only been here for five minutes. When you interviewed, I didn't think I'd need to warn you about India.'

'It's fine,' I said. 'To be honest, I'm just relieved that this house is warmer than the one in London.'

A mental image of that house came to me. It had been at least five storeys, including a basement, and rendered in immaculate white stucco. I could barely afford even to park in that area of London, so I couldn't begin to imagine how much a house of that size must be worth. Ten million pounds? Twenty? I remembered standing awkwardly in the chilly black and white tiled hallway with its décor of gleaming marble, polished stone and gigantic mirrors, and shivered. It had felt colder inside there than it was outside.

'We wouldn't have it any other way,' replied Angela. 'Especially Marilise – she likes to be cosy. I was only up in London for a couple of days, and it wasn't worth firing up the central heating for the entire house, so most of it was arctic.'

'The sitting room was toasty, though,' I said, remembering the room, which overlooked the quiet square of enormous Georgian mansions outside. A fire had blazed away in the large, iron grate and the space was completely different from the austere hallway. It was painted a deep shade of red with a thick, cream carpet and two invitingly squashy sofas and I had been immediately more at ease. Angela had plied me with tea and chocolate chip shortbread while explaining a little about the set-up at this house, in Somerset. She was the housekeeper and her husband, Greg, looked after the grounds and did all the little "bits and bobs" around the house.

'It's the nicest room in that house,' said Angela, finally sitting down next to me and taking a macaroon herself. 'I pretty much live in it when I have to go down to London on business.' She must have seen me looking curious, because she added, 'I'm a chartered accountant as well as doing all the dusting.'

I thought I had managed not to let the surprise show on my face, but she must have been used to people underestimating her and smiled gently. 'People do find my role unusual, but it works for me, and I love this family.'

We had, of course, talked about Marilise's needs and what my job would entail, but I was eager to find out more about the people I would be living with over Christmas, particularly my patient.

'So Marilise is nearly ninety, how wonderful.'

'That's right, dear, and she's been fit as a fiddle until recently, but she's had a series of infections and viruses which have slowed her down. The family normally goes up to London for Christmas as Nick can't bear being here for it. But Marilise isn't well enough to travel this year. I've been doing all her non-medical care – we've had nurses who come in for that side of things – but it's getting too much for me with the rest of the house to look after and now Christmas coming. There are bound to be guests turning up and I can't be pulled in so many directions, although I would still like to be involved with her care, and I'll cover you when you're not working. Hence the details the agency gave you, for day-to-day nursing care and companionship. I was very impressed by your CV; you're exceptionally experienced. Most of the applications were from people with only a year or two's work behind them, and that didn't seem the right choice for Marilise.'

I nodded. I had been a nurse for nearly twenty years and reached the level of band six specialist ward nurse.

'Yes. And I probably would have continued in hospital work, but my husband fell ill.' I sipped my tea slowly before continuing. It hadn't been necessary to divulge all this at the interview, but I felt instinctively that I could trust Angela with the story of my past. 'It was a short illness, and I looked after him until... the end.' Angela gave me such a sweet and sympathetic smile that I had the courage to continue. 'That's when I retrained as a companion-ship care nurse, and that's what I've been doing ever since, living with patients in their homes to provide treatment and support.'

I didn't add that a large part of the reason I did this was because I couldn't bear to live in the house that Paulo and I had bought together. That was rented out, and if I had time in between jobs, I either gritted my teeth and went back briefly to my childhood home to stay with my mother, father and sister, or took a trip away.

'It sounds as though you've had a difficult time,' said Angela, pushing the plate of shortbread towards me again. 'But the agency said we were very lucky to have the opportunity to employ you, with your excellent reputation and willingness to work over Christmas. Don't your parents want to see you?'

'They live in Somerset as well, so I can visit them on my days off,' I said, hoping that this noncommittal response would not invite any more questions on the subject of my family. 'I think the agency passed on my request for the Saturday before Christmas specifically, as that's when my sister is getting married.'

'Oh yes, of course,' said Angela, beaming. 'How nice, a winter wedding! You said you were going to be a bridesmaid?'

'Yes,' I replied shortly, then rushed on before the wedding

talk set in. 'Is Marilise happy to have a nurse come to work with her?'

'She is,' said Angela, smiling fondly. 'She's a lovely person, very gracious. She's bona fide royalty, you know; we all call her Marilise and she wouldn't hear of anything else, but her full name is Princess Marie-Elise Colombo della Rovere. The royal family was abolished between the wars and she came to London with her parents, then met her husband when she was a deb in the fifties. He was the one whose family owned the London house and all this.' She waved her hand around. 'But he never got over the fact that although he had the money, it was all from trade – dog food, it was – whereas it was she who had the real pedigree.'

This was a world known to me only by the occasional flick through a society magazine at a patient's house, and it did sound intriguing.

'She must have some fab stories.'

'She does, but not many people to share them with these days, so if you're willing to listen, she'll be only too glad to tell. Her son, Nick's father, died about seventeen years ago and the dowager widow, Astrid, who was his second wife, not Nick's mother, has all her time taken up with India, the garden and her fiancé, Philip, who lives in Texas.'

I laughed.

'My head's spinning already! It sounds very complicated.'

Angela nodded.

'It always is with these families,' she said sagely. 'But you don't need to worry about any of that; you'll pick it up as you go along.'

'I hope so,' I replied. 'And Marilise was happy to employ me without meeting me first?'

'She trusts my judgement,' said Angela, picking up the plate of treats and giving me little choice but to take yet another. 'And you'll fit in perfectly at Lyonscroft. We're very lucky to have found you.'

I smiled. Despite the dog, the bush, Nick's grumpiness and the Addams family joke, I felt just the same.

'Oh, look at the time!' exclaimed Angela. 'Marilise should be waking up around now – shall we go upstairs?'

Glad to be getting started on the real reason I had come to Lyonscroft, I rose quickly and followed her out of the room, eager to find out what my princess patient would be like.

THREE

We walked briskly down the passageway towards the pretty entrance hall and up the stairs.

'Should I take my shoes off?' I asked, almost afraid to step on the pristine cream carpet.

'Goodness, no,' said Angela. 'I give this carpet a good clean every day and even that dog hasn't yet managed to leave a stain I couldn't tackle.' She paused, her hand on the banister, and lowered her voice slightly. 'Between you and me, I'd prefer shoes off, but Nick can't bear it – reminds him of his father who was a man who liked to tell other people what to do. As long as you're comfortable, wear whatever you like on your feet.'

I nodded.

'Thanks. I usually wear soft plimsolls when I'm working, and they stay pretty clean, but I adapt to whatever the house rules are.'

At the top of the stairs, she turned right, and I followed her past two or three closed doors then down a couple of steps, where the passage opened out and became a small, light-filled landing. She knocked gently on one of the doors and opened it slowly, without waiting for an answer.

'Are you awake, my dear?' I heard her ask, then, apparently receiving an answer in the affirmative, she pushed the door open further and said, 'I've brought your new nurse-companion to meet you.'

She turned and beckoned to me, and I followed her into a large bedroom, very different from most of the spaces I was used to working in. The cream carpet flowed into the room, interrupted only by an exquisite pink and green rug that lay at the foot of the bed, with a sofa upholstered in similar hues standing on it. All the other furniture was white and very elaborate, with lots of curls and scrolls, leaves and flowers carved into it. It wasn't a style I would ever have chosen but at this scale, and in the setting, it looked fabulous. Over the top, yes, but so fresh and feminine I would have defied anyone not to be delighted by it. The wallpaper was the same cream as the carpet, with a delicate pattern of widely spaced pink and green stripes, and the floor-length curtains, in the same chintzy fabric as the sofa, were held back from tall windows by thick, pale green, tasselled ties. I took all this in quickly as Angela approached the tiny figure sitting upright in the bed, an embroidered unrumpled white silk coverlet over her legs and two fat pillows behind her back. She put down the book she had been reading, removed her glasses and smiled at me.

'Welcome to Lyonscroft, Nurse Wilde,' she said, her slightly accented voice clear, if a little fragile, with a slight accent. 'I am so very pleased to meet you.'

She held up her hand and I stepped forward quickly to take it. She clasped my hand between both of hers and looked intently at me with deep brown eyes.

'It's a great pleasure to meet you,' I replied. 'And please, do call me Laura.'

'I shall, and I am Marilise. I know that Angela will have made the perfect choice in you.'

She smiled warmly at the other woman.

'Thank you,' said Angela. 'Now, I'm going to leave you two to get acquainted. Will you take your swim today?'

'No, I don't think so, thank you. I don't think Laura needs that on her first morning and anyway, I want to conserve my energy for tonight; there is a party, is there not?'

'Only if Laura says you're well enough to go,' said Angela in a teasing voice.

'Ah, I'm sure she will find that I am,' replied Marilise, her eyes dancing. 'And does the spooky family theme still hold?'

'No,' said Angela firmly. 'India has confessed that the matching costumes idea was abandoned ages ago.'

'So she told you,' said Marilise, some regret in her voice. 'It would have been amusing, no, if we had all appeared in our Halloween outfits at their pretty Christmas party?'

'You knew?' asked Angela. 'And did you know that it would have meant Laura here dressing up as a walking wig?'

Marilise gave the most mischievous grin I have ever seen on anyone over the age of five.

'And she was game, was she not? India texted me.' She held up a phone that had been concealed by the bedclothes. 'We would not have made you go through with it, Laura, but I know we are going to get on fine.'

'Hmm,' I said, smiling though I made my voice stern. 'I may have decided that you were not strong enough to attend and, sadly, we would both have had to stay home.'

'I can see you're in good hands,' said Angela, nodding in approval. 'I'm going now. I have to make sure I have everything ready – tomorrow's Stir Up Sunday.'

She left the room, and I perched on a small, exquisite chair next to Marilise's bed. She reached over and patted my hand.

'India and I were having a little fun; I hope you don't mind?'

'Of course not,' I said, meaning it. 'I'm looking forward to being here with you all.'

'Have you met my grandson yet, Nikolai? Or *Nick*, as he insists on abbreviating his beautiful name.'

'Yes, I have. I helped him rescue his dog from some undergrowth.'

She chuckled.

'Of course. I'm not surprised to hear that he would prioritise my nurse's time on saving that Steve. Sometimes, I think the dog is the most important one of us, as far as Nikolai is concerned.'

'I'm sure that's not true,' I said doubtfully, remembering what Nick had said in the kitchen.

'It may well be,' replied Marilise. 'He is a wonderful man, that much I can promise you, but so determined not to give his heart to people, not even – or maybe especially not – his own family. I'm afraid my son – his father – was a cruel man, and after my daughter-in-law died, well...' She clicked her tongue and shook her head. 'All Christoph cared about was that he had someone to pass the houses and the wealth down to. His interest in his own son began and ended there.'

'That's so sad,' I said. *Maybe this kind of privilege wasn't such a blessing as it seemed.*

'It is sad, but not so uncommon,' replied Marilise. 'I was lucky that my own father revelled in his daughters. But what about your family? Do you not wish to spend Christmas with them, rather than looking after an old lady?'

I hesitated. Usually, when patients asked me about myself, I kept my responses simple and unremarkable, but my sister's wedding had upset me more than I cared to admit, and Marilise had a comforting strength about her that made me feel it would be safe to be truthful.

'Please,' she said. 'I would very much like to know. You have a sadness about you, Laura, which is unusual in one so young. I carry plenty of sorrow myself, but I have had several decades more to accumulate it. We are to work closely together, intimately, no?' I nodded. 'Then I would be glad if you can speak as freely to me as I will to you. That would burden me less than your silence, if that helps?'

I swallowed.

'Well, I was widowed, three years ago, just before Christmas,' I said, stumbling slightly over my words. Marilise squeezed my hand and nodded. I carried on. 'I think I understand a little how Nick feels, although our circumstances are very different. I can't imagine daring to love someone again, knowing how painful it is to lose them.'

'I see,' said Marilise, and I was grateful that she hadn't argued with me, or offered any platitudes. 'And your family?'

'My parents and sister live not far from here. They–they think that I should have moved on by now. They don't like to think about Paulo – my husband. And now my sister's getting married, very close to the anniversary of his death.'

My mouth snapped shut. I had said enough, and I was worried that I might cry. What a horribly unprofessional start this was. But Marilise didn't seem remotely bothered.

'So they are not respecting his memory, or your grief?' I shook my head. 'I don't blame you for finding somewhere else to be.'

'I am happy for Steph – that's my sister,' I burst out. 'But it's too hard to be steeped in it all. And there's a *lot*.'

A whisper of that mischievous grin touched her lips again.

'Ah, there is a splendid word, maybe you think it fits her: *bridezilla?*'

She rolled the word around her mouth with relish, and I laughed.

'Poor Steph, she wants everything to be perfect, but she can be scary about it at times.'

'And you and I know,' said Marilise, 'that life is not perfect, nor is love, but that does not take away from its wonder.'

Tears pricked at the back of my eyes. I had been pushing

that wonder away, I knew that, but now I spoke a bit too brightly.

'Well, I love the life I have. I meet so many different people and have freedom and flexibility – I'm not sure most can say that.'

'I certainly could not,' replied Marilise. 'Not now, not ever, really, but I had my family and this beautiful home and that, for me, was enough. But we are all different.'

I wanted to tell her that I was not different, that, if I was being honest, a home and a family of my own was what I longed for. But this was a truth I could barely admit to myself, let alone someone else. If I were to say it out loud, it would feel as if I were being somehow disloyal to Paulo. This life I had created honoured his memory and gave me some relief from my guilt over his death. It also protected my barely mended heart from being torn to shreds all over again. I changed the subject.

'What would you like to do this morning? We still have an hour or so before lunch.'

'I normally swim, as you heard, but not today. I do want to go to the party tonight, and that means lots of rest. Perhaps you could help me dress, and then I would like to sit quietly down-stairs and read.'

'Of course.'

Letting her guide me as to how much aid she needed, I helped Marilise wash and dress. She wore a smart pair of black wool crepe capris with a neat cotton shirt and a rich purple cashmere cardigan, which had little pearls for buttons. She then applied a little make-up, and I helped her brush and arrange her hair.

'There, Laura, I think I will do.'

'I think so,' I replied. 'You look nicer than I do when I'm going out, let alone spending the morning around the house with my family; maybe I should start making more of an effort.'

She surveyed me seriously.

'Your clothes may be casual and comfortable, but you have good taste, I can see that. The cut suits you and the colours are flattering. But I never regret making that little bit of effort. Speaking of which, please could you find the small pearl earrings in that box on the dressing table?'

I opened the box as directed and found it was full of earrings, all neatly pushed into padded velvet slits. Several were pearl, but I selected the pair I thought might go well with the cardigan buttons and held them up.

'These ones?'

'Clever girl. I said you had taste.'

I felt absurdly pleased as I helped her put them in, then took her arm to support her. We moved slowly, but she took care to step properly, not shuffle as so many older people do. As we came out on to the small landing, my bags were waiting for me outside another door.

'Ah, good,' said Marilise. 'Someone has brought them up. I asked for you to have that room; it's near me but, more importantly, it's one of the nicest rooms in the house. It's the one my sister always used to stay in, and she wouldn't have anything but the best.' She laughed gently. 'I also have a "bridezilla" in the family; one day I will tell you about her.'

We moved towards the stairs.

'I look forward to it,' I said. 'Maybe we can exchange notes on how to manage them.'

'I found living in another country to be an excellent solution,' said Marilise, holding firmly to the banister with the other hand. 'But maybe that is too drastic.'

I refrained from comment, but couldn't deny it sounded tempting. Steph from a distance of a couple of thousand miles would be much easier to handle. We reached the bottom of the stairs and Marilise directed me to a small, light-filled room, its walls lined with bookshelves and French windows that looked over the gardens. I settled her in an armchair and made sure she had her book.

'Can I get you some tea or coffee?' I asked, hoping I could remember the way back to the kitchen.

'No, no,' she replied. 'I'm going to text Angela.' She pulled out the phone again and lit up the screen. 'I have things to talk to her about, anyway. Now, you must go and see your room and unpack; come back for me just before lunch, if you would.'

'Of course,' I said and left her sitting peacefully as I went to make myself at home in Lyonscroft.

FOUR

I returned to Marilise's room, where I made the bed and tidied up. As I stepped out and pulled the door shut behind me, a whirlwind of a woman came tearing down the corridor towards me. She was tall, with curly light-brown hair escaping from the combs that caught it up above her temples. She was wearing a floor-length, flowing silk skirt in melding browns and ambers, and a dark green cardigan knitted from the chunkiest wool I had ever seen. She seemed to be trailing several scarves, tied to her hair and wrapped around her neck, and the whole effect was of some beautiful autumnal wood nymph that had been blown in by the wind.

'Are you Nurse Wilde?' she asked breathlessly, seizing my elbow.

'Yes,' I replied. 'Is everything all right?'

Judging by her wild-eyed look, I was worried that something had happened to Marilise.

'Oh yes, unless you count my appalling manners in not being here to greet you,' she said. Her dark blue eyes widened as she gazed at me imploringly. 'I'm awfully sorry, but Victoria has just rung and announced that she's sending Sofia to stay *tomorrow...*' She trailed off as I frowned, trying to remember who everyone was. 'Oh dear, oh *dear*, of course you haven't the faintest idea who I'm talking about.'

But nursing, like teaching, makes you good with names and I smiled.

'Isn't Victoria Nick's sister, and Sofia her daughter?'

'Thank God!' she exclaimed, making me jump. 'I *knew* Angela would find somebody competent, and here you are. I'm Astrid, by the way – Nick's not terribly wicked stepmother.'

I had suspected as much.

'I've met India,' I said. 'She's your daughter, isn't she?'

'That's right. Was she riding a horse?'

'She was the first time, yes.'

'There you go, always down at the stables or fiddling around with something equine. I suppose I'll have to drag her back up to the house to help.'

'What needs doing?' I asked. 'Marilise doesn't need me right now, so maybe I can help?'

Her eyes widened again, as if I had suggested sprouting wings and flying.

'*Would* you? I need to get Sofia's room ready, do the bed and so on. Poor girl, I do so want to make her feel welcome.' She started marching off and I followed quickly as she turned into another bedroom. This one was smaller and much simpler than Marilise's, but still twice the size of the master bedroom in my own house. It had a pale pink carpet, walls papered in a pretty pattern of little green sprigs, and smart walnut furniture. Astrid opened a wardrobe and started pulling out bedlinen. 'Bloody Victoria, sending poor Sofia here on a moment's notice for the whole of Christmas, because she wants to swan off to some Caribbean island with her second husband, who runs the hedge fund for the billionaire who owns the damn island and who doesn't want to have his stepdaughter hanging round.'

My head was sent into a spin by all this information about a world I had no concept of. I had no idea what a hedge fund was, and I could barely imagine an island-owning billionaire, other than Richard Branson. Maybe it *was* Richard Branson? Given the culture shocks I had already endured, it wouldn't surprise me. So I asked the only question I could come up with.

'How old's Sofia?'

Astrid flung the sheets – now hopelessly tangled – onto the bed and turned to me, her face red.

'Eight! Just eight years old, poor little mite.'

I picked up the sheets and started shaking them out.

'That is young to be left by her mum, but at least she's with family.'

'*Family,*' chuntered Astrid, seizing a pillow. 'We barely know the child. Ah well.' She suddenly threw the pillow down and turned to me, her face breaking into a smile that made my spine tingle with its sweetness and warmth. 'Don't mind me, love. I get fired up sometimes. Truth is, I'm *glad* to have Sofia coming. You probably already know that we never spend Christmas at Lyonscroft, and rarely so many of us together, so having a child here might buck us all up into making it a *proper* Christmas. And, of course, it'll probably be my last one here.'

'You're getting married, aren't you?' I asked, taking the other corner of the duvet she was trying to stuff into its cover. She stopped briefly, glanced at me, then continued.

'Yes, that's right. My fiancé, Philip, is from Texas, so that's where we'll go in the New Year. Amazing for India – so many horses.'

I detected a certain strain in her voice – would it be quite so amazing for her as for her daughter?

'Do you like horses, too?' I asked.

'Not really,' she replied. 'I like gardening. I'll probably have to build some raised beds out there to get anything to grow...' She trailed off, then continued brightly. 'We'll see – all an adventure, I expect! Right, well, that looks more welcoming.'

We surveyed the bed which did, indeed, look cosy now with its fat duvet and two plump pillows. 'Angela's already done a dust round, so I think I'll go and cut some greenery for a little display on the dresser. Thank you for your help, Laura.'

'My pleasure.'

She swept off down the stairs as I went back to my room. I picked up my bags and pushed open the door. Immediately, I could see why Marilise's sister had considered this the best room in the house, although it was more a suite than a room, with two distinct sections. On one side, making full use of a deep bay window, was a sitting area, with inviting armchairs, a coffee table and two low bookcases. On the other side stood the bed, a high four-poster with an open top and elegant drapes and opposite that was a fireplace with a marble surround and wide mantelpiece upon which stood an ornate clock and two pretty vases, both stuffed with tall evergreen branches. I supposed that this thoughtful touch had been provided by Astrid. The colour scheme was of the palest duck egg blue and ivory and, after my busy morning, had an immediately restful effect that was very welcome, even if I couldn't help thinking back to the hospital wards I had worked on for so many years, and how they could benefit from even a fraction of the money it must have taken to decorate this gorgeous room. I quickly unpacked my clothes into the large wardrobe and set out my toiletries on the glass-topped dresser, wishing I had decanted them into elegant bottles, as the plastic packaging from a local pharmacy seemed to be letting the side down. Opening a door in the corner of the room, I found a bathroom, not as large as the one downstairs, but still three times the size of mine in the house I had shared with Paulo. We hadn't been short of money, or wanted for anything, but our lifestyle – if you could call it that – was distinctly modest, funded as it was by the salaries of a nurse and an electrician. But we had been so content with our cosy home, our 'staycation' holidays and our ancient car that felt like it only kept going out of good will. Our bathroom had been on the elderly side but perfectly fit for purpose. The fittings in this one were clearly modern, and pristine, but were in keeping with the age and style of the house, including a free-standing rolltop bath with high ends that curved gently down towards the middle. There was a separate shower and two sinks, side by side, as well as floor-to-ceiling fitted wooden cupboards. Suffice to say, these were not my normal nurse's quarters, and it was as if I had wandered into some sort of Cinderella story, or period drama, as I went back into the bedroom and gazed out of the windows. They overlooked the front of the house and allowed me to appreciate the perfect symmetry of the front gardens, although the sight of the woods to one side made me shudder as I remembered my inelegant crawl to 'rescue' Steve. A knock at the door brought me back to the present.

'Come in!'

'Hello again,' said Nick. 'Angela, who seems to think that my job is so pointless that I can be sent on errands at any given moment, asked me to let you know that lunch will be ready in about fifteen minutes.'

'Oh, thank you. Sorry you were disturbed – I'll learn the household routines quickly.'

He shrugged.

'She's got a point. She and Greg manage this entire house, Astrid has the greenest fingers this side of Kermit the frog, you're a nurse... Designing apps does feel kind of pointless next to all that talent and dedication, but then there are upsides to being totally dispensable. Beyond errands, no one asks much of you.'

Yet another side to this complicated man: self-deprecating to an extreme that made me a little uncomfortable.

'What sort of apps do you design?' I asked, hoping to find something there to bolster him.

'Anything I'm asked to,' he replied with another shrug. 'The current one is for an online pet food shop; the one before that was a wheel spin game for a soft drinks company so you can win free stuff when you use their app rather than going to the website.'

'I see,' I said, trying not to look as though I agreed that his job might seem, well, unfulfilling, if not exactly pointless. 'Did you always want to do it?'

He snorted with laughter, and I felt embarrassed. I was like a maiden aunt asking polite questions about which I knew nothing.

'Funnily enough, I didn't dream of it as a child, but then I wasn't allowed to dream of anything other than taking over this place and managing the family properties. As soon as my father died, I handed all that over to other people and led an even more pointless existence until I realised that I was reasonably good at this and that people would hire me. What do you think, that I should start having ambitions to be a firefighter, or an astronaut?'

His sarcastic tone riled me; I was only trying to be polite, after all, and I *did* have an important job to do, an important job that this conversation was keeping me from.

'Why don't you join the Foreign Legion?' I suggested, rather more tartly than I had meant to. 'You'd look rather good riding into the distance on a camel.'

And before he could reply, I slipped past him and hurried downstairs to find Marilise.

FIVE

A few minutes later, I helped Marilise into the dining room, another grand affair with a large mahogany table, surrounded by at least fourteen chairs, a massive sideboard and the tall sash windows flanked by floor-length curtains. I seated Marilise at the end of the table, then, noticing that she looked a little unwell, discreetly took her pulse as the rest of the family started arriving.

'Please have a glass of water,' I said, pouring one. 'How are you feeling?'

'I have been better,' she admitted, sipping the water. 'But I probably need to eat and drink.'

'Is the doctor coming this afternoon?' I asked quietly.

'Yes, she is, so let me enjoy my lunch before she tells me something else I have to be careful of.'

I smiled.

'From your notes, I think it's only extreme sports and excessive alcohol that you have been warned against so far, so you're not doing too badly.'

'I suppose not,' she said. 'But I am not fond of being told not to do anything, even things I dislike.'

'Sounds familiar,' said a laughing voice behind me, and I turned to see Nick. 'Maybe if no one had insisted I had to play lord of the manor, I'd be striding around the countryside right now, a hunting rifle in one hand and a list of tenants in the other.'

Marilise chuckled, but I could barely summon up a polite smile. These arrogant, privileged rich boys were right up my sister's street, but I had no interest in them at all, and I was surprised that Araminta had described Nick in such glowing terms. I turned back to Marilise.

'All right then, I'll see you later.'

'What do you mean? Are you not having lunch?'

'Yes, but I thought I'd be eating in the kitchen.'

'Don't be ridiculous.'

I turned to see Nick scowling at me.

'I beg your pardon?'

'Of course we all eat in here together and always have – well, since my father died. Sit down.'

I took the seat he indicated next to Marilise, feeling stupid yet again. How was I to have known? From the way Steph and her best friend Dorothea talked about 'the help' and frowned on me having a job at all, let alone one they considered so menial, I had rather assumed I might be eating 'below stairs', although no one I had encountered so far at Lyonscroft – even Nick – had given even the vaguest impression that that might be the deal. I reddened as I contemplated my gaffe, then was comforted to feel a furry head and wet nose push against my hands under the table.

'Hello, Steve,' I said, pushing my chair back slightly to see him. 'Have you come for some lunch, too?'

'Not even he is consigned to the kitchen at mealtimes,' said Nick, in a softer tone of voice, sitting down beside me. 'Sorry, I didn't mean to be rude, but you hit a nerve. My father was a terrible snob and a stickler for people "knowing their place" as he put it. I hate it. As we've already established, you're a much better person than me, anyway, and would be far more missed if it was you galloping off on the camel.'

He gave me a sudden grin, and his handsome face went from brooding to merry in an instant; I couldn't help but smile back. Everyone was seated now, including Greg, to whom I was briefly introduced, and Angela asked us all to help ourselves from the array of dishes in the middle of the table. I served Marilise first, birdlike portions that I hoped were enough to fuel her properly, then myself: tiny roast potatoes, purple carrots and salmon en croute that made my mouth water just looking at it.

'I grew the carrots,' said Astrid proudly. 'They're a heritage variety and should be delicious; I hope you like them.'

'Will you be able to grow them in Texas?' asked Greg. 'You've done a fine job with these.'

Astrid looked worried.

'I think so,' she said. 'Although I'm not sure how much time I'll have. We'll see.'

Angela looked as though she were about to say something, then changed her mind and we ate in silence for a moment.

'Oh, Nick!' said India suddenly, producing a large, red envelope. 'This came for you. Sorry, it's a bit squashed. I took it from the postman at the top of the drive when I was riding.'

She passed the envelope to him, and he opened it, pulling a face when he saw the contents. I glanced across at what looked like a very smart invitation, in embossed black lettering on a card with gilded edges and smoothly rounded corners.

'What is it?' asked Astrid.

'It's the invitation to that Christmas charity concert at the Montgomerys',' he said. 'I've been expecting it, but I was hoping they'd forget all about it. No such luck. I tried offering them a donation, but they've refused to take it unless I go in person; they said I owe it to the charity to show my face.'

'What charity is it?' I asked.

'Blood cancer,' replied Nick. 'My mother died of leukaemia, so I've always supported it, and they know that it's a surefire way of getting me there.'

'And poor Nick doesn't want to go and spend the evening being forced together with poor Minty, any more than she wants to be forced together with him,' said India. 'Maybe you should borrow Laura's Cousin Itt outfit and go incognito.'

'Araminta?' I asked. 'Who I met?'

'That's right,' replied Nick glumly. 'It's her parents holding the concert and they've decided that she and I are the perfect match, despite the fact that neither of us agrees with them. Until one of us is married to someone else, they don't look like giving up, and there's no way I'd inflict myself in matrimony to anyone. Maybe I'd better rethink the Foreign Legion, after all.'

Talk turned to the family in question, and I checked on Marilise and finished my delicious lunch, thinking how glad I was that I had chosen my nomadic lifestyle and singledom; with men like this around, apparently permanently dissatisfied despite the silver spoon, knife and fork they had been born with, I was much better off.

When we had finished eating, I took Marilise back upstairs to prepare her for the doctor's visit and her afternoon nap. I stayed to speak to the doctor, who, after we ran through the medications I would be administering, explained that Marilise needed plenty of rest, but should otherwise do whatever she felt strong enough for, including that evening's party.

'Being sociable is a sort of medicine for certain patients,' she said. 'I'd love to prescribe it for many more. Just watch her pulse, encourage her to eat little and often, and she'll benefit.'

After she went, I drew the curtains and promised to wake Marilise in plenty of time to get ready for the evening, then I went to complete my next mission: familiarising myself with the layout of the house. Most of my jobs were in suburban semis or sheltered housing, but this was a different matter. If I was to look after Marilise properly, I would need to know where everything was so that I didn't have to rely on her or other family members to constantly point me in the right direction.

I was relieved when the first person I bumped into downstairs was India.

'Hello, are you going to the stables?'

'Yes, do you want to come and see my horse? He's called Firefly and he's so beautiful. He...'

I could see that the horse chat could run on, so I politely cut her off.

'He sounds glorious, and I'd like to see him at some point, but right now I was hoping that you might have a moment to show me where the pool is. I know I'll be taking Marilise every day and I'd like to check it out first.'

India looked a little disappointed but smiled politely.

'Of course, come with me.' She led the way towards the kitchen, chattering all the time. 'I think Firefly would be the perfect addition to the Christmas show this year at school, but the Head doesn't agree. She says it would be a donkey or nothing and that there isn't room for artistic interpretation of the Bible story. When I asked her why, then, it was okay for Camilla Tytherington-Smythe to have more lines than anyone else as an innkeeper when there wasn't one of those in the Bible either, just because her father's a governor, she told me that if I argued, I'd be demoted to third shepherd.'

She paused for breath, and I laughed.

'I'm amazed you're still doing a Nativity. I think I was about four in my last one.'

'Oh, it's not only the Nativity,' said India darkly. 'It's a whole Christmas spectacular and the entire school – primary and secondary – has to take part one way or another, whether they're some *pretend* Bible character, a cheery elf or a dancing snowflake. I was hoping to skulk at the back of the percussion section with a tambourine if I couldn't ride Firefly, but the Head said I had to be a shepherd and look after all the little ones dressed up as sheep. I wouldn't mind, but they're so snotty at this time of year, I spend half my time wiping noses.'

'Sounds delightful,' I said, grinning. 'I'm sure you'll get your reward in heaven.'

'Long time to wait,' grumbled India. 'At least, I hope it is, I suppose. I wonder what part they'll give Sofia.'

'She's joining your school?' I asked in surprise.

'Yes. Victoria's dumping her so fast to belt off to the Caribbean that there are still three weeks of school left. She sweet-talked the Head into taking her for the last bit, even though Mum said she wouldn't mind having her here. I've met her a few times, she's a nice kid, quiet. Maybe she won't mind Camilla Tytherington-Smythe having all the best lines,' she added bitterly.

For most of this conversation we had paused outside a door just past the kitchen, but now India opened it.

'Anyway, this is the pool, come in.'

I don't know what I had expected, but it wasn't this and I gasped as I stepped through.

'Impressive, isn't it?' said India. 'Apparently, Nick and Mum had it built after his father died, a sort of revenge because he had thought there was nothing more vulgar than a swimming pool in a house and had always refused to install one, even though Nick was a promising swimmer when he was younger.'

'This is some revenge,' I said, gazing round at the sight before me. An extension had been added to the side of the house with the most incredible gabled glass roof that ran for nearly its entire length. Huge bifold doors opened out onto the garden, and it must have been glorious in summer, or heavy rain or, well, whenever! The pool itself was large and blue and the square floor tiles surrounding it were smooth, creamy porcelain. At one side stood a sort of circular pergola, containing a bubbling jacuzzi and on the other side there was a fountain, surrounded by shallow steps. There was also a seating area with luxurious chaises longues and a low table. It was like something out of a film and like no swimming pool I had ever visited. My most recent experiences hadn't even been in municipal pools, which I disliked for the chill, the almost guaranteed verrucae and the reek of chlorine. I had, however, done some work using hospital hydrotherapy pools, which tended to be tiny, brightly lit and strictly utilitarian in design.

'I bet you were dreading getting your swimsuit on every day when you heard about that part of the job,' said India teasingly. 'I would have been. Still feel the same?'

'You're right,' I replied. 'It wouldn't normally be my first choice of activity on a winter's morning, but this is going to be a treat.'

'I've brought Marilise a couple of times myself,' she went on. 'Nick had those steps by the fountain installed so that she could get in easily. Come over this way.' She led me around the side of the pool to two glass doors. 'This is the sauna, which she doesn't like, but this one' – she tapped one of the doors – 'is the steam room, which she adores.'

'It will be good for her heart, too, in small doses,' I said. 'I'm beginning to think I should be paying the family to be here, rather than the other way around.'

We started to walk back around the pool.

'Look, I'm sorry about the Cousin Itt thing,' said India. 'I was being silly. I'm glad you're here, and I'm glad Sofia's coming. It should cheer Christmas up a bit, even if...'

She stopped abruptly.

'Even if what?' I asked.

She stared at me, doubt in her eyes.

'You can trust me,' I said. 'I won't pass anything on, unless I think you're in danger. I'm a nurse, I'm good at keeping confidences.'

She sighed.

'Thank you,' she said, looking at me again and then giving a small nod, as if she had decided to trust me. 'I was going to say, even if Philip, Mum's fiancé, turns up.'

'You don't like him?'

'No. I don't think he's good enough for Mum, he doesn't treat her kindly. Just because she's a bit scatty and gets lost in her gardening, then panics about doing enough for everybody. Obviously, I never met Nick's father, but he sounds horrible, too. I think she's got pretty bad taste in men.'

'She must see something in him, if she's going to marry him.'

'I think she's convinced herself that it's the best thing for me. He has lots of horses and of course I'd love to be amongst all that, but I'd never want her to sacrifice herself for me. I'm happy here, but I think Mum's worried that Nick's going to sell, although he'd see right by us, I know he would.'

I didn't mention the conversation I had been there for in the kitchen earlier, when Nick had indeed announced his intention to sell Lyonscroft.

'I'm sure he would,' I said, although I wasn't at all sure how loyal he would be to the family he didn't seem to believe loved him. 'Do you see your father?'

She nodded.

'Yes, sometimes, although he's often away with work. He's horsey, like me, but he stopped riding a few years ago after an accident. Now, he photographs horses.'

'What, like portraits?' I asked in surprise.

India grinned.

'Sometimes, but mostly he takes pictures of them in action. He's at all the big events: the Olympics, the Horse of the Year show, important races all over the world. He does reportage stuff as well, taking pictures behind the scenes; people trust him.'

'It sounds very interesting,' I said in a neutral voice, sensing that there was more to this story than India had indicated. For a moment, we stood in silence, looking at the glistening pool, then she spoke.

'It is. I've gone with him once or twice, but I don't like leaving Mum on her own. She knows that and I think it's another reason she's marrying Philip, so that she's not a burden to me. But she's not!' She turned her face to me, as if imploring me to believe her. 'We want each other to be happy so much that we end up doing or not doing things to try and help, and then neither of us gets what we want. It's so stupid. If only...'

I waited without interrupting or prompting for her to carry on. I knew all about 'if onlys' and 'might have beens' and how they can make you feel stuck in life. She darted another look at me and continued.

'If only Mum and Dad had made it work when I was born. They did the same thing, *I* think: tried to do what they thought the other one wanted, and I don't think either ended up happy.' With a sudden movement she turned away, but not before I had seen the tears in her eyes. 'I'm going for a ride,' she said abruptly, and strode out of the pool room, leaving me staring at the blue waters and trying not to think too much about my own life and what it might be like now *if only* I could have saved Paulo.

SIX

I spent the next couple of hours completing some paperwork – I have to keep detailed records on my patients – and finding out where other things I would need in the house were. There was a utility room off the kitchen, and I was familiarising myself with the washing machine when I looked out of the window and saw Astrid in the garden, staring at some roses – all stalks now, of course – a pair of secateurs in her hand. She hadn't put anything on over her clothes and despite the cardigan, I thought she must be freezing. Various coats were hanging by a door that led outside, so I pulled one on and grabbed another for her, then opened the door and stepped out, the dank November air immediately wrapping itself around me and inserting its cold fingers down my collar and up my sleeves. Astrid didn't seem to notice my approach, so I coughed and stamped a little as I drew nearer, hoping not to startle her, but she still did not turn until I said her name, and then she did so with a jump.

'Sorry,' I said. 'I didn't mean to disturb you, but I saw you out here and thought you might be cold.'

I held out the coat, which she stared at in bewilderment, not seeming to know what it was or what to do with it. I shook it out and draped it over her shoulders; only then did she draw it around herself and give me a half-smile.

'Oh, thank you, yes, gosh, I hadn't noticed, but I'm freezing. Do you think these roses need trimming?'

I looked at them doubtfully. I knew nothing about gardening, but it didn't feel helpful to announce that right now.

'No,' I said, sounding as confident as I could. 'They're just right. Why don't we go inside? We need to start getting ready for the party.'

'Oh, yes, all right,' said Astrid vaguely, and followed me back into the utility room, where we removed our coats.

'Is everything all right?' I asked casually, going back into the kitchen. 'Only you looked kind of worried out there.'

That was putting it mildly.

She turned to me and tried to smile.

'Yes, I'm worried about absolutely everything, but so glad to have you here to help with Marilise. She does need more care now and it was too much for us.' Her voice took on a slightly wild tone. 'Now, if you could persuade Nick not to sell Lyonscroft, provide a happy Christmas for Sofia when she arrives, decide on the best choices for India and conjure me up an outfit that won't embarrass everyone for this evening, that would be ideal.'

She pushed her hands into her hair and bared her teeth in what was supposed to be a smile but looked to me more like extreme anxiety. I wanted to put my arms around her and reassure her that everything would be okay, but I wasn't sure how appropriate that would be. Instead, I did what I do best and went practical.

'As far as I can see, the only thing we can do immediately is work out what to wear this evening. It's not costumes anymore, but is there a dress code?'

'No, but it's the first event of the season locally, so everyone will pull out all the stops. I haven't bought a new party dress since about 1997, and I doubt I'd fit into that anymore. Do you think I could wear this?'

'It's nice,' I said firmly. 'But you might feel more partyish with a different top. Should I come and help you look? I've got about ten minutes before Marilise is expecting me.'

Astrid clutched at my hands.

'Would you?' she whispered urgently. 'I'd be so grateful.'

We went to leave the room, when who should come in but the lord of the manor himself, wearing nothing but a pair of black chinos, with his hair damp from the shower and wafting some delicious peppery cologne. For a moment, I froze; nurses are used to bodies, but in my line of work I don't often get to see one as toned and muscular as this. He must have kept up his youthful hobby of swimming, with a side order of weights. My reverie was quickly broken when he spoke, his voice tight with irritation.

'Have either of you seen Angela? This shirt needs ironing.'

'I can do that for you,' said Astrid immediately, reaching out for it. Mindful of the minutes ticking away, and my hackles rising at this man who apparently couldn't wield his own iron, I broke in.

'We've only got a few minutes to find you something to wear, so we'd better go up.'

'But what about his shirt?'

In my head I was shouting *well, what about it? Can't he iron his own bloody shirt?* but I managed to keep that particular thought internal.

'I'm sure it can be sorted out later,' I muttered, furious that this domestically challenged manbaby might stop poor Astrid finding something she would feel comfortable wearing that evening. I got the strong impression that her needs came very far down everybody's lists, including her own. Nick glared at me, and I looked back at him as coolly as I could, until he surprised me by giving a sudden bark of laughter.

'Oh! You think I can't iron my own shirt?'

I shrugged.

'It's not that,' he said. 'I don't expect anyone to do it for me. But Angela is very strict about the iron, what water goes in it and so on, and I don't want to muck it up. That's why I need her; I don't usually iron anything, so when I have to, I can never remember the rules.'

Astrid's shoulders dropped in relief.

'Oh well, I can't help you with that,' she said. 'I once put some lavender essential oil in it to make the sheets smell nice and she was cross with me for weeks.'

'Look, here she is now,' I said gratefully, seeing her come through the door at the end of the corridor. 'Should we go and look in your wardrobe?'

Astrid and I hurried upstairs and she took me into her bedroom, another grand affair but impossibly messy. There were clothes, books and magazines scattered everywhere, and the bed was unmade.

'Sorry about the state of it,' she said nervously, twitching the duvet and making it look worse than it had before. 'I never seem to get time to sort it out.'

I didn't comment, instead going to the large wardrobe and opening it. To my surprise, it was stuffed with clothes.

'Sorry again,' said Astrid, coming to stand next to me. 'I hardly ever shop, but I also find it hard to throw anything away. Some of this is my mother's, and most of it doesn't fit, I don't think.'

I glanced at my watch discreetly; I only had a few minutes until I needed to be with Marilise.

'Well,' I said, 'your skirt is beautiful, so why don't we find a top that would work with it?' Panic gave me laser focus. 'Look, what about this?'

I pulled out a pearl grey silk blouse with long sleeves.

'Oh!' exclaimed Astrid. 'That was Mum's, I forgot it was there. I couldn't possibly wear it, I'll only spill something down it.'

'Try it on,' I said firmly. 'I promise that I am an expert at getting out stains, so it doesn't matter if you do.'

I could see her looking with excitement at the gorgeous garment and I pushed it towards her.

'I need to go. Please, at least try it on.'

She took it and I hurried out of the room, hoping that she would dare to do this one nice thing for herself.

I tapped lightly on Marilise's door, then pushed it open. She was still asleep, so I moved quietly around the room preparing the things we would need when she awoke. Checking my watch, I was about to gently wake her when I heard her say my name, and hurried over to the bed.

'Laura,' she said again, clutching for my hand. 'Is it time to go? Have I overslept?'

'It's fine,' I reassured her, helping her to a sitting position. 'No rush at all.'

She smiled at me.

'I have always loved to get ready for parties. When I was young, my sisters and cousins and I would spend hours preparing, purely for the joy of doing it, as much as to look nice, which of course we also liked. We would sometimes have a drink of schnapps, weakened down with water on my mother's instructions, fruity in the summer and minty in the winter. We were impossibly giggly before that, anyway, and it made us worse.'

'It sounds like fun,' I said. 'My friends and I, sometimes, never even made it out because we were having so much fun getting ready.'

That felt like a long time ago.

'Well, we will not do that tonight. The Westmans throw very good parties, and I wish to go.'

'Of course.'

I helped her out of bed and through the steps needed before she could get dressed, then when she was ready in her robe and underwear, she directed me to the wardrobe.

'I have a gown I have been looking forward to wearing again for many years, Laura. You will find it on the right-hand side, the red one.'

Carefully, I moved aside the fragile clothes until I found a beautiful, beaded, cranberry dress and lifted it out, heavy on its hanger.

'This one?'

'Yes! That is the one. I wore it once to an ambassador's reception and she was pea green with envy in her navy silk. Carefully now, don't snag the beading.'

I helped her into the dress, and she leant on me as I did up the zip and hook and eye fastening, then tugged gently until it sat straight.

'It's a perfect fit!' I said with delight, helping her to the mirror so that she could admire herself.

'Of course,' she said calmly. 'My body may not work the way it once did, but I have not lost or gained an ounce. Good. Now, my make-up.'

I watched as she applied powder, eyeshadow, mascara and lipstick, each in heavy golden packaging, their glamour putting my plastic-cased drugstore buys to shame. Maybe it was time I treated myself. Then I brushed her hair and put in two circular clips she handed me.

'I am all but ready,' she said. 'Now, what about you?'

'It won't take me long,' I answered. 'Don't worry, we won't be late.'

'If only I did not need so much help,' she sighed. 'We could have got ready together with some schnapps, like the old days.'

I smiled.

'Maybe we can do something about that next time.'

'Maybe, now go, go, or we'll be late.'

She waved me away as she took a few steps to an armchair and retrieved her phone. I hurried across to my own room, checking my watch. Only fifteen minutes before we were supposed to leave. Twisting my hair into a quick knot, I jumped in the shower, then pulled on the simple black dress and low heels I had with me for such an occasion. *Probably even more boring than the ambassador's navy silk*, I thought, and grinned wryly at myself in the mirror as I ran a brush through my hair and swiped on some make-up. I looked presentable, and that would have to do well enough.

'I'm ready,' I said, going back into Marilise's room.

'Hmm,' she said, looking up from her phone and surveying me. 'The dress is classic and fits you well, but you lack a certain pizzazz, my dear. Don't you have any other jewellery? The necklace is pretty but so simple for a party.'

I put my hand to the single teardrop pearl that I always wore.

'It was a present from my husband,' I replied, the familiar lump coming to my throat. 'I prefer to wear it.'

'Very well, but here.' She took her stick and moved the few steps to her dressing table, waving away my offer of help. 'I'm sure I have something – ah, yes!'

She took out a side hair comb with a dazzling spray of jewel flowers and beckoned impatiently at me to sit on the stool. Steadying herself on my shoulder, she put down her stick and with a deft movement, swept my hair up at one side and pushed the comb in firmly.

'Now look,' she commanded, pointing in the mirror. 'Much better.'

She was right. With my hair pulled away from my face and the sparkling hairpiece adding instant lift, I looked party ready. I smiled.

'It's beautiful, thank you.'

'Good. Now, we must go.'

We went downstairs and found only Nick waiting in the hallway. He stood up as soon as he saw us coming down the stairs, wearing his shirt now, which had been immaculately pressed.

'Marilise, you look sensational,' he said, smiling warmly, then turning to me, 'As do you. Are you ready to go?'

'Thank you,' I replied. 'Yes, we're ready.'

'The others have gone on ahead,' he explained. 'We needed two cars, anyway.'

He offered his arm and Marilise moved to lean on him as I followed them outside. He had brought his car around to the front of the house and helped Marilise into the back as I took the passenger seat. The journey was a few minutes and when we arrived, I was left in no doubt at all that the Halloween theme was long forgotten and the Westmans were thoroughly embracing Christmas. The front gate at the bottom of the short drive stood open and was wrapped in twinkling golden fairy lights. The lights continued on either side of the gravel drive, like two sparkling gilded streams, studded with illuminated candy canes, at least twenty on each side, which stood at jaunty angles as they lit the way. The house itself, a long, low, traditional farmhouse, was strung with thousands more lights, all in the same warm hue. There were silver icicles hanging from every window and, on the roof, a huge star rippled with multi-coloured lights that seemed to dance in the darkness. Nick pulled up and stopped near the front door.

'Everyone else is using the field to park,' he said, pulling on the hand brake. 'But Joanie Westman said we could park here so it was less of a hike for the guest of honour.'

'Guest of honour, am I?' cackled Marilise. 'I should think so, too, although I think I'm outshone by these decorations. Tasteless, of course, but at least you know it's Christmas. Maybe we should do the same at Lyonscroft?'

I felt, rather than saw, Nick's shudder.

'Not sure the electricity grid is up to it,' he said lightly, then got out of the car. I followed suit and we helped Marilise out.

'No more help now,' she said firmly, leaning on her stick. 'I like to walk into parties like a proper guest, not some old lady in need of an arm. It's good manners. How I leave, of course, may be a different matter.'

I stepped back slightly, casting my eye over a herd of spangled wicker reindeer that had been arranged on the other side of the front door. Nick rang the bell and, when the door was opened, a blast of warm, cinnamon-scented air and the strains of 'Sleigh Ride' hit me in the face and the heart. I gasped as I was transported back to my first Christmas with Paulo in our house, when we had gone all out, determined to give all our senses a festive treat. He had rigged up a system that played that same song every time you stepped in the front door, and my love of scented candles meant that the house smelt of gingerbread and cranberries, even when they weren't lit. We had looked up recipes for spiced cakes, spent hours untangling lights and dragged home a tree that was a foot too tall and wide for our small living room and necessitated moving out several items of furniture to squeeze it in. We had sat admiring it, once it was bedecked with dozens of baubles, basking in the glow of the fairy lights and candles, sipping our third attempt at eggnog, the first two being too disgusting to drink, if hilarious to make. It was there that we had sketched out our hopes and plans for the future, including how many children we might have, little knowing that in a few short months it would all be snatched from us and life – and Christmas – would never be the same again.

'Laura?'

I jumped as Nick said my name. He gestured for me to go into the house in front of him and I quickly caught up with Marilise. The woman who had opened the door gave me a broad smile and offered her hand.

'Lovely to meet you, I'm Joanie, come in! Hello, Nick. Everyone else is through there getting stuck into the prosecco. What can I get you all to drink?'

'You know me,' said Marilise.

'Of course,' said Joanie. 'The champagne's on ice and waiting for you. Bubbles for you, too?' she asked me.

I hesitated, then said, 'I'm working, so something soft, please.'

'Nonsense,' said Marilise. 'Have some champagne. I'm your boss, and I insist.'

I might have put up more of a fight, but I could see Marilise paling already, and I wanted to get her sitting down somewhere she could enjoy the party without having to put in too much effort.

'Looks like I've got my instructions. Champagne would be delicious, thank you.'

'I will stick to non-alcoholic,' said Nick. 'Designated driver tonight.'

We went through into a huge living room that oozed faded glamour. The walls were papered in a red and cream pattern and the window frames, dado rail and cornicing were painted black. Three enormous and very comfortable-looking sofas stood around a tiger print pouffe that was about the size of my bathroom and various other chairs and small tables were scattered about. A fire blazed and the mantelpiece bore a dramatic arrangement of dried wildflowers. A Christmas tree that must have been eight feet tall stood near a door, smothered in tinsel, lights and a riot of decorations, from grand gold-tasselled baubles to wonky, glitter-smeared loo rolls that could only have been made by a small child. In all, there was a complete mish-mash of styles, colours and patterns, but so artfully done that it worked to make the room look stylish and inviting. Joanie directed me towards an armchair she had been saving for Marilise. I settled her in and pulled myself over a chair so that I could sit with her. A couple of minutes later, Nick approached with our drinks. He gave a flute to Marilise, who was already in deep conversation with a young man who had come over, and offered me the other glass.

'Thank you,' I said, taking it. 'I must say, I'm glad I'm not wearing that Cousin Itt outfit.'

He grinned.

'Might have been a bit warm. Talking of outfits, you've done a kind thing for Astrid.' He nodded over to where she was chatting in a group of people, looking happy and animated and unusually glamorous in the shirt I had picked out earlier. 'I'm not sure how happy she is at the moment, and she never takes time for herself, always worrying about everyone else.'

'I hope she'll be all right in Texas.'

Nick frowned.

'What do you mean?'

'Sorry, I was just thinking aloud. It seems like a big move – a big change.'

'But one she's chosen to make.'

I heard a sharp edge to his voice and tried to use a soothing voice. I didn't want to aggravate my new boss.

'I've only been here a day, so it's not up to me to comment. I'm sure it will be fine.'

But Nick wouldn't let it go.

'But you have noticed something? I'd rather you just said.'

I sighed. I'm hopeless at keeping things to myself if I think I might be able to help.

'Just that I'm not sure if moving to Texas is the right thing for Astrid – or for India.'

'But she'll love the horses, that's what Astrid keeps saying.'

'Yes, but you said yourself that she's always thinking about everyone else. I get the impression that she's very much last on the list when it comes to the whole 'moving to Texas' plan. It makes things very... convenient.'

'Convenient?'

Dear me, did I have to spell it out in words of one syllable? I'd already said far too much. I sipped my champagne and said nothing, trying to pretend Nick wasn't glaring at me with distinct hostility.

'I suppose you mean convenient for me?' he snapped.

I looked up at his handsome face, surprised to find an expression of confusion, even pain, where I had been expecting to see anger. I reached out a hand to touch his sleeve, but he shook me off.

'You think it would make selling the house easier, I suppose?' I shrugged, wishing I had never got into this conversation. 'But if Astrid wasn't going to leave, I'd never sell it from underneath her,' Nick spluttered. 'Surely she knows that?'

'Look, I don't know,' I said. 'Maybe just talk to her. She loves you very much, that's clear, and she wants to try and help you be happy.'

'By freeing the way for me to sell that bloody house. Ugh, it's always been a millstone: keep it, sell it, someone misses out.'

What an unhappy man, I thought. *And what complicated feelings these piles of bricks bring out in us.* I knew I wasn't the best person to give advice on the subject, not having been able to either live in or sell the house I had known so much happiness in with Paulo. I turned to Marilise, who was now talking to Joanie, the woman who had opened the door to us earlier. I waited for a lull in their conversation, then asked if she would like something to eat, glad that the life I had chosen was, despite its paucities, one which asked few difficult questions of me.

. . .

After about an hour and a half, most of which I spent quietly sitting and watching the party with its range of revellers, including a tiny child who couldn't have been more than three and spent most of her time dancing before falling asleep on a pile of cushions, Marilise put her small hand over mine and said:

'I think I'm ready to go home now, if you are. If possible, I prefer a French exit: as quick and quiet as possible.'

I laughed.

'Is that what it's called? I like those, too. Okay, I'll go and find Nick.'

I weaved my way through the people, spotting Astrid, who was looking flushed and relaxed as she sang along to a jazzy version of 'Jingle Bells' now playing, and Angela, who was studying the beautiful Christmas tree with Greg. I found Nick in the kitchen, drinking tea and playing snakes and ladders with three tired-looking children. I paused for a moment, watching them.

'Not another snake,' said the smallest, after throwing the dice. I could hear the tears threatening as she spoke, 'I'm *never* going to get to the end.'

'Maybe it's time for a new rule,' said Nick.

'Another one?' asked one of the older children, grinning.

'Another one,' said Nick firmly. 'What do you all think? Maybe yellow snakes mean something special... I've got it! Yellow is for "hello": if you land on the head of a yellow snake, all you have to do is say "hello" in a nice, hissy voice, and you stay where you are. If you refuse to greet the snake, you have to slide down it.'

'Yes!' said the little girl, and then made her voice growly: 'Hello, Yellow Ssssssnake!' She turned to Nick. 'Was that okay?'

'Splendid,' he said solemnly. 'That means you're still in the lead, well done.'

He leant over to ruffle the older boy's hair and caught sight of me.

'Marilise is ready to go,' I said. 'Sorry to break up your game.'

'No worries,' he said. 'I was losing horribly to these three, anyway.' He turned to them with a little wave. 'See you for a rematch soon!'

SEVEN

When we got back to the house, I helped Marilise to bed, then finally headed that way myself. Sitting on my bed in my pyjamas, I lit up my phone for the first time in hours. Big mistake. I had forty-seven WhatsApps from Steph, showing increasingly horrible bridesmaids' dresses and with no apology at all for having left buying them until so late. The truth was, she had been so preoccupied with her own dress, shoes, headband, earrings, tights – well, you get the picture – that what her army of bridesmaids was going to wear had barely occurred to her, and now the choices were limited as they had to be off the peg and available in enough of a range of sizes to fit us all. And with the wedding budget nothing but a distant memory, she was trying to do the whole thing on the cheap. I zoomed in on one horror, which she had labelled 'my favourite' and tears sprang to my tired eyes. Not only must I go through a wedding at this impossibly difficult time of year, but now she was proposing that I wore a tight, beige-pink shiny satin dress with one shoulder – in December! – and a sort of frilly flounce of lavender tulle at the bottom. I would look like a cheap chocolate truffle someone had sat on. Thank goodness for Minty, who had sent a cheery text saying how glad she was to have met me and to let her know once I was settled at Lyonscroft. Meeting her had been the one saving grace of the appalling evening I had spent at my parents' house the night before I left to come here. Given how tired I was, I should have known better, but I let my thoughts drift back to that night.

As I pulled up outside, I had berated myself for my poor timing: there were several cars there already, which meant that the self-named 'Steph's Set', aka my sister's seemingly innumerable bridesmaids, most of whom I barely knew, were out in full force, and the bridal crafting party I had been hoping to avoid was still going. I had dallied with the idea of backing down the drive to make my escape, but as I threw the gear stick into reverse, the front door opened and my mother appeared.

'Laura!' she hallooed, waving frantically and spilling prosecco down her silk Boden tea dress. 'We're all still here!'

Oh good, I remember thinking, putting the car back into neutral and heaving on the handbrake with resentment. *No escape, then.* I climbed out of the car and plastered a smile on my face.

'Hello, Mum, you look lovely.'

She clashed her cheek against mine and squeezed me to her with one arm, the other stretched out to try and preserve what was left of her drink.

'All the girls are here, come and get some bubbles and join in, it's such fun.'

'I'll just grab my stuff...' I said, with the feeble hope of buying myself some time, but my mother was wise to such ruses.

'Daddy will get that for you later. Come straight through, everyone will be thrilled to see you.'

Doubtful of that, but outmanoeuvred, I let her lead me

inside and through to the dining room, where the large rose-wood table was buried in pastel tissue paper, little organza bags, tiny terracotta plant pots and lengths of ivory crochet yarn. Eight young women sat around the table chattering at the tops of their voices. I had no idea what any of them were saying, or how any of them could know, either, but it didn't seem to matter as the same words flew out over and over again:

Adorable!

So clever!

The prettiest!

I stood awkwardly for a moment until Mum's piercing tones managed to override the lot of them.

'Steph! Your sister's arrived!'

Steph's pretty, heart-shaped face, a little gaunt now thanks to her punishing pre-wedding diet, shot up from poring over what looked suspiciously like a cross stitch of two doves and a heart, and her baby blue eyes widened warily before she pasted on a gleaming – very expensive – smile and stood up.

'Laura,' she said graciously, coming over. 'How lovely to see you.' She drew me into her chilly embrace and hissed in my ear, 'If you're going to join us, no talk about your patients, okay? This is a *happy* occasion.'

I pulled away and gave a small smile, nodding as my face went hot. When Paulo died, my mother and sister were scandalised – not so much by the injustice and sadness of my young husband being snatched from me so cruelly, but by the destruction of their world view that everything – but particularly love and marriage – should be *nice* and tidy and unsullied by ugly inconveniences such as death. When I moved into companionship care nursing, they refused to talk about it, no matter how much I tried to explain that it didn't necessarily mean end-of-life care, and was an immensely rewarding, fulfilling and often joyful job.

'Why can't you be the sort of nurse who helps doctors?' my

mother had wailed, while Steph had doubled down on her efforts to snare a husband rich enough to do away with the need for her to work at all, eventually finding him in the shape of Hugo, her sweet but spineless now-fiancé.

'What would you like to do, Lor?' boomed one of the women, who I recognised as Dorothea, an old schoolfriend of Steph's, who had married Hugo's older brother and was delighted to have someone else coming into the fold who would spend her days shopping for hats and eating vast cream teas rather than doing anything as boring and pedestrian as going to work.

'Er, do?' I answered, my eyes roving over the table with increasing panic.

'Yes, *do*,' replied Dorothea. 'All the bridesmaids are making things. That's why you're here, isn't it?'

I had known, of course, about this event, but had been hoping to turn up too late, once everything was finished or everyone had consumed too much prosecco to cut in straight lines, whichever came first.

'Of course it is,' I said, forcing a smile. 'Erm, what is there?'

'You can crochet a flower hair clip, make confetti cones or start on the table decorations.'

I looked at her helplessly. I am deft with a syringe, handy with bandages, and my wound stitching is second to none, but present me with any sort of crafting and my fingers turn into sausages and I can only produce items that a five-year-old would be ashamed of.

'Maybe you'd better help me put sugared almonds into the favour bags,' piped up another woman, who was tiny, with bright blue eyes and a mass of glorious titian ringlets. She giggled. 'Ooh, sorry, we haven't met! I'm Araminta and I'm awfully tiddly after all those bubbles. I kept dropping stitches and my crochet roses looked like the greenfly had got to them, so they put me on sugared almonds, but I keep losing count.'

Steph and Dorothea tutted in unison.

'Five per bag,' said my sister, her mouth tightening. 'And a mix of colours.'

'Oops.'

Araminta grinned sheepishly at me as she emptied out three little bags, and it was at that moment I decided I liked her.

'I think that job would suit me, too,' I said, sitting down. 'And maybe you could help me catch up on the prosecco, Dorothea?'

Huffing, she went off to the kitchen.

'How did you dare?' whispered Araminta, putting four pale green sugared almonds into a bag and pulling the drawstrings. 'I'm terrified of her. More sister-in-awe than sister-in-law.'

'Well, she *is* chief bridesmaid,' I whispered back, opening the bag again, redressing the balance of colours and adding another nut. 'So, she should expect to be kept busy.'

'Don't you mind that it wasn't you who was asked to be chief bridesmaid?' asked my new friend. 'Being Steph's sister?'

I shuddered.

'Not at all. The official line is that it might be insensitive, seeing as I lost my husband, but my sister has never been sensitive about anything that didn't suit her. I think she's more worried that I might bring bad luck with my widowhood. I consider it *good* luck, in this case.'

Dorothea plonked a glass of, well, plonk down next to me on the table and returned to decorating a large blackboard with rather uneven chalk pen hearts. I took a welcome swig.

'Sorry, I didn't mean to be catty,' I said insincerely. 'Steph just wants everything to be perfect. How do you know her?'

'I don't really,' replied Araminta, eating a sugared almond absentmindedly. 'Hugo's my brother – and Giles, who married Dorothea earlier this year, is my other brother, so I wasn't given much option.'

Now, it was my turn to giggle.

'Gosh, with these two as sisters-in-law, Christmases are going to be fun.'

'It's all right, I'm going to elope with someone unsuitable and hope they disown me,' she said, grinning. 'What about you, though?'

'I always work over Christmas,' I said, and explained what I did for a living. 'In fact, I came tonight to tell them that I've got a new job, but I'd better pick my moment so I'm not accused of ruining things.'

'I shouldn't worry about that,' said Araminta airily. 'I've been blamed for that so many times that my family's almost disappointed if I don't play up. Where's the job?'

'Just up the road, a place called Lyonscroft.'

'With the Princes?'

'That's right. I'll be working with Marilise. Do you know them?'

'You bet I do – I've known them my entire life. Nick's one of my oldest friends.'

'He's her grandson, isn't he? Owns the lot?'

'That's right. His father died young and Nick inherited, not that he's interested in any of it. I'm not even sure if he's in the country at the moment; he isn't very often.'

'What are they like?'

'The ones you'll be living with are great. There's Astrid, Nick's stepmother, who spends most of her time up to her elbows in the garden, and her daughter India, who's fifteen and completely crazy about horses. Say something about fetlocks or saddle soap when you meet her, otherwise she won't even notice you've arrived. I'm not sure about her father, but she was born after Nick's father died.'

'How are you getting on with those almonds?' Dorothea's strident voice cut across what Araminta was saying, and we both jumped.

'One, two, three, four, five,' we counted loudly in unison,

while Dorothea narrowed her eyes at us and moved on to bully one of the others about her tissue paper crumpling technique.

'Go on,' I said, once she wasn't looking. 'What about the others?'

'Angela and Greg are amazing and will look after you like a daughter,' she continued. 'And Marilise is marvellous, all diamonds and furs, even if she's only going to the garden centre. I'm sorry she's not so well these days,' she said, her face clouding over. 'But I'm glad she'll have someone as nice as you to look after her.'

'Thank you,' I replied. 'I'm looking forward to meeting her. Angela said she has lots of stories.'

Araminta brightened.

'Oh, she does! She's a European princess, you know, from some teeny country on an island somewhere in the Black Sea where they abolished their royal family decades ago. She's got lots of glamorous stories about palace life before she had to move here, and plenty more from then. I'm sure you'll love her.'

I saw Dorothea advancing again and quickly snatched up a little chiffon bag and dropped in some almonds.

'What about Nick? You said you were old friends?'

'We are. There are plenty of pictures of us capering around the grounds of Lyonscroft when we were little, having a terrific time. Until that horrible father of his sent him off to board, that is, then I only saw him in the school breaks, if he was allowed to come home.'

'Allowed by the school?' I was confused, not understanding what the rules of boarding school might be.

'No, by his father. He never liked Nick much, or Victoria, his sister, for that matter.' She shrugged. 'Just wanted an heir, I think, and when that job was done, he pretty much washed his hands of the lot of them.'

'How sad.'

She nodded.

'He's nothing like his father, thankfully, but he also doesn't want anything to do with the house, which scandalises this lot.' She jerked her head to indicate the other women in the room. 'They can't think of anything nicer than inheriting a smart country pile and a London pied à terre, regardless of how much – or how little – your parents loved you. Poor Nick's a very eligible bachelor round these parts.'

'Nothing like that between you and him, then,' I asked, the prosecco and Araminta's openness making me nosier than I would usually be with a complete stranger.

She snorted.

'No,' she said firmly. 'Everyone's been trying to push us together for years, but there isn't that vibe between us, and there never will be. Anyway' – she lowered her voice – 'I'm having a terrific time playing the field. They don't approve, because they think I should be looking for a husband, so don't tell them, will you?'

I held up my little finger, and she crooked it with her own.

'Pinky promise,' I said. 'As long as you tell me more another time.'

'Will do,' she agreed, and hastily stuffed a few more bags, as my mother approached.

'Thank you for your work tonight, girls,' she said, picking up the box of completed bags and looking around for more. 'Is that it? Oh well, maybe you can finish them off tomorrow, Laura.'

I looked around the room: most people had left while Araminta and I were talking, so I gathered myself.

'Actually, Mum, I'm only staying over tonight. I've got to head to a new job tomorrow.'

'What!' she shrieked, and I pressed myself back in my chair, steeled for the inevitable fallout.

'What is it?' demanded Steph, marching over. 'Is that all you two have done of the almonds? You can finish them tomorrow, Laura.'

'She won't be doing *that*!' hissed my mother, fanning herself with a pattern for a satin ring pillow. 'She won't *be* here.'

'Won't *be* here!' parroted my sister, accepting an emergency glass of prosecco from Dorothea, who was enjoying every second. 'Of course she'll *be* here, what do you mean?'

'I won't, I'm afraid,' I cut in, knowing that this one could run and run. 'I've accepted a nursing job. I'll be nearby, though, about nine miles away, so I'll be able to do all the wedding stuff.'

'But what about *me*?' wailed Steph, snatching the pattern from Mum and handing it to Dorothea, who flapped it around the bride-to-be's rapidly reddening face. 'What about supporting *me* at the most special time in my life?'

I briefly thought of reminding her about how little she had supported me, ever, but squashed the words down.

'You'll have Dorothea for most of that,' I said calmly. 'As your chief bridesmaid. And I'll be here for the hen and the wedding itself, of course. They said it was fine for me to take the whole day.'

'And who are "they"?' demanded my mother. 'These employers who want to take you away from your family at such a special time of year and such a special occasion?'

It seemed unfair that they, rather than I, seemed to be getting the blame, but I wasn't going to argue.

'They're called the Princes,' I said. 'They live at Lyonscroft.'

'Not Princess Marie-Elise Colombo della Rovere?' gasped Dorothea, turning the makeshift fan on herself.

'That's the one,' I said cheerfully. 'Although I've been told to call her Marilise.'

'Did *you* have anything to do with this?' she said, turning on Araminta, who was making a paper aeroplane out of a page torn from a bridal magazine.

'How could I have?' she protested, launching the plane, which promptly nosedived into a bowl of dried rose petals. 'I only met Laura tonight.'

'I wouldn't put it past you,' snarled Dorothea before returning her attentions to Steph, who was pretending she was about to faint. 'Come on, darling, you've had an exhausting evening. I'll help you to bed and then I must get home to Giles.'

She shot another venomous look at Araminta who, seemingly oblivious to her ire, was picking up empty prosecco bottles to check for dregs, before Dorothea steered Steph out of the room.

'I'd better go as well,' said Araminta, giving up on the final empty bottle. 'Shall we swap numbers?'

We did so, then I waved her off in a taxi before returning reluctantly inside. As I entered the dining room, my mother, slumped in a chair, looked up at me.

'*You* speak to her, Charles.'

My poor father, dragged away from his book, looked at me sympathetically.

'What's all this about, then, Lor?' he said, absentmindedly eating a handful of sugared almonds. There wouldn't be any left for the guests at this rate.

'Nothing much,' I said, and started to tidy up the table. 'I've got a nursing job over Christmas like I always do, that's all.'

Dad looked helplessly at Mum, who tutted.

'But this Christmas isn't just Christmas, is it? It's Steph's wedding; she thought you were going to be here with her every step of the way. And so you should be. We all know that it's a difficult time of year for you, but...' Her voice began to rise. 'You're being *very selfish*.'

There it was. Out loud. What my mother and sister truly thought: that grieving for my husband, finding events such as weddings and Christmas difficult to handle, was selfish. The truth was that they branded anyone who didn't put them at the centre of everything, or who threatened to move the spotlight for even a moment, as selfish. Steph had even intimated that it was some failing on my part that Paulo had died when he did:

you're a nurse. Couldn't you at least have got him through Christmas so that it wasn't spoiled? I have been branded as selfish repeatedly throughout my life, which has shaped it. I went into nursing, one of the most selfless careers there is, to prove something, but now I was older I was beginning to realise that what I needed to be was *more* selfish, rather than less, for my own protection.

'I'm sorry that's how you feel,' I replied. 'But I did find something close to home, so I'll still be able to help.'

My father came over and put an arm around me.

'It's such a shame that Christmas is tough for you now. You loved it so much when you were a little girl.'

My eyes filled with tears and I relaxed a little, to lean against his reassuring sturdiness.

'You did,' said Mum, her voice softer. 'You were transfixed by the presents under the tree, but you didn't want to guess what they were, so you would never touch them, just stare, and then when it came to opening them, you'd do it so, so carefully.' She chuckled. 'Steph couldn't wait to rip the paper off to get at what was inside, but you'd peel the tape slowly in the hope of preserving the paper, and enjoy unwrapping gifts almost as much as finding out what they were.'

I nodded.

'I know.' My voice broke, and Dad gave me an extra squeeze. 'I'm sorry about never being here, but I'm still trying to cope.'

'We all miss Paulo,' said Dad, wiping his own eyes.

'We do,' said Mum. 'But you're such a wonderful woman, Laura, we want to see you happy. When will it be time to let him go and move on with your life? It's been three years, nearly.'

It had, but whilst other people saw three long years, they had been to me like the blink of an eye, and every time I found that I was enjoying something – particularly Christmas – the guilt at not being able to help Paulo threatened to overwhelm me and I turned to work as a salve.

'I'm happy for Steph, really I am,' I said. 'But I'm also fine with my life as it is.'

'Fear can make moving on as difficult as grief can,' said my father. 'But only you can know at what point being fine with your life isn't enough and find the courage to face it.'

I shrugged. Mostly I felt numb, and that worked for me.

'I have to leave early in the morning,' I said. 'I'll try not to wake anyone up.'

I had gone upstairs to my bedroom, where the sight of my bags on the bed, brought up unobtrusively by my kind father, threatened to push me into tears.

Now, in the beautiful bedroom at Lyonscroft, exhausted from all the events of the past twenty-four hours, which had been crowned by Steph's texts, I pulled up my knees and dropped my face against them, silent tears soaking into the duvet. I might have stayed this way until I fell asleep, had a weight not suddenly landed on the bed and the same comforting muzzle as earlier pushed its way into my hand.

'Hello, Steve,' I muttered, pulling him to me. 'I bet you wouldn't stand for any of this. Maybe you could be ring bearer in a frilly collar and take the attention from me.'

The door, which Steve had pushed to gain access, opened wider and Nick's face appeared. I gave a little yelp and scrubbed at my teary eyes. Nick flushed red and beckoned awkwardly to his dog, trying not to come any further into the room.

'Sorry about him,' he said. 'Come here, Steve.'

The dog's response to this was to collapse next to me with a loud sigh and shut his eyes.

Nick edged a little further around the door.

'Steve!' he hissed but was magnificently ignored.

'It's all right,' I said, hearing my hoarse voice and wishing he would just go. 'I don't mind if he stays.'

'Are you all right?' he asked.

I rubbed a hand over my no doubt blotchy face.

'I'm fine, just tired – it's been a long day. It's okay if he stays, if you don't mind.'

He nodded.

'Of course. He may be stubborn and wilful and get stuck in bushes every three days, but I do know...' He hesitated. 'I do know how helpful he can be. Good night, then.'

He left the room abruptly and, putting my phone to one side, the messages unanswered, I switched off the light, burrowed my fingers gratefully into Steve's soft fur, and went to sleep.

EIGHT

The next morning when I woke up, Steve had gone, and my spirits had lifted. I had slept well and now here I was at the beginning of a new job with a patient who was definitely going to be interesting, in an amazing house filled with characters. I dressed quickly and went downstairs to the kitchen where I found Angela bustling around, pots bubbling merrily on the Aga and the kettle boiling. Greg was sitting at the table, devouring a large plate of bacon and eggs.

'Good morning!' I said, and they returned the greeting.

'Now, you sit down with a cuppa,' said Angela, pouring me one. 'I'll only be a few minutes. What would you like? There's a full English, porridge, toast, cereal, yoghurt...'

'Are you sure?' I asked. 'I was expecting to get my own breakfast, and Marilise's, too.'

'I'm sure,' she said firmly. 'What people seem to expect of nurses! You're here to look after Marilise, and that means it's important to keep your own strength up and not waste it doing other people's jobs. I daresay you'll find living here will ask more of you than you expect, so don't you worry about me making you breakfast. Now, what would you like?'

I grinned at Greg, who had been making amusing faces throughout his wife's speech, and said, 'Well, in that case I'd love some porridge, thank you.'

I sat down and sipped my tea.

'There's no arguing with her,' said Greg, wiping a piece of bread around his plate and eating it with evident satisfaction. 'And she's right, anyway, of course.' He winked at Angela, who batted him with a tea towel. 'Do you normally get all the meals for your patients, then?' he asked.

'Yes,' I replied. 'And not only that. Usually, it's just me and my patient in their home, so I do everything on top of their medical and personal care: cooking, cleaning, shopping; whatever's needed. If I'm lucky, they'll have a cleaner who comes in once a week, or meals on wheels delivered, but those things are a luxury.' I smiled at their horrified faces. 'I enjoy it, I like looking after people, but I will admit that it can be very tiring. I feel very lucky to have come here this Christmas.'

'I think you're a wonderful young woman,' said Angela, pulling out a tray and putting on bowls and cutlery. 'And it's us who are the lucky ones. Now, this is all ready to go up, if you are?'

I put my half-drunk tea onto a space on the tray and picked it up, then went upstairs. There was a small table outside Marilise's room which was perfect for resting the tray on while I opened the door. She was still sleeping, so I moved about the room quietly but making enough noise to rouse her, as she had instructed me to. 'I have enough naps during the day,' she had said. 'So I like to be awake at eight to enjoy a bit of the morning.'

Sure enough, a few minutes later, she began stirring, and I went over to help her sit up.

'Good morning, Laura,' she said with her sweet smile. 'Have I slept very late? I was tired after that fabulous party last night.'

'Not at all,' I reassured her. 'You're right on time.'

After I had helped her to the bathroom, we sat either side of a polished circular table by the window to have breakfast.

'What a view,' she said, nibbling at her toast. 'I have never grown tired of it in all the years I have lived here.'

I could see why. Beyond the immaculate frosty lawns and through the morning mist you could make out undulating hills in the distance. Dozens of birds came and went to the feeders hung in the bare trees, and I could hear wood pigeons gently cooing.

'Here,' said Marilise suddenly, opening a small cabinet next to her and taking out a bag of seed. 'Open the window and put this on the sill; sometimes, I get a little visitor.'

I did as she had instructed and, sure enough, a few moments later, a little robin appeared. He pecked at the seed, then looked straight at us, his head on one side, as he ate.

'Isn't he sweet!' I said. 'The gardener's friend, isn't that what people call them?'

'My friends, too,' said Marilise. 'We saw so many of them at the palace when I was young, we used to tame them so they would come and sit on our hands to take treats. One year my dear father took photographs of all us children with them perched on our fingers. He may have been an important man with all the jewels and luxuries imaginable, but he loved a simple robin, and a child's joy in it.'

'Christmases there must have been incredible,' I said, trying to imagine the bygone days of a sumptuous palace and a royal family now destroyed, its members dispersed around the world.

'Oh, they were! It always snowed at that time of year, and we drove our nursemaids crazy by spending hours playing in it, then crying because we were so cold and wet. They would bring us inside and change us into dry clothes, scolding us for our folly, and then we would sit by the fire and our parents would come, bringing sweets and little pastries that cheered us up and made us want to go and play in the snow again.'

I laughed.

'I guess children are the same no matter what!'

'Exactly, although we of course had the luxury to be naughtier than many.' Her face grew solemn. 'We did not have to work from a young age, help put food on the table, or worry about losing our home. Or so we thought. It was a blessed time.'

'How old were you when you had to leave?' I asked.

'Seventeen,' she replied. 'One night my mother shook me awake, told me to put on as many clothes as possible, with my jewels stuffed into my underwear. I was allowed one suitcase, and I remember the feeling of panic, not because I feared what might happen to my family – I was too ignorant and protected for that – but because I could not take all my belongings with me.'

'How awful,' I said, tears coming to my eyes as I imagined the horror of their nighttime flit.

'Yes, but we were so lucky, so lucky to be able to come to England and continue a very spoilt life, even if it was not the same. We lived at the Ritz for two years, the Ritz! We do not deserve sympathy. Many people are displaced and do not have the comforts that we took for granted. Anyway, I prefer to remember the happy parts of my life, and Christmas is among those.'

'Well, I'm very glad to be spending this Christmas with you,' I said. 'And I'm sure that even if we can't replicate the Christmases of your childhood, we can still make it a very happy one.'

'Not if Nick's got anything to do with it,' said a cheeky voice from the doorway. It was India. 'Mind if I join you?' She lifted up a bowl. 'I had a glorious ride this morning on Firefly and everyone else has finished breakfast.'

I pulled another chair over to the table and she sat down.

'So, how are we going to persuade Nick to get this house

looking more festive?' she asked, gobbling down porridge. 'I don't think there are any decorations here at all.'

'I did have an idea,' I said slowly. 'I don't think it will take too much in the way of actual decorations, mostly paper and paint and some imagination.'

'I'm sure we can supply those,' said Marilise. 'What is your idea?'

'Well, I was thinking about Sofia arriving later today, and worried that she will already be feeling upset. It would be nice to have something to welcome her. I know it's not December yet, but I thought we could do a sort of Christmas countdown, using the house – make it into a giant advent calendar.'

'That sounds brilliant,' said India. 'How are we going to do it?'

I smiled at the 'we'.

'I don't think we can have it all ready in one go, but I thought to get started we could put today's date in one of the windows. She would have to go and find that window from inside the house and there will be some sort of Christmassy surprise there to welcome her. Then maybe we could all take turns doing different windows for different people.'

Marilise clapped her hands with joy, and I could see the carefree little princess still within her.

'This is beautiful, Laura! I will enjoy thinking of ideas, so much.'

'It's a great idea,' said India, nodding. 'Let's tell the others about it at lunchtime.'

'Do you think Nick will mind?' I asked. 'He did specifically say that he doesn't want to be involved in decorating the house.'

'Well, he won't *have* to mind,' said India. 'It's a super idea, and he doesn't have to join in if he doesn't want to, he can ignore the whole thing. It's not like we're stringing tinsel up all over the place.'

Right on cue, we glanced at a movement outside in the

garden and saw Nick striding across the lawn, Steve gambolling around him.

'I worry about my grandson,' said Marilise with a sigh. 'He is lonely, anyone can see that, but he pushes everyone away, even his family, who care so much for him.'

'He is lonely,' agreed India. 'But he brings it on himself, always rushing off around the world and refusing to put down any roots. Everyone's always trying to set him up with women, but he won't have it, at least...'

She stopped suddenly and we both looked at her.

'At least, what?' asked Marilise. 'You can speak plainly here.'

I nodded, curious as to what her thoughts were.

'I was going to say, "at least not for more than a night", but that's a bit gossipy of me.'

Marilise shrugged.

'Maybe, but I think it is true, and it makes me very sad. He is such a warm-hearted man – he would make a perfect husband and father – but he runs from it all.'

'Maybe he's happy that way,' I ventured. 'My family think it's wrong of me to move from job to job and refuse to contemplate marriage again, but I like my life.'

Marilise and India both stared at me, identical sceptical expressions on their faces, but didn't comment. Instead, India said:

'You know, you should go to that concert with him. You can be a sort of bodyguard and I'm sure Minty would be glad, too. It would get her family off her back.'

I raised my eyebrows and was glad not to have to reply when a knock came at the door and it was pushed open.

'Is it all right to come in?' asked the doctor.

'Perfect timing,' I said, standing up. 'We've just finished breakfast.' I turned to Marilise. 'I'll see you for our swim at eleven, then? I might get started on that advent calendar.'

'Marvellous,' she replied. 'I'll see you then and we can continue plotting to get some Christmas cheer into this house.'

As I carried the tray downstairs to the kitchen, I reflected on the irony that it was I, who had avoided Christmas for three years now, who was the one bringing it to Lyonscroft.

I sorted out the breakfast things and drove into Taunton where I knew there to be the most beautiful toy shop. I could have stayed for hours but restrained myself to buying just one furry friend for the first day's advent calendar. I didn't know Sofia, of course, but the lady in the shop agreed with me that it was a toy any eight-year-old girl would love. Goodness knows I'm nearly thirty years older and I was tempted myself. I returned to the house a little later than I had aimed to, so was relieved to be greeted by India, whose imagination had clearly been caught by the whole 'advent calendar' idea.

'I know you have to take Marilise swimming, but come and see what I've done.'

She led me into a room I hadn't seen before, a light, bright sitting room with peach walls, a rust-coloured carpet and a soft grey sofa and armchairs. A table stood under the window, and she led me to it to show me a large sheet of paper with a beautifully painted '1', decorated with festive flourishes of bright green holly leaves with red berries.

'I thought we could go up from one, rather than put the dates, that way it won't matter if we miss a few.'

'It's perfect,' I said. 'You understood what I meant, and I agree about the numbering. Look what I've bought Sofia as the first present – do you think she'll like it?'

I opened the bag to show her.

'Aw, it's adorable! I'll have it if she doesn't want it!'

I laughed.

'Well, you'll be behind me! Right, I'd better go and put this away; I'll wrap it later. Do you want to pick the first window? You know the house much better than I do.'

She agreed and I ran upstairs to find my swimming costume and collect Marilise.

Our swim was delightful. The pool was beautifully warm and, as well as helping her with the exercises she had been given by her physiotherapist, I sat and allowed the fountain to cascade over my shoulders as Marilise paddled about on her own. When I could see her starting to tire, I suggested going into the steam room for a few minutes and then, after a cooling shower, we went to lunch.

'How was your swim this morning?' asked Angela as we sat down.

'Very good,' replied Marilise. 'Although Laura here is a harder taskmaster than you when it comes to my exercises.'

'Which is exactly why we need her!' replied Angela. 'Somebody needs to be strict with you.'

The light-hearted conversation continued until the subject came around to the charity concert.

'Bridget Montgomery rang earlier,' said Astrid. 'She pretended to be interested in a recipe I told her about not long ago, but she wanted to know if you were going to that concert, Nick.'

He groaned.

'The formal invitation only came yesterday – give me a break.'

'You might as well accept,' said India. 'You know you're going to in the end. But I had a brilliant idea yesterday!'

I looked over at her sharply. Surely she wasn't going to...

'I think that you should take Laura with you as your plus one,' she continued. 'It might put Mrs Montgomery off the matchmaking, for a while at least, and Minty would be pleased.' She turned to me. 'You know her, don't you?'

I nodded.

'Yes, she's one of my sister's bridesmaids, about as eager for the job as I am, but it's her brother she's marrying.'

'Your sister's marrying Hugo?' asked Nick.

'That's right,' I said. 'Have you been invited to the wedding?'

'No,' he replied. 'Minty and I were great friends, but I never really... *gelled* with her brothers.'

'I don't blame you,' I said indiscreetly. 'Hugo's nice enough but so proper and old-fashioned in his outlook. He pities me more because I have a career than because I'm a widow. I haven't met Giles, the eldest brother, but he's married to Steph's best friend, Dorothea.'

'Whether he wants to be or not,' said Nick. 'She's a very determined woman, by all accounts. Now, we're all taking bets on how long it will be before she turfs out the Montgomerys senior and has the run of that amazing house.' I giggled. It was kind of malicious of us to talk like this, but a relief to find out I had allies. 'And I think India might be onto something,' he continued. 'If you can be spared, and if you could bear an evening at the Montgomerys—'

'Which will actually be fun,' interrupted Astrid. 'They've got some super musicians coming and they're excellent hosts, never stint on the food and wine.'

'Maybe I will go instead,' said Marilise, her eyes twinkling, and everyone laughed.

'I'd be honoured to have you on my arm,' said Nick. 'But I don't think you'd be a very good decoy in these particular circumstances.'

'No, no,' she replied, smiling. 'You take young Laura, we can spare her for one evening, can't we, Angela?'

'Absolutely,' said Angela warmly. 'You and I can catch up

on that gin rummy tournament, although I'm losing so badly, I'm not sure there's much point.'

'Looks like a done deal,' said India, smirking.

I hesitated.

'Well, I suppose I could, but it sounds very smart. I'm not sure I have the right clothes.'

'Now, now, none of that,' said Marilise. 'I have wardrobes full of frocks that never get worn, we can find something for you. I will gladly lend it if, in exchange, you will promise to tell me all about the evening. It would be too much for me, but I would love to hear who was there, what they wore, what music was played.'

I looked around the table. Although I was unsure about spending the evening with Nick, I had to admit that it *did* sound like fun – something that had been lacking in my life for a long time.

'Okay, I'll come,' I said, and was met with a ripple of approval. 'Maybe you should come as my plus one to Steph and Hugo's wedding, in return.'

I was only joking, but Nick stuck his hand over the table for me to shake.

'Done!' he said. 'One good turn deserves another. Now, we'd better make sure we swap notes so we make a convincing couple.'

I couldn't think of a *less* convincing couple: the handsome tech whiz with his royal blood and playboy lifestyle going out with a boring nurse who had one foot in the past and whose idea of excitement was discovering a new bedpan disinfectant. But I nodded and smiled; after all, if I could be helpful, then I would be.

'What time does Sofia arrive?' I asked, changing the subject.

'Around three,' replied Astrid, the familiar look of worry suffusing her face. 'Greg's picking her up at the airport. Oh dear, I do hope she'll be all right here.'

'Airport?' I asked, confused. 'Isn't her mum dropping her off?'

'Oh no,' replied Astrid. 'They've been for a very quick visit to Switzerland from the USA – where they live, you know – and they've put poor Sofia on a flight here while they head to the Caribbean.'

'Are you allowed to do that?'

'Apparently so.' Astrid pursed her lips, her disapproval evident. 'You pay for an "Unaccompanied Minors" service, then wave them off. Poor child, I hope she's not too overwhelmed when she finally arrives.'

'Oh! We haven't told you about Laura's idea,' said India, then quickly outlined our plan for turning the house into an advent calendar. 'Marilise is in on it as well, but we were hoping everyone might like to do a day or two.'

Amongst the excited agreement from Astrid, Angela and Greg, I sneaked a glance at Nick. The expression on his face was completely neutral, and I was glad that at least he didn't seem annoyed. Suddenly, his eyes flicked towards me, and I flushed and looked away, caught in the act of staring.

'I think it's a great idea,' he said, and when I glanced up, I saw that he was still looking directly at me. 'Looks like we've been sent a Christmas angel this year.'

The heat rose again in my face; I couldn't tell whether he was being sarcastic or serious.

'I agree,' said Marilise, putting her hand over mine and smiling. I smiled back, gratefully. 'I think that Laura is exactly what we all need at Lyonscroft.'

NINE

We were all waiting for Sofia when she arrived from the airport with Greg. We didn't want to overwhelm her, so only Astrid went out to greet her, then brought her through to the cosy living room where India had painted the advent calendar number. As soon as she was ushered gently through the door by Astrid, my heart went out to her. Slender and pale, with smudges under her eyes, she had the same thick chestnut hair as her uncle, but her eyes showed none of his brittle confidence, just terror. Angela, doubtless feeling the same as me, immediately rushed forward.

'Come and sit down, duck, and I'll make you some hot chocolate. You must be exhausted after that flight and it's getting so cold now. I make it for your great-grandmother all the time, so I'm something of an expert.'

'That is very true,' said Marilise. 'I like mine with plenty of sugar, maybe you do, too?'

Sofia allowed herself to be sat down in a chair and managed a whispered 'thank you' when Angela put the mug in front of her.

'Do you like horses?' asked India, receiving a tiny nod in

response. 'Oh good, I'll take you to meet Firefly – that's my horse – later today or tomorrow. You'll love him and he'll love you, especially if you give him a carrot.'

'I like dogs, too,' said the little girl, glancing over at Steve, who was in his customary position beside the Aga. I watched as Nick's face lit up. I was impressed when he spoke gently.

'Well, that's Steve, my dog, and when he's not snoring in front of the stove, he's great fun. Do you remember meeting him when you came here before?'

'I think so,' said Sofia. 'He stole Mummy's glove, and she was cross.'

Nick roared with laughter.

'I'd forgotten that! Yes, my dear sister was deeply unimpressed. Steve thought she'd brought him a new toy. I've got to think of some things to put in his stocking for Christmas, so maybe you can help me?'

She nodded and a smile crept onto her face.

'I'd like that.'

Seeing that she had already finished her hot chocolate, I took my turn in making her feel at home.

'Hi, Sofia, it's lovely to meet you. I'm Laura and I'm here to help Marilise. I've only been here for a day, so I'm still finding out where everything is. Maybe you and I can help each other settle in a bit?'

She turned her huge, frightened eyes towards me and again I saw that glimmer of a smile.

'I'd like that. I know where the swimming pool is, but Mummy wouldn't let me go in when we were here before.'

'Well, this time you must,' said Marilise. 'I swim with Laura every single morning, and we would love you to join us.'

'We would,' I said. 'I'll make sure I call you tomorrow. But for now, we've prepared a little welcome surprise for you.' I threw a questioning glance at India, who gave me a thumbs up. I continued. 'We decided it would be fun for all of us to have an advent calendar, one that we can start today, even though it's not December yet. And we would like you to discover what's behind the first window.'

She looked around and frowned, for a moment seeming to forget her fear and exhaustion.

'Where is it?'

'Ah, well, that's the clever part. You're in it.'

'In it?'

'That's right. This Christmas we are going to make the whole of Lyonscroft into one great big advent calendar, with surprises for everyone behind the doors and windows. All you have to do today is find the number one.'

India stood up and reached for Sofia's hand, then led her outside with me and Nick following. We all looked at the elegant front of the house, with several of its windows lit up, our eyes scanning for the poster.

'There it is!' shouted Sofia, her voice now full of excitement. She pointed to an upstairs window.

'Well done,' said India. 'Now, you have to find the right room.'

The two girls ran back inside, with Nick and I jogging after them, up the stairs and round to the right, where Sofia's surprise was waiting for her in her new bedroom. Once inside the pretty room, she ran straight to the window and let out a little squeak when she saw the wrapped present there. She reached for it, then drew her arm back.

'Can I open it?' she asked. 'Or do I have to wait for Christmas?'

'You don't have to wait,' I said. 'This is a welcome present for you.'

She picked it up and carefully pulled open the paper. When it revealed the adorable stuffed reindeer, which was wearing a little red fluffy coat, she squealed with delight and hugged it to her.

'*Thank* you!' she said, holding it away to get a good look, then cuddling it again. 'I love him.'

'What do you think you'll call him?' asked Nick.

I looked over at him and, although he was smiling, his eyes held a strange expression. If I'd been pushed to name it, I might have said pensive, or even gone so far as sorrowful.

'His name is Reddo,' she said. 'Because of his red coat.'

'Good idea,' said India. 'Do you want to come to the stables now? We've got plenty of time.'

'Yes, please,' said Sofia. 'Can Reddo come, too?'

'Of course,' said India, and they walked to the door. Suddenly, Sofia stopped and pointed to her suitcases.

'Those are mine. Is this my room?'

'That's right,' I said. 'Do you like it?'

Astrid had been busy since we made up the bed, and now as well as a beautiful arrangement of winter greenery on the dresser, she had added a small pile of books on one bedside table and a stack of notebooks next to a large pot of different pens and pencils on the other.

'I love it,' said Sofia, reaching her hand out to touch the pretty duvet cover. 'Mummy doesn't have any colours in the house, other than boring grey and beige and white, even in my room. This room is just the sort of room I want.'

'Well, it's yours for all of Christmas,' said Nick, and I could hear the emotion in his voice. 'And whenever you want to come and visit again.'

The little girl's face lit up and she hugged Reddo tightly.

'Thank you.'

'Come on,' said India. 'Firefly will be wondering where we are, and we have to get a carrot from the kitchen on the way.'

The two girls ran out, leaving Nick and me standing in the bedroom.

'Poor little kid,' he said. 'I think she's more of a nuisance to Victoria than anything, messes up her perfect life and colour scheme. I do *not* understand,' he added fiercely, 'why people insist on having children they don't want.'

For a moment, I saw the sad little boy whose only function in life had been to inherit, rather than having been born to be loved and nurtured and enjoyed. I spoke carefully.

'Maybe people don't always realise what the reality of having a baby is, and that the baby will grow up.'

'Or all they want is for the baby to grow up and stop being a bother.'

I had an inexplicable urge to reach out to this man, to hold him and tell him until he understood it that he was loved, very much so, by the people who lived in this house. All he had to do was accept that love. But instead, I made a noncommittal noise and said, 'I think Sofia feels happy here already. There's not much you can do about her home life, but you can show her that she's welcomed and wanted at Lyonscroft.'

He looked at me sharply, then turned away to look out of the window, wrapping his arms tightly around himself. When he spoke, his voice shook with emotion.

'And then she'll leave, like everyone else. So, what's the point?'

He was asking the wrong person. Hadn't I decided, too, that the pain of loss outweighed the joy of love and that I was safer alone?

'I don't completely know,' I said slowly, and he turned to look at me again, his face anxious. 'But part of it is in the happiness you can bring someone else, as much as get for yourself, and in knowing that people carry that with them, even if you're not there to see it.'

'So, you're saying I'm selfish?'

Maybe a touch self-absorbed, I thought, but I wasn't going to say that after two days in this man's employment.

'I didn't mean that,' I replied. 'Just trying to help. Anyway, I'd better go and find Marilise.'

For a second, I could have sworn that he pouted, then the smooth, bland expression I had seen before wiped all emotion from his face.

'See you later.'

I ran back downstairs, knowing Marilise was looking forward to hearing all about Sofia's reaction to the present, and determined to push thoughts of the guarded, wounded Nick from my mind.

The next day, when it was time to take Marilise for a swim, I called Sofia as I had promised. As the three of us splashed about, she chatted about Reddo and Steve and Firefly, and I was glad to see her so much happier already.

'I like swimming, too,' she said. 'But not on my back. I won't be able to come with you again until the weekend, though, because I've got to go to school tomorrow.'

'Why aren't you there today?' I asked, having completely forgotten about the arrangement.

'They thought I needed a day to get over the jetlag,' she replied, then she lowered her voice conspiratorially. 'I don't, I feel fine, but I didn't say.' Her eyes darted between me and Marilise and a note of worry entered her voice. 'You won't, will you? Say anything?'

'Of course not!' said Marilise. 'I think it is sensible, anyway, to have one full day to settle in, do you not agree, Laura?'

I nodded solemnly.

'I certainly do. No need to rush these things.'

I was about to ask her who she thought we should do the second advent calendar window for, when, before I could properly understand what was happening, Steve dashed into the room barking madly and hurled himself gleefully into the water. All three of us screamed. Sofia, near the side, clutched onto it, and I went straight over to Marilise. Steve doggy paddled around, his tongue lolling out of the side of his mouth and giving him the most comical expression of delight. Confident that Marilise was all right, I started wading over to the dog, who was having none of it.

'Come *here*!' I said, trying to grab his collar, but he swam away, far more agile in the water than me. If he had been a person, he would have been screaming with laughter. I turned to Marilise and Sofia in despair, half laughing myself, when Nick came striding into the room.

'Steve!' he bellowed.

Steve took no notice and swam around in a little circle, looking pleased with himself.

'For God's sake,' muttered Nick, taking off his shoes and socks and rolling his jeans up. He stepped onto the first shallow step behind the fountain. 'Steve, come here!' Nothing. 'Laura, would you mind getting around behind him and sort of shooing him towards me?'

He darted a look of frustration towards Marilise and Sofia, who were now clutching each other and giggling. Stifling a smile myself, I swam around behind the dog and started half flapping, half splashing him. He looked balefully at me, then Nick, but did start to head towards his master. When he got there, he scrambled up the steps, evaded Nick's grasping hand and shook himself vigorously. By now all three of us in the water were in stitches, and the more furious poor Nick looked, the funnier the whole thing seemed. Eventually, he managed to grab Steve's collar. He stood there, barefoot, his shirt covered in splashed water and his jeans soaking. He looked from Steve to us and back to his dog again and I was worried that we were all in for a telling-off. But suddenly, unexpectedly, the thunderclouds rolled back and he, too, grinned, then started laughing.

'This stupid dog!' he howled. 'Every day there's something, it's ridiculous. Well, I'm glad you three have enjoyed the show – I'm off to find a towel and ring the pound.'

He went off, still smiling and shaking his head, unable to be properly cross with any of us, let alone his precious dog.

'Come on,' I said. 'I think we'd better get out and dressed, it's nearly lunchtime.'

'He won't really send Steve to the pound, will he?' asked Sofia, her little brow wrinkling.

I grabbed a towel and wrapped it round her, giving her a hug at the same time.

'Of course not, he was only joking. Anyone can see he adores that dog and it's about the only thing he trusts; it's rather touching.'

'I see you have the measure of my grandson,' said Marilise. 'He trusts that the dog loves him back, unconditionally, and that is where we see the true Nikolai.' She sighed sadly. 'If only he could feel that from us.' But then her expression lightened in the way I had seen Nick's do, a wicked glint coming into her eye. 'Maybe we should try getting stuck in bushes or falling asleep in front of the Aga every five minutes.'

This made Sofia laugh, and we headed upstairs to get dressed, discussing the different ways we could 'be more Steve'.

After lunch, while Marilise was having her afternoon nap, I was writing up my notes when my phone rang: Steph. I was tempted not to answer, but that always makes me more nervous than just getting it over with, and I knew that if she had something to say or ask, then she wouldn't give up because of one dropped call.

'Hi, Steph.'

'Ah, hello, Laura. How's life at Lyonscroft?'

My mind roamed over the last few days.

'Busier than I had expected, but good. How are the wedding preparations coming on?'

'Yes, I wanted to talk to you about that.' *I thought you might.*

'You didn't get back to me about bridesmaids' dresses, so we've made a decision and they're all ordered. We went for the peach satin in the end.' *Of course you did.* 'Now, I wanted to talk to you about the hen night. Dorothea said she'd emailed you all the details, but you haven't transferred the money yet, so I'm chasing.'

'Sorry, yes, it's been hectic here. I'll make sure I do it later.'

'Please do. Now, there's something else I've been thinking about.'

'Yes?'

'As soon as Hugo and I have tied the knot, we're going to get pregnant.'

'Are you?'

The words popped out of my mouth before I could stop them, but thank goodness I managed not to add anything else, such as 'how?' or 'are you sure?' Her breathtaking self-confidence would sweep away all doubt; the thought of any kind of fertility struggle wouldn't be allowed to take up residence in her head, and while I truly hoped it would happen as instantly as she seemed to have planned, I had painful memories of my own inability to get pregnant, and the monthly disappointment and two early miscarriages Paulo and I had suffered.

'Of course. Statistically there's an eighty-five per cent chance of us being successful within the first year, but I'm sure it won't take that long.'

'Right, great.'

'Anyway,' she bulldozed on. 'I've had an excellent idea. I think that you should retrain as a maternity nurse.'

'Excuse me?'

'And then when Baby comes, you can come and live in and help look after both of us. You're not going to have children any time soon – if ever – yourself, are you? So, it's a perfect solution.'

Tears filled my eyes and started splashing down my face. I clasped my hand to my mouth and held the phone away while I gasped with the effort not to let her hear me cry and tried to gain some sort of composure. *A perfect solution?* What, that she had a servant on hand and that I would be lucky enough to pick up the crumbs from her table? As if looking after someone else's baby would be compensation for everything I had lost? I wanted to scream this at her down the phone, try to penetrate that rhinoceros hide of hers to elicit some shred of sensitivity; she *knew* what I'd been through. What she didn't know was that, despite my chosen life, now and then I ventured onto a bridal website – and not to look at the bridesmaids' dresses. Or that I gazed at babies when I was out and about, the longing to have my own child so powerful that it sometimes exhausted me. But I couldn't say any of this to Steph. I knew what would happen if I did, and it wasn't worth it. First, she would laugh disbelievingly. Next, tell me I'd brought things on myself. I'd be accused of attention seeking and, ironically, selfishness. Then she'd get my mother involved to say it all again, until I was so worn down that I agreed I was a terrible person and was, in fact, grateful to them for their intervention. I have ways of dealing with my family, but direct confrontation was pointless. I could hear Steph squawking away on the end of the phone, so I took a deep, juddery breath and brought it up to my face again.

'Sorry,' I said blandly. 'Dropped the phone.'

'I see. Well, I've got to get on. I'll leave you to look up the courses, shall I?'

'I'll have a think. Bye, Steph.'

I threw the device down on the table and rolled my eyes. Why, *why* couldn't I stand up to her? I was so confident and capable in my job and my everyday life, but when it came to family, I was – there were no two ways about it – scared. Become a maternity nurse. Well, that was not a career path that had ever crossed my mind. I had wondered from time to time about changing direction jobwise, but whenever I started to look into it, I felt as though I was betraying Paulo's memory and cutting the final link I had with him. Which was, of course, what my family wanted me to do. In their own clumsy, but well-meaning, way they thought it would be better for me to do something else, which was doubtless part of the conversation when they came up with this latest scheme. *Let's help Laura to help herself.* Pushing the phone call out of my head, I returned to my paperwork, finding comfort there.

TEN

When I had finished, I went downstairs to make a quick cup of tea before it was time to wake Marilise. I found Sofia in the kitchen alone, reading.

'Hi there,' I said. 'Are you okay in here on your own? I've come to make a drink. Can I get you anything?'

She looked up; her eyes were red. My stomach clenched in sympathy, and I went to sit beside her, putting a hand on the back of her chair. To me, she looked like a child in need of a hug, but I didn't want to make her feel uncomfortable by gathering her up the way I wanted to. Sofia, however, had no such reservations. She immediately slid her arms around my waist and pressed her face into my shoulder and, as I wrapped my arms around her and muttered soothing words, I could feel her sobbing. After a few minutes, she pulled away and drew the back of her hand across her face. I dug in my pocket for a tissue and handed it to her.

'Oh, sweetheart,' I said. 'I'm sorry you feel so wretched. Are you missing home?'

She nodded and gulped, then said, 'Sort of, yes, and I miss Mummy, and I'm scared about starting school tomorrow.'

'I would be, too,' I said, and she looked surprised.

'Really? Mummy said it was silly because it was just school, and I've been to school before.'

Raising an internal eyebrow at Mummy's rather harsh take on the matter, I considered my next words carefully.

'Well, people feel differently about these things. But I felt scared coming here, even though my whole job is about going to new houses and meeting new people. I'd never been to *this* house, or met *these* people, so of course I was worried.'

'But are you happy now?'

'Very,' I said firmly, if not a hundred per cent truthfully. 'I'm much more comfortable now I'm getting used to it, and everyone has been very kind and welcoming. I'm sure school will be the same, and you know that India isn't far away. Maybe she'll even be able to check in on you during the day.'

I made a mental note to mention it to India, having no idea of how the school was laid out, or what their rules were about senior girls visiting younger ones.

'I hope so,' said Sofia, giving me a wan smile. 'I like India. And Firefly.'

'I'm going upstairs now to see Marilise,' I said. 'She often likes to play a game around this time. Would you like to join in?'

'Yes, please!' said the little girl, a real smile now coming to her face. 'Do you think Marilise would like some of those ginger snaps we had yesterday?'

'I think that's an excellent idea.'

A few minutes later, we were going quietly into the bedroom and, before long, all sitting around the table in the window munching ginger snaps and playing Snakes and Ladders.

'Do you like the ginger snaps?' asked Sofia, nibbling what must have been her fifth. I wondered what her mother would think about this intake, but she seemed to have sent little in the way of instructions for her daughter's care, so either she assumed we knew what we were doing, or she wasn't bothered. Either way, unlimited sweets seemed like the way forward for the time being.

'I like them very much,' said Marilise, then groaned as she landed on a long snake and had to go back about thirty spaces. 'But at this time of year what I used to love to do was bake Linzer cookies with my sister. Of course, the recipe was Austrian, not local to us, but we loved them so much. We would eat almost as much jam as we put in.'

She gazed out of the window, and I thought she looked rather tired. Turning to Sofia, I said, 'Would you pop over to my room quickly? I left my thermometer on the dressing table.'

When she had left the room, I asked Marilise how she was feeling.

'Tired,' she said. 'I do not like to admit it, but your nurse's eyes see it, so what is the point in pretending?'

Sofia came back with the thermometer and sat quietly looking out of the window while I did some basic checks.

'I don't think it's anything that an early night won't solve,' I said, and Marilise chuckled.

'You think an early night will solve the fact that I am nearly ninety years old?'

I grinned.

'Well, maybe not, but I think you'll feel – ooh – at least eighty-five in the morning.'

'Eighty-five! I'll take that.'

'Good. I think you should have your supper up here; I can join you.'

She hesitated.

'Yes, yes, you could, but I wonder if you would mind seeing if Angela is able to come up for a little while if I eat now? I know she is so busy, but I miss her.'

'Of course,' I said, secretly pleased, because it meant that I would be able to put a plan of my own into action. 'I'll go and find her. Come with me, Sofia, I need your help with something.'

A few minutes later, Angela was on her way upstairs with a tray of morsels she thought might tempt Marilise, and I turned to Sofia.

'Right, miss, we have a job to do!'

'What is it?'

I took out my phone and tapped away, then turned the screen towards her.

'This is a recipe for the cookies Marilise said she liked to make as a girl. We need to see if we can find the ingredients and get baking – I think she should get tomorrow's advent calendar surprise.'

Gleefully, Sofia began hunting through the cupboards for the ingredients, which were mostly pretty simple. After ten minutes, we had amassed everything we would need and were feeling very pleased with ourselves. My phone started running out of battery, so I ran out to the hall, where I had left a charger in my bag. I was heading back with it when Nick came down the stairs.

'Hello,' he said. 'What are you up to?'

I explained quickly and he smiled.

'Sounds like a good idea.'

'You could join us, Uncle Nick,' said an eager little voice, and I turned to see Sofia, who had followed me out to the hall.

'Oh no, I don't think so,' he replied. 'I'm sure I wouldn't be any good at it.'

'Okay,' said Sofia dully and, taking the charger out of my hand, returned to the kitchen. I frowned.

'Is there a problem?' said Nick, arching an eyebrow at me.

I knew I shouldn't overstep, that it was in no way appropriate for me to challenge him, but maybe it was my irritation at having been unable to stand up to my sister earlier that compelled me to speak. Even so, I spoke more sharply than I had intended.

'That little girl wants to spend some time with you, and I'm surprised you don't have more empathy for her.'

'Empathy?' he asked, an edge to his voice.

'Yes. You say that you weren't wanted here; well, how do you think you're making Sofia feel? Her mother has already abandoned her over Christmas, and she needs to feel that her uncle is happy to have her here.'

'Everybody else is doing a good job as far as I can see,' he replied rather sulkily. 'Sofia will be leaving again in a couple of weeks, so I don't see the point of playing happy families.'

'So, you're going to let the hired nurse, an old lady and a fifteen-year-old girl do all the heavy lifting?'

'There's Astrid, don't forget, and Angela and Greg. More than enough people.'

'Well, I would bet that the one person she needs to care about her this Christmas is *you*, her nearest blood relative. Her mum's brother. But I'm sure you know best,' I added tartly, and turned on my heel to walk back to the kitchen. By the time I got there, I was mortified. What on earth had come over me to make me speak to him like that?

'Are you okay?' asked Sofia, her face looking worried and drawn again.

'I'm fine,' I said. 'Let's get on with the baking.'

As we tipped the butter into the scales, the door opened, and Steve came in.

'Hello,' I said. 'Your master's not here, I'm afraid.'

'Yes, I am,' said a voice, and in came Nick. He avoided my eye and looked at Sofia. 'Sorry, of course I want to help. Now, what can I do?'

The smile that spread over Sofia's face was like the sun coming out.

'We have to cream the butter and sugar first – can you do that?'

'I have no idea,' said Nick. 'But I can give it a try.'

A most unexpected scene of domestic harmony then ensued as we combined the ingredients for the dough, giggling as we tried to work out how much an eighth of a teaspoon of ground cloves was, then deciding it probably didn't matter too much. When the time came to roll and cut the dough, I picked up my phone.

'Come on, we need a Christmas playlist, it can only make these cookies taste better.'

I searched for the cheesiest mix I could find, and soon we were stamping the Linzer out in time to 'Wonderful Christmastime'.

'What's your favourite Christmas song?' asked Sofia. 'I like "Holly Jolly Christmas" best.'

'Mine's easy,' said Nick. 'It's "Little Saint Nick", of course. I do like having a song that reminds everyone how saintly I am.'

He put his hands under his chin and fluttered his eyelashes, making Sofia squeal with laughter.

'It's almost impossible for me to decide,' I said with an exaggerated sigh. 'I love them all.' It was true, I did, and this was the first time in three years that I had voluntarily put on Christmas music.

'Well, you have to,' said Nick in a mock stern voice, pretending to threaten me with a wooden spoon. 'It's the Christmas law, right, Sofia?'

'Right,' she said, and put her hands on her hips. 'Come on, pick a favourite.'

I paused. My first instinct was to say whatever came into my head, but it didn't feel right to be untruthful. Sofia, just eight years old, had been so brave about coming here over Christmas and Nick, I knew, had been brave in a different way to come to the kitchen after my telling-off and join in wholeheartedly. It was my turn to be brave.

'It's always been "Sleigh Ride",' I said. 'My husband rigged something up one year so that it played every time I came into the house, and I never got sick of it.'

'Where is your husband?' asked Sofia. 'Aren't you spending Christmas with him?'

'No,' I said, keeping my voice steady. 'Sadly, he was very ill and died a few years ago. But there are lots of nice things that help me remember him in a happy way, and "Sleigh Ride" is one of them.'

This was, of course, untrue. I had done everything I could to avoid any memories of Paulo, happy or unhappy, but as I touched my necklace, an image of him laughing at my delighted surprise the first time I walked through the door and set that song off appeared in my mind. Maybe it was time to let the memories, good and bad, surface.

'Shall we put it on?' asked Sofia. I glanced at Nick, who had nothing but sympathy in his face, then grinned.

'Yes, let's, and then we'd better get these cookies in the oven before Angela comes down and needs the kitchen. I think we'd better do the jam in the morning, when they're completely cool – if we can all make it down a little early?'

They agreed, and we put the cookies in to bake, then I said, 'Go on, you two, you've done enough for one day. I'll do this bit of washing up and see you for supper soon.'

Sofia ran out, happily shouting that she was going to go and see Firefly and India, but Nick sat down at the table.

'You were right,' he said, running his finger through a scattering of flour. 'All I could think about was not getting too friendly with Sofia because she'd be going home before too long. I'm glad I joined you.'

'So am I,' I said. 'I guess we all have feelings we'd rather avoid, but maybe facing up to them is better in the long run.'

He stood up then, looked at me for a long time, then gave a brisk nod.

'That could be true.'

Then, calling to Steve, he left the room, leaving me slightly flustered and wondering what other feelings we both might need to face up to over Christmas.

ELEVEN

The next morning, I was impressed when both Nick and Sofia turned up before breakfast to sandwich the Linzer cookies together with jam.

'Marilise will be ever so pleased,' said Angela, who was making breakfast. 'Where are you going to put the number?'

My last job before going to bed last night had been to paint a large number two on a sheet of paper.

'I thought in the window of the sitting room,' I said. 'Then we can take her outside on a pretext at lunchtime.'

This plan was agreed to and when lunchtime came, we sprang into action.

'Marilise,' said Sofia, her face wreathed with excited smiles that were a total giveaway. 'I wanted to ask you something about one of the windows, but you can only see it from outside. Can I show you?'

Knowing something was up, Marilise smiled gently and agreed. We all trooped out of the front door and stood looking at the house.

'It's that one!' said Sofia, pointing to the sitting room

window where my large – and now, I could see, rather wonky – number two was displayed.

'Oh!' said Marilise. 'The next part of the advent calendar! For me?'

'Yes!' said Sofia. 'Come in and see your present.'

We all went back inside and showed Marilise the pile of cookies.

'Oh, my goodness,' she said, and swayed slightly on my arm. I quickly helped her to sit down.

'Are you all right?'

'Yes, yes, more than all right, I am delighted,' she said, brushing a tear away. 'It is such a long time since I saw these – for a moment, I'm afraid I was overcome.'

The worried look had crept back on to Sofia's face and I squeezed her shoulder.

'It's okay, that's a good thing.'

'Very, very good,' said Marilise. 'You have made me feel very happy. Maybe, after lunch, we can all share these, and I will show you some photographs I have of Christmas when I was a girl. Nick, maybe you could fetch the albums, if I tell you where they are?'

I looked at him to see what his reaction would be. Did he want to see pictures of his grandmother's past Christmases, or would he make some excuse about a work call and vanish? But he surprised me.

'I'd love to,' he said, and his eyes flickered over towards me.

After lunch, we all made ourselves comfortable in the sitting room: Marilise in her chair, Greg, Angela and me on the sofa, Astrid and India perched on the window seat and Sofia flitting from chair to footstool to floor. Nick brought in a pile of photograph albums, bound in blue silk. He placed them on a small table next to Marilise and she picked up the first one and opened it, turning a few pages.

'Ah, yes,' she said, smiling. 'This is Christmas when I was eight years old, the same as you, dearest Sofia.' Sofia beamed. 'We had a lot of snow that year, even more than usual, and here you see my sister, Leonore, and I wearing the beautiful outfits my mother bought for us.'

She held out the album with shaking hands and although I made to take it from her, Nick was faster. He gazed down at the photo, then showed it round to us all. Two little girls with pretty, mischievous faces smiled out at us through the years. They were wearing capes with fur-lined hoods and long velvet skirts with shiny lace-up boots peeping out from underneath. India pointed at one of the children.

'She looks like you, Sofia!'

We all leant in for a closer look and saw that she was right.

'Let me see,' said Marilise, and she took the album back and examined the photo closely. When she looked up, she had tears in her eyes. 'It is true, you are so like my darling Leonore. Beautiful girl,' she whispered, but we did not know if she meant her sister or Sofia; maybe both. 'Come now,' she said, turning the page. 'I think there is a picture of the tree... Ah, yes! Here it is, and another of us with our parents.'

Again, we looked, admiring the beautifully decorated tree with its real candles and piles of wrapped presents underneath.

'There's another family resemblance,' I said, pointing to Marilise's father.

'And I have said that many times,' said Marilise. 'But now maybe you will believe me, Nikolai. Look.'

He peered at the picture and a strange look came over his face. For a moment, I wondered if he would be the next to well up, but he blinked quickly and the moment was gone.

'He's very handsome,' he said, and the weak joke moved the conversation on.

We looked at the albums for another twenty minutes or so, until Greg checked his watch.

'I'd better get going,' he said. 'I need the windows of this house sparkling clean if you're going to be making them all into an advent calendar and the light fades so early these days.'

I also checked my watch and looked up at Marilise's happy but pale face.

'I think it's time for your afternoon nap,' I said. 'Can we look at these some more later?'

She agreed readily, and I took her upstairs, along with the precious albums, which I thought she might want to look at again if she woke up early.

I went downstairs and headed straight to the kitchen, thinking that I could do some chores and take them off Angela's list. Nick was in there, crouching down over Steve, in his habitual sleeping place. Nick looked up at me as I came in. His face was grey and his eyes panicky: something was very wrong.

'What is it?' I asked. 'Are you okay?'

He shook his head.

'No,' he said, his voice sounding strangulated. 'It's Steve, he's not well.'

'What's happened?' I asked, looking at the dog, who was lethargic – even for him – and seemed slightly cramped up.

'I think he ate something horrible when I took him for a walk. He often picks up disgusting things, but I can usually make him drop them, or sometimes he's sick straight away. You – you couldn't take a look at him, could you?'

'Well, I'm not used to dogs as patients, but I don't mind trying. Has he eaten or drunk anything since you got back from the walk?' Nick shook his head. I knelt down and reached out a hand to stroke Steve's head. He half opened one slightly rolled eye in response. I stroked his body and could feel him trembling, and his heartbeat felt irregular. I gently pushed his lips up. 'Are his gums normally this pale?' I asked Nick, who had gone rather pale himself.

'No – oh, I don't know. I don't think so. What do you think?'

'I think you were right. As I said, I am not a dog nurse, but it looks like poisoning. I think you should call the vet.'

As he started fumbling for his phone, Steve's whole body contracted and then he was violently sick.

'Have you got that number?' I looked up at Nick, but he had frozen, shock and fear etched on his face. 'Give me the phone,' I said calmly. 'And please get some kitchen towel and a small plastic box.'

The screen of the phone was lit up and Nick had already found the vet's number, so all I had to do was press 'call' and in a few moments I was speaking to a kind man at the surgery, who assured me that the vet would be with us within the hour and gave me instructions as to what to do until then. I thanked him and hung up, then took the things I had asked for from Nick.

'Okay, the vet will be here soon. We need to clear this up, of course, and I know it's gross, but we should put some in that little box for the vet to see. I'm going to go and get us both some gloves.'

'Can you give him anything to help?'

'No. All we can do now is look after him until the vet gets here.'

I ran to get some disposable gloves, and we cleaned up. Then he was sick again, so we cleaned up again.

'Thank you so much for helping,' said Nick, as I mopped Steve's face with wet paper towels. 'I've never seen him this ill.'

At that moment, Angela came into the kitchen.

'What's going on?' she asked, and we explained. 'Oh, poor chap,' she said. 'Thank goodness he has a real nurse to look after him. You stay here and I'll look out for Marilise this evening.'

I opened my mouth to protest, not sure that I could do more

than anyone else, especially once the vet had been, but Nick was faster.

'Thank you so much, Angela,' he said, his voice quivering with emotion. 'It's such a relief to have Laura here. I-I couldn't bear it if anything happened to Steve.'

I nodded.

'Yes, thank you. Let's see what the vet says.'

We didn't speak much for the next forty-five minutes. When he heard the knock on the front door, Nick leapt up and rushed from the room, returning almost immediately with the vet.

'What's up, fella?' he said and crouched down to examine him. I handed him the box so that he could inspect its contents and, after a few minutes, he stood up.

'All right, I think what young Steve here has, is a case of acorn poisoning. Could he have ingested any this morning?'

'Yes,' said Nick. 'He does sometimes pick them up, but I didn't know they were poisonous to dogs, and I don't think he's ever eaten one before.'

'First time for everything,' said the vet cheerily. 'The good news is that we've caught it fast and he's been sick.'

Nick, back on the floor next to his dog, stroked his head.

'There you go, boy, you're doing well.'

Steve licked his hand feebly.

'See, he's picking up already,' I said encouragingly.

'That's right,' said the vet, starting to unpack various items from his bag. 'I'm going to give him some fluids and charcoal immediately and I could take him back to the surgery with me overnight, or you can look after him here, if you prefer. He'll need monitoring all night and might need some more medication.'

'I'd rather keep him here,' said Nick. 'Laura is a nurse and has been amazing so far.'

The vet glanced at me, and we gave each other the faintest whisper of a smile.

'That's fine,' I said. 'I can monitor his temperature and heart. Anything else?'

'Help me with these subcutaneous fluids now,' said the vet. 'You can give more in a few hours, if you're all right with that?'

'Absolutely,' I said, and watched closely as he slipped the needle in.

Twenty minutes later, he left, with instructions to call immediately if we were worried. A steady stream of visitors then ensued, and everyone had to be reassured that Steve would make a full recovery.

'It would be terrible if Steve died,' Astrid confided to me when we were out of the room for a while. 'We all love him, but he's so terribly important to Nick.'

'He'll be fine,' I assured her. 'He's a big dog and the vet said that acorn poisoning isn't usually too serious at this time of year, because there aren't many left. You'll need to keep an eye on him next autumn, though.'

Astrid looked glum.

'Next autumn I'll be in Texas.'

I squeezed her hand.

'One day at a time, eh?'

By eleven o'clock, the rest of the household had gone to bed, and it was Nick, Steve and me left in the warm kitchen. Greg had found a camp bed, which Angela had fitted out with a sheet, pillow and duvet so that Nick and I could take turns sleeping. Steve would need his next lot of fluids at about one in the morning, so I took the first sleep. I thought it would be impossible to fall asleep lying on a camp bed in the kitchen with Nick sitting a couple of feet away, but, to my surprise, I dropped off quickly and was all too soon being awakened by a gentle hand on my shoulder and Nick's voice saying my name.

'Laura, I'm sorry, but it's time to wake up.'

I'm used to having to get up throughout the night to attend to patients and sat up, alert to my surroundings.

'How's Steve doing?' I asked quietly.

'Really well, I think,' said Nick. 'He seems pretty chilled. He's woken up a couple of times and tried to get up.'

'He might need a wee,' I said. 'I think we should help him outside before I do the next lot of fluids.'

Nick woke Steve as softly as he had woken me, and the big dog did indeed start to get to his feet. We helped him to the door and out into the freezing garden.

'This can't have been what you were expecting,' said Nick between chattering teeth.

'No,' I agreed. 'But a nurse's life is always one of surprises; it's one of the reasons I love the job – no two days are the same. I had a patient once with a pet lizard, which was hardly ever in its cage. It sat with him a lot of the time, but it liked to watch me in the kitchen. I got used to it after a while, but I can't pretend I missed it when the job finished.'

Nick chuckled. Steve was ready to go in now, and staggered back to the Aga on wobbly legs, where he lay down again.

'There you go, boy,' I said, patting his head. I got a feeble tail wag in return. 'Now, I'm going to give you a little injection – it won't hurt, and you'll carry on feeling better.'

I inserted the needle and sat down on the floor with the bag.

'This won't take long,' I said to Nick. 'Why don't you get some sleep?'

'I don't feel tired in the least,' he said. 'Would you like a cup of tea?'

'I'd love one,' I said. 'Something without caffeine, though, please.'

A few minutes later, Steve's fluids were nearly done, and Nick and I were both sipping from steaming mugs.

'I'm sorry about your husband,' he suddenly said. 'You're so young to be...'

I was used to people trailing off when they talked about this.

'Widowed,' I supplied. 'Yes. And thank you. He had a bacterial infection that got complicated, so it was very unexpected. I was looking after him at home and then he took a turn for the worse. By the time we got him into hospital, there wasn't much anyone could do.'

'I'm sorry,' Nick repeated. 'It must have been tough nursing him.'

I put down my mug and removed the needle from Steve's back, then started packing away the bits and pieces, glad of something to keep my hands busy.

'It was,' I replied. 'Very. I was glad to be with him, but when my help wasn't enough, well...'

Now, it was my turn to trail off. I had probably said enough, anyway. The warm kitchen in the early hours of the morning with the three of us there was a safe little bubble, and it would have been easy to pour my heart out. Instead, I changed the subject.

'When are Astrid and India leaving for Texas?'

'In the new year. You said – you said that you didn't think she wants to move.'

I looked at him sheepishly.

'I'm sorry, it wasn't up to me to say that.'

'No, I'm glad you did. I've been so focused on my own feelings about them leaving... I know Marilise won't be here forever' – his voice cracked, then he took a deep breath to continue – 'and now Sofia's here and she's so sweet, but she'll go back to Victoria. Steve is my only constant, but earlier today – well, yesterday, I suppose – I thought I was going to lose him as well.'

'Everybody leaves.'

He looked up, his eyes hollow.

'Exactly.'

'And you're trying to get a handle on that by being the one who leaves first, as if that will stop it hurting. Aren't you punishing them, and shortening even further the time you have together?'

'But they're leaving me!' he exclaimed. 'I'm making it easier. I don't want to hang around being a nuisance to people. I had enough of that with my father. That was always the easiest way to get his approval: stay away as much as possible.'

His voice was bitter, and I couldn't blame him.

'But the family is here at Lyonscroft now,' I said. 'They love you. That supersedes however much of a nuisance you are.'

'My father certainly didn't,' he said. 'He didn't want me at all, other than to inherit. He just had to get me to eighteen, and it was easier to outsource that to schools and nannies.' He spoke in a casual, almost offhand way, but the whiteness of his knuckles as his fingers tensed into a fist betrayed his hurt. 'I suppose it might have been better if my mother hadn't died; maybe she loved me, but I don't know.'

Another one who left him, I thought, but I didn't speak, and neither did he, for a moment. When he did, the detachment had drained from his voice.

'I *know*,' he said fiercely. 'I *know* I'm being childish and that I'm lashing out before they can hurt me, but it's useless, isn't it? I mean, the hurt's still there.' The fist sprang open and he slapped his hand down, making me jump. His voice softened. 'How does one cope? How did you cope when your husband died?'

I laughed drily.

'I'm not sure you should be learning lessons from me.'

'What do you mean? You seem so... together.'

'I'm not,' I said, looking up at him, finally. His face had lost all trace of its customary humour, or of the pain that had twisted it just now, and instead taken on a sincerity that was hard to resist. For the first time in three years, I wanted to pour my heart out. Maybe it was meeting another person who struggled with risking their heart, who was wounded by loss, who had shown me their vulnerability.

'I'm not. Together, that is. I've not been so very different from you. Since Paulo died, I've spent my time moving from house to house, always working and living in the short term. I've slapped down a boundary that says no one gets close, gets in, and I've covered it all with an unarguably noble veneer of helping others.'

'What about your family?'

'My family means well,' I said. 'But they're not very... sensitive.'

'So, you avoid them?' I shrugged. 'You're punishing them, even though they love you?'

'Ha, not sure that depriving them of my company is exactly a punishment,' I said.

Nick folded his arms and stared at me, then grinned.

'So, we have plenty in common, then,' he said.

'Hmm, very clever,' I said, not willing to admit that he was right. 'Now, isn't it time you got some sleep? Steve will be fighting fit in the morning and you're going to need all your energy to keep up with him.'

He took the bed, and I made another mug of herbal tea and settled down near Steve with my book, but my mind kept wandering from the story and over to the sleeping man, who was beginning to intrigue me.

TWELVE

Nick and I swapped places again once more during the night, and had no further concerns about Steve, who was peaceful throughout. In the morning, I stirred awake, feeling unusually stiff, then instantly remembered where I was. Sitting up and pushing my hair away from my face, I saw Nick kneeling next to Steve. For a moment, my heart sank: *was the dog okay?* But then Nick turned to me, a smile of pure happiness on his face. I can only say in my defence that my – well – defences must have been down, due to having just woken up, but for a fleeting moment, I could have pulled the owner of that gorgeous, smiling face right onto the uncomfortable camp bed with me. Thankfully, my nurse's instincts proved stronger than any other, and I pulled myself together.

'How is he?' I asked.

'He looks so, so much better,' said Nick. 'The difference is incredible. He's trying to stand up, but I was hoping he might be able to do it without my help.'

In response, Steve suddenly staggered to his feet and stood there swaying slightly, looking absurdly proud of himself.

'I'll take him out,' said Nick, and I seized the moment to

straighten myself out and put the kettle on. It was still very early, and dark, and the lack of sleep would haunt me all day, but I, too, was overjoyed that Steve had made it through the night and looked to be well on the road to recovery. He was an undeniably daft dog, but he had a sense of kindness and understanding that he was generous enough to extend to all of us. I wouldn't forget in a hurry that first night when he had come to sleep on my bed.

When they came back inside, I had made a pot of tea and was boiling some white rice.

'Just getting your breakfast ready,' I said to Steve. 'The vet said you have to have chicken and rice for the next couple of days, little and often.' I took a plate out of the fridge. 'And look at this delicious chicken Angela cooked for you last night, you lucky thing.'

A few minutes later, he was eating eagerly, and drinking as well, as Nick and I watched him.

'Laura, I can't thank you enough for what you've done,' said Nick. 'You've helped save his life and been so nice about it. You didn't even mind cleaning up after him.'

'I was happy to help,' I said truthfully. 'Though... that's twice I've rescued him now.' I smiled.

'I suppose it is. Well, in that case – and please don't say no, which I guess would be your first answer – can I do something for you in return?'

He was right, I normally would refuse to have a favour returned, but his insistence made me think again.

'Well, there is something, actually. I wonder if you might reconsider getting involved in decorating the house for Christmas. I think it would mean a lot to your family – and I'd like it, too. I know you said they could go ahead, but I don't think they will without you.' I paused. 'I know it's a lot to ask, but there's a good chance I'll need to climb a tree in pursuit of Steve, or abseil down an old well or something to get him out, so could you take that into account?'

He laughed, as I had intended.

'That is true. I know I seem like a right Scrooge where Christmas is concerned, but it's this house. We haven't spent Christmas here since Dad died. We always decamp to London, but Marilise wasn't up to the journey this year. My father hated what he always called *"the commercialisation of Christmas"* in a disgusted tone of voice, and he refused to sully the house by putting up any decorations, even a tasteful wreath on the front door. When I came home from boarding school, I was already dreading the holidays with that man. When everyone else had been talking so excitedly about the plans their families had, the ways they were going to deck out their houses and all their special traditions, it was particularly tough to find the house as drab and chilly as ever.'

My heart went out to the disappointed little boy that I could still see in him, and I thought of all the over-the-top, fun Christmases I had spent with my family as well as with Paulo.

'I'm so sorry, that sounds awful.'

'It was. Astrid used to do what she could for me and Victoria – she'd take us out secretly for a special lunch and to see the lights and displays in Taunton, and I'll always be grateful to her for that. She also insisted on presents and lots of special food, so it's not like Christmas was banned altogether. Although I'm sure it would have been if that man had had his way.'

Did he ever refer to him as 'Dad'? 'That man' didn't seem to have earned the title.

'Astrid's so kind. She's always trying to make everybody happy. I'm glad she managed to, at least a little bit, for you and your sister.'

'She did.' He frowned. 'I must talk to her about Philip. I cannot have her marrying another tyrant. Anyway. He used to say, "Thank God carol singers can't be bothered to come up the drive, I couldn't stand all that caterwauling and they would have had a wasted journey: I wouldn't have given them a penny." I think the real reason they didn't come was because they knew exactly what he was like.'

Tears came to my tired eyes.

'But music is the best thing about Christmas. How awful to have that denied you.'

'You really love it, don't you?' asked Nick, and I nodded, the tiredness and emotion leaving me unwilling to risk speaking. 'Then I'm glad you're coming with me to the concert at the Montgomerys. They may be a pain, but they put on a magnificent evening; you'll love it.' I nodded, and then he added, 'And it turns out I'm looking forward to it myself this year.'

Before I had a chance to think about what he might mean by this, let alone formulate a reply, the kitchen door opened and Sofia came running in, followed by Angela.

'Is he all right?' asked the little girl, eyes only for Steve. 'I've been thinking about him all night.'

'Yes,' said Nick. 'He's done brilliantly. You can see for yourself.'

Sofia flung herself down on the floor and stroked the dog gently. In response, he opened his eyes and gave her hand a lick.

'Oh! He *is* better!'

'Well done, you two,' said Angela. 'Did he eat any of his chicken?'

'All of it,' said Nick, pointing to the empty bowl. 'And he can have some more in about two hours.'

I stood up.

'Right, I'm going to go and jump in the shower, and then I'll go and see Marilise.'

· · ·

Twenty minutes later, I was pushing open her bedroom door. She was already awake and sitting up in bed.

'Good morning,' I said, drawing the curtains. 'Have you slept well?'

'Not at all,' she replied. 'Call it the nonsense of an old woman, but I have been so worried about that dog. I kept waking up, wondering how he was, and wishing I could do something to help.'

'Steve's fine,' I said. 'Nick and I stayed with him all night and now he's doing well – getting up a bit and eating and drinking.'

Her hand flew to her heart.

'Oh, what a relief! He is a nice dog, but I was more worried about what the effect would be on Nick if he were to die. Until that boy learns to lean into the love of his family, Steve is his greatest comfort. Now,' she continued, 'I would like to go downstairs for breakfast today, please. I feel too far removed from all the action.'

I sent a quick text to Angela to let her know, then helped Marilise with her morning routine before we made our slow way downstairs. Breakfast was eaten in the kitchen, and when we arrived, everybody was there. Astrid jumped up to help Marilise to her chair, and I accepted a cup of coffee gratefully from Greg. Initially, the talk was all of Steve and his recovery; we had to tell the story of the whole night and how we had looked after him. When that topic was finally exhausted, and I was beginning to think that Steve was the most high-maintenance patient I'd ever had, Nick spoke.

'It's nearly December,' he said. 'And I was thinking that it's time to decide how we're going to decorate the house.'

A little murmur of interest went around the table, and I could see people darting looks at one another – all except Marilise, who was smiling at me. 'It hasn't been done for decades, so there's no traditions to constrain us. In fact, the only tradition I've ever known was that the house *wasn't* decorated, so we want to throw that one out, for sure.'

'Can we have a tree?' asked India. 'There's room for a huge one.'

'Done,' said Nick. 'Anyone else?'

'Reindeer,' said Sofia, hugging Reddo, who came everywhere with her. 'Not real ones, I suppose, but some big ones outside.'

'Reindeer, tick!' said Nick.

'For my part,' said Astrid, 'I'd like dozens and dozens of lights. That's what Christmas is about, isn't it, bringing light to the darkness?'

Nick smiled.

'Definitely lights, they're on the list.'

'It will make me very happy to see Lyonscroft dressed up beautifully for Christmas, as she was when I was a young bride,' said Marilise. 'I am sorry that my son was so aggravated by the festive season and did not make happier memories.'

'Nick's turning it around now, though,' said Astrid. 'The new memories will overwhelm the old.'

'I believe this, too,' said Marilise. 'But I have some old memories that may contribute. The decorations that were in the photographs we looked at yesterday – I think, as long as they have not been moved or disposed of many years ago, that some of them are packed away in the attics. Angela, if you do not mind helping me, I would like to insist that Laura takes the afternoon off to help Nick with this endeavour.'

'Me?' I said. I wasn't sure how I felt about that.

'You,' said Marilise firmly. 'You have so much Christmas spirit longing to be let out. Please, help Nick.'

I nodded silently and took another piece of toast as Marilise told Nick exactly where she thought the boxes were. I was always glad to be a tourist in other people's Christmases, and I was delighted that Nick had decided to get involved in the seasonal transformation of the house, but since Paulo died the thought of hanging a single decoration myself had always floored me. But now I had to admit that I could feel a stirring of excitement in my stomach. Thoughts of where the tree could stand and of which lights would look best where floated unbidden into my head, and I knew exactly the life-sized reindeer that Sofia would adore. I used to have one myself, named Noddy, who stood outside our front door with a red bow around his neck. I had given all our Christmas decorations to the charity shop when I had frantically cleaned out after Paulo's death, trying futilely to soothe my grief with action. But maybe I could do it, I thought. For Marilise, for Sofia, for India, yes. I could frame it in my mind as helping them, then maybe it would be possible. But a little voice whispered in my head: *Just for them? Or for you, too? And for Nick?* I couldn't deny that, as much as I tried to think of it as altruistic, the opportunity to go all out for Christmas brought a thrill to my heart, even when images of Paulo in his final days were still so strong. Could I reconcile the two? And could I keep denying that the idea of bringing some Christmas cheer to Nick, which might help the healing of the sad little boy that lived inside him, was the most tempting thing of all?

THIRTEEN

After lunch, Nick showed me where the stairs to the attic rooms were, behind a door not far from my room. I peered up them.

'So, this is where all the family history is?' I asked, as we creaked our way up.

'Well, all the bits people have got fed up with,' he said. 'There are probably a lot more photos lurking up here somewhere, and my school reports.'

'Ah, now those I *would* like to see,' I said teasingly. I put on a posh accent. 'Nikolai is a clever boy but must learn to apply himself and discipline that scattered mind so that he can put it to some useful purpose.'

He laughed.

'How did you know? Actually, one master wrote that I had great potential, but should stop squandering it on fripperies.'

'Ouch.'

'At the time, yes, but it's the fripperies that keep the heating running; app design pays surprisingly well.'

'And it's probably not really a frippery, is it?' I asked, stopping as I came to the top of the staircase and was faced with a long corridor, lined with doors. 'I wouldn't know where to start – it must need a lot of specialist knowledge.'

Nick shrugged.

'I suppose so, but it's frivolous compared with, say, nursing.'

'I doubt your schoolmaster would have been much more impressed if you'd said that was your ambition,' I said. 'My family asked me for years why I didn't train to be a doctor instead; I never could make them understand that if you have a vocation, then that's that.'

'For what it's worth,' said Nick, looking me deep in the eyes, 'I think it's an amazing way to spend your life.'

Despite the chill of the passageway, I felt rather warm all of a sudden.

'Thank you,' I said quickly. 'Now, where should we start looking for those decorations?'

'Marilise said they would be in the furthest room, and thinks there are two tea chests,' said Nick, starting off down the passage. He opened a door at the end, and we peered in.

'It's awfully murky,' I said. 'Is there a light?' We both groped around for a switch. I found one and quickly flicked it. 'Ah, that's better.'

The room was stacked with boxes and chests, and a large armoire stood to one side. There was also a beautiful wooden rocking horse, which I approached to stroke its real horsehair mane.

'Isn't he beautiful?' I said. 'Sofia would adore him.'

Nick came and stood next to me.

'Victoria and I used to play on him when we were kids,' he said, his voice nostalgic. 'I thought he was long gone. We used to argue over his name. I thought he should be called Silver, after the Lone Ranger's horse of course, but Victoria was insistent that his – or rather *her* – name was Snuzzle, after one of her My Little Ponies.'

'I loved those!' I exclaimed, an image instantly coming to my mind of the colourful pony figures I had played with endlessly as a child.

'So I can't count on you to back me up with "Silver", then?' asked Nick teasingly.

''Fraid not,' I said, shaking my head and putting on a doleful expression. 'It's Snuzzle all the way for me.'

'My sister's toys are probably up here somewhere as well,' said Nick, continuing the fun. 'We could look them out and you can keep yourself busy when you're not, you know, doing that nursing stuff.'

'Great idea!' I said, injecting my voice with girlish enthusiasm. 'We can look for your Ken dolls at the same time.'

'*I* did not play with Ken,' said Nick in a tone of offended dignity. '*I* was loyal to Action Man. Now come on, let's find these decorations or we'll have Marilise to answer to.'

Still giggling, I helped looked for the tea chests. It had been a long time since I had had such a silly, light-hearted conversation and I could feel how much it had lifted my spirits. I probed to see if the guilt was about to follow, but it didn't. I might have thought more about it if Nick had not suddenly said, 'Do you think it's these?'

I went over.

'Yes, they look just the thing. Let's open them up to check.' The lids weren't pressed on too tightly and we were easily able to pry them off with our fingers. 'Oh yes, this is them!' I exclaimed, taking a small object wrapped in tissue paper and carefully opening it. Inside was an exquisite teardrop shaped glass bauble, delicately gilded with swirls and tiny dots. 'It's stunning.'

'Even I'm beginning to look forward to decorating a tree with these,' said Nick, opening another package to find a similar bauble, but in cranberry-coloured glass and in the shape of a pinecone. 'Come on, let's take these down.'

The chests weren't particularly heavy, and I could easily

carry one back downstairs to where Angela and Marilise were sitting looking at the photograph albums again.

'You found them!' said the old lady, her face lighting up.

'Exactly where you said they would be,' said Nick. 'We'd better get going to the shops for everything else – you could go through these while we're out.'

'No,' said Marilise. 'Much as I would love to see them again, I wouldn't dream of unveiling such treasure when India and Sofia are at school and cannot join in. I will be patient, and we can do it all of us together, when we have a tree for them to live on.'

The drive to Taunton wasn't long and we were soon walking to a pop-up Christmas shop I had found via a quick Google search. The town, already charming, had its lights up and a festive display in every window. As we walked past a little food and drink van parked next to an enormous, lavishly decorated tree, a waft of cinnamon and peppermint hit me and I stopped dead.

'Ooh, look,' I said. 'Christmas hot chocolate.'

'Do you want to get one?' asked Nick.

Any December of the past three years would have found me saying a firm 'no', wrapping my arms tightly around myself and walking away, trying to hold back the tears. But today, looking at Nick's warm smile and remembering Marilise's joy in finding her forgotten ornaments, a rush of festive spirit washed over me.

'I'd love to,' I said. 'Will you join me?'

'Why not?' said Nick, and we walked over.

'What can I get you?' asked the friendly man behind the counter.

We studied the menu.

'It's hard to choose,' I said. 'But I think I'll go for the

Christmas Cracker. Cinnamon, ginger and popping candy sounds too good to turn down.'

'And I'll have an Old Saint Nick,' said Nick. 'White chocolate with caramelised orange, and named for me, too.'

'Excellent choices,' said the man, and a few minutes later, we were presented with huge mugs, topped with whipped cream.

'Oh dear,' I said. 'I thought we'd be able to drink them on our way to the shop.'

'Take a seat,' said the man, his eyes twinkling for all as though he was one of Santa's elves and gesturing towards a small table beside the tree. 'Enjoy the season, the hot chocolates and each other; no need to rush.'

His comment made me feel a little shy, but now that we had our china mugs, there wasn't much option other than to sit down.

'Maybe we should send Marilise a selfie,' I said, half joking. 'She'd be glad to see us getting into the spirit of things.'

'Let's do it,' said Nick unexpectedly, and took out his phone. We held up our mugs and grinned. He showed me the photo. 'Happy with that?'

'Yes, it's a good one,' I said, and it was. With the tree behind us, our cold, rosy faces and our elaborate hot chocolates, we looked like an advertisement for Christmas.

He pressed send and we sipped our drinks, which we agreed were both delicious.

'So... what should we get?' asked Nick. 'Now that I've agreed to this, I want to go all out, but I've got no idea what to buy.'

'Well, you chose the right person to come shopping with,' I said. 'I already have an image in my mind, but your father wouldn't like it at all.'

'Marvellous,' said Nick. 'Maybe that should be our theme.

Forget, oh, I don't know, candy cane stripes or Nordic Christmas, ours should be "He would have hated it".'

'Hmm, I'm not sure we've *quite* imbued you with the Christmas spirit,' I replied, 'but we're definitely getting there.' I finished the last of my hot chocolate. 'Shall we head off?'

He nodded and we handed our mugs back to the vendor and went to the shop. It was an incredible sight, even from down the road. Around the window of the large storefront was greenery a foot wide and thick, laced through with every colour of tinsel you could imagine, from metallic gold, silver and bronze, through all the colours of the rainbow and even an iridescent white, which I immediately added to my mental shopping list. The window itself had an enchanting display of a winter forest at night, with frosted trees surrounding a party that was being set up on tree stumps, figures of woodland creatures placed to look as if they were scurrying to and fro. Mice carried trays of food, hedgehogs poured drinks and squirrels sprang from tree to tree with strings of lights. A beautiful deer watched through the trees while a fox arranged presents and two owls swooped overhead.

'Is this the sort of thing you were thinking of?' said Nick jokingly.

'Yes, that's right,' I replied. 'I thought four or five Christmas trees and we could do away with the furniture for a few weeks. A small sacrifice to make.'

Laughing, we went inside the shop. Even I was momentarily overwhelmed; it was a Christmas explosion. Where to start? Part of me wanted to panic and run away, but I couldn't let everybody down and besides, another part of me was thrilled by the prospect of this glittering emporium. I looked at Nick and he turned to me.

'The five-year-old in me *loves* this,' he said. 'The thirty-five-year-old is terrified.'

'Well, it's the five-year-old we've come to indulge,' I said.

'He deserves to make up for all those missed Christmases. Where would he start?'

'Candy canes,' said Nick decisively. 'I've always liked them, they're so cheerful. I'd like a few of those about the place.'

'Candy canes it is,' I said, and moved into the shop. 'Look, there's a whole area dedicated to them. You can have indoor or outdoor lights, tree decorations, giant versions, tinsel, even a candy cane front door cover to fit over your own. Pretty much anything you can think of, but with red and white stripes.'

'I'm starting with this,' he said, picking up a glittery foam cane that must have been three feet high. 'In fact, I want two, one for either side of the fireplace in the sitting room.' He picked up a second one and stood there grinning at me. 'And now,' he continued, 'I want that candy cane Nutcracker figure, but I've already run out of arms.'

'Can I help?' asked a perky voice. I turned to see a young woman dressed as an elf, with a name badge that said 'Twinkle'.

'You can,' I replied. 'I think we're going to need somewhere to put things while we shop.'

'No problem at all,' she said. 'I'll allocate you an area. And let me take these,' she added, removing the candy canes from Nick and somehow managing to collect up the huge Nutcracker at the same time.

'Back in a mo,' she chirped.

'With Twinkle on board, this is going to be even more dangerous,' I told Nick. 'Are you sure you don't want to get out now, while you still can?'

'Absolutely not. I'm beginning to enjoy myself. Now, tinsel.'

For the next hour, we capered around that shop like children, picking out everything we would need. We hadn't planned on buying any tree decorations, given that we had Marilise's, but they proved far too tempting, so Nick announced that we would simply have two Christmas trees: Marilise's in the hallway and the second in the living room. We paused for the occasional serious discussion over whether we needed a person-sized gingerbread man (regretfully, we decided not) or if there should be two or three deer (three, of course) and I thought how much I was enjoying myself. Had I been wrong to try and cut Christmas out of my life, or was this just good timing? Eventually, we were finished. Even Twinkle had to admit that it wasn't necessary to choose anything else.

'You two have done very well,' she said, and we basked in her approval. 'There is *one* tiny thing, though.' We frowned. What could we have missed? She pointed upwards. 'You're standing under the mistletoe, and you know what that means.'

A tall, thin elf passed by at that moment, paused and said in a singsong tone:

'*Mistletoe kiss. Mistletoe kiss. Brings Christmastime magic and Christmastime bliss.*'

Before we knew it, several other elves appeared and began chanting the same thing.

'They want you to kiss,' said Twinkle in a stage whisper.

'Yes, I think we realised that,' said Nick drily, and looked at me, then raised one eyebrow. 'May I, Nurse Wilde?'

Swept away by the fun of the afternoon, my senses reeling as Christmas spirit flooded my heart again, I nodded. He bent his head and kissed me on the lips, a light kiss but long enough to set off fireworks and it was all I could do not to reach out and pull him closer, feel his body against mine, deepen the kiss and see where it took us on that heady, unreal December afternoon. But it was over as quickly as it had started and we were blushing and grinning for the clapping elves, who no doubt set people up twenty times a day and never wanted the scene to become any steamier than a festive peck.

'We'd better pay and sort out how to get this lot home,' said Nick, and we went with Twinkle to the till. The total was several hundred pounds, and I looked at Nick nervously. Did his newfound Santa status reach as far as his wallet? Apparently, it did, because he handed over his credit card without complaint or panic, merely asking about home delivery and once that was arranged for the next morning, we headed back to the car. There was a new energy between us, and when we passed the Salvation Army band playing 'Sleigh Ride', I didn't cover my ears or rush away but smiled to remember happier times and to wonder what the future might hold.

FOURTEEN

We stopped off on the way back to Lyonscroft to order the Christmas trees, again for delivery in the morning, and got back as everyone was sitting down to supper.

'Did you get everything?' asked India. 'Mum told us where you've been all afternoon.'

'We may have picked up a few little trinkets,' said Nick casually, reaching for the butter.

'That's right,' I chimed in, adopting the same tone of voice. 'Some small and tasteful lights – one string – and a bauble or two.'

'I don't believe you for one second!' said Marilise, her voice full of delight. 'I think you have bought out the shop.'

Nick and I glanced at each other and grinned, and the fireworks fizzed again.

'Yes, you've nailed it,' he said. 'It's all arriving tomorrow, with the trees, so I hope you're all flexing your fingers to help put it up. Good of them to deliver on a Saturday.'

'Try and stop us,' said Angela. 'I love Christmas decorations. Did you remember to get hooks, tack and tape as well?'

We looked at each other again, but this was more of a damp squib than fireworks.

'We didn't even think about it, I'm afraid,' I said. 'I can pop out in the morning and get some?'

'No need,' said Greg, grinning. 'In our experience, those are always forgotten, so I stocked up. Ange and I figured that if we didn't need them, then they'd come in useful for something else.'

That little drama dealt with, we chatted over the girls' week at school. Sofia seemed to have settled in remarkably well. Her summary was that 'the teachers are kind and there are chickens', which struck me as high praise. They were both involved in the end of term show, and it appeared that all teaching had been abandoned in place of rehearsals. Sofia was pleased to have been cast as a snowflake, and India seemed to be having the time of her life sneaking sweets to her little charges and reading horse magazines while she was waiting to rehearse her bit.

'Honestly, it's not that difficult – all I have to do is look a bit scared when Felicity Duckrington-Gamble pops up as the angel Gabriel, then say, "Let us go to Bethlehem now" and herd the younger ones off. I could do it without any rehearsal at all and spend all that time with Firefly.'

'I expect it's good for you,' said Astrid glumly. 'Things you don't want to do often are.'

'Now, who would like something sweet?' chimed in Angela. 'I've got some mince pie flavoured ice cream I thought might be interesting.'

Through the intrigued mutters, Sofia's voice came through, quiet but clear.

'I've never eaten a mince pie.'

Every head in the room swivelled towards her. It was Angela who got her act together first.

'Never had a mince pie? Why on earth not?'

'Mummy doesn't like them, she says they're "*pointless calories*", whatever that means.'

'My sister has a lot of living to do,' said Nick, rolling his eyes. 'There's nothing pointless about a mince pie. Do we have any, Angela, that she could try?'

'Sorry, no. I have everything ready to make them, but I haven't got around to it yet.'

'Then the ice cream will have to do – for now. They're even better hot and *with* ice cream,' Nick continued.

'Brandy butter for me,' said Astrid, and Greg nodded.

'What about custard?' said India, her eyes shining. 'Yum!'

'No, no,' said Marilise. 'They are perfect with the slight tang of crème fraîche.'

Sofia laughed.

'I can't wait to try them in all the different ways.'

'Not all at once, I hope,' said Nick. 'Although if you're going for that challenge, I might have to join you.'

After supper and before taking Marilise up, I hung around the kitchen and helped Angela tidy up. Nick was fiddling with the coffee machine.

'Go next door,' she insisted. 'You work hard enough.'

'Actually, there's something I wanted to ask you. Seeing as Sofia has never had a mince pie, I thought it would be the perfect thing to put in the next advent calendar window. If you don't mind me doing it, I'll knock some up tonight so we can do it in the morning.'

'Oh, you are a lovely, kind girl,' said Angela. 'But I don't mind doing it, it won't take long.'

'I'd like to,' I said. Now I'd started on Christmas I didn't want to stop, and Christmas baking is only just below music on my list of festive favourites. 'And anyway,' I echoed her words. 'You work hard enough.'

'Laura's right,' said Nick, smirking in satisfaction when the coffee machine finally obeyed him. 'I'll give her a hand.'

My stomach leapt. He was going to stay and help me? My mind flew back to the kiss and I got flustered, nearly dropping the bowl I was drying. I hoped my voice would sound normal.

'Great!' *Nope, squeaky.* I cleared my throat. 'I'm sure it won't take long. I'll be back down when I've finished Marilise's routine with her.'

Throwing the bowl in a cupboard, I scuttled away, my face burning, and barely managed to pull myself together to do my job that evening.

By the time I bid Marilise good night, I was feeling calmer and returned to the kitchen with every intention of making a quick batch of mince pies and keeping up the jolly festive banter of the afternoon. The kitchen was far away enough that we could listen to some Christmas songs without disturbing anyone, and I got out my phone to find a playlist. But, when I opened the door, Nick had beaten me to it, and I was met with the ethereal strains of 'Once in Royal David's City'.

'Oh, it's beautiful,' I said. '*Carols from King's?*'

He nodded.

'Yes, I went once, years ago. I thought it would get us prepared for the Montgomerys' concert. It's not just Christmas pop you like, is it?'

He looked anxious.

'No, absolutely not. I love carols. I was in a nurses' choir once, I loved it.'

'You should do it again.'

'Maybe.' I shook myself. 'Come on, let's get these mince pies going or we'll be here all night.'

Angela, in her kindness, had laid out everything we would need, so it was a case of making pastry, rolling and cutting it and adding the mincemeat and pastry lids. The kitchen was warm and peaceful, a contrast from the busy town earlier. The only noises were the gentle music playing and the occasional snore from Steve, who was most put out not to be allowed any pastry offcuts, as he was still on a simple diet. Nick and I chatted easily; he was still very enthused about the decorations we had bought.

'I think you've come round to Christmas,' I said, sliding the pies into the oven. 'Aren't you going to miss it when this place is sold and you're sipping a cocktail on the beach come the twenty-fifth, rather than shivering in the Somerset chill?'

'Doesn't sound too bad,' he said. 'But I have to admit that I'm beginning to understand all that stuff about Christmas being about the people.' He stepped closer to me and my heart picked up its pace. 'You have icing sugar on your face,' he said, and rubbed my cheek with his thumb. The fireworks decided to prove that, up until now, they had been nothing but a warmup act. 'I liked kissing you earlier,' he went on. Unwilling to risk any more squeaking, I nodded. 'Although I could have done without all those bloody elves standing around. Maybe we could try again, just the two of us?'

And then he came closer still and his lips met mine. I kissed him back, hesitantly at first as thoughts whizzed through my brain: *Don't mix work and pleasure! This is the first person you've kissed since Paulo! He's moving to LA!* But each thought was extinguished as quickly as it came, as if from a touch by a fairy's wand – *poof!* – and I allowed the kiss to deepen, my arms snaking around his back, our feet interlaced. He started to kiss my neck, twining his fingers into my hair, and I think the ensuing scene would have been highly unsuitable for Steve's eyes, had the oven timer not chosen that exact moment to chime. I laughed reluctantly and, my whole body trembling, grabbed the oven gloves to remove the mince pies.

'Can't we leave them?' murmured Nick, lifting my hair and kissing the back of my neck. 'I'm sure they'd be fine.'

'Sadly not,' I replied, opening the oven door. 'Angela would never forgive us if we burnt them.'

'Fair point,' he said, and stepped away so that I could put them on the cooling rack. Truth be told, I wasn't wholly sorry to have been put on a cooling rack myself, so to speak. Incredible though the kiss had been, and tempting though it was to let it continue, I had spent three years grieving and shying away from anything that reminded me of Paulo. Hell, I had actively avoided Christmas and Valentine's Day, but the thought of meeting another man had never entered my consciousness. My hand went reflexively to my necklace. I fussed with the pies for as long as I could, then turned around. Nick was leaning on the table, a tender smile on his face.

'You're going to turn in now, right?' he said. 'And I'll see you in the morning?'

Thank goodness I didn't have to explain.

'I am, yes.'

'I've enjoyed making mince pies with you,' he said. 'You're doing a very good job of immersing me in Christmas. Right, I'll take Steve out for a final run.'

He called to his dog and, as he passed me, kissed me once more, very briefly, on the lips.

'Good night,' he said. 'I look forward to seeing you in the morning.'

I went upstairs feeling dazed, not knowing what my head thought but knowing that my heart was singing and with a smile on my face that couldn't be suppressed.

FIFTEEN

When I awoke the next morning, I was still grinning. I lay for a moment letting the events of last night return to me and reliving every spinetingling moment. My hand went automatically to my necklace, as it so often did, and I cautiously probed my feelings about Paulo. To my surprise, they were less raw than usual and felt, oddly, both combined with yet detached from my bubbling happiness over what had happened with Nick. And what of Nick? I was well aware that I still didn't know him very well, that he was planning to move goodness knew where in the world, but somehow those thoughts failed to take hold. All I could think of was how he had opened up to me about his father, how wholeheartedly he had thrown himself into making Christmas special for his family, how tender, then passionate, his kisses had been. I sighed. *Not much point in trying to disentangle it all now*, I thought. *Let's see where today takes me.*

I hopped out of bed, took a quick shower and went in to see Marilise, who was already sitting up in bed.

'Good morning!' I said, going to open the curtains. 'Oh, look. It's snowing, how gorgeous!'

'I do love the snow,' she replied. 'Is it that which has put you on such good form this morning, Laura? You are so cheerful.'

I beamed at her, part of me longing to perch on the side of her bed and spill out the whole story, but although she probably wouldn't have minded in the least, it wouldn't have been remotely appropriate or professional.

'There is something uplifting about snow,' I said. 'And I'm looking forward to putting the decorations up today.'

'Christmas has crept back into your heart,' said Marilise. 'I'm glad. Did you make your mince pies?'

'The mince pies!' I exclaimed in horror. 'I forgot all about them.'

'Don't worry,' said Marilise. 'I don't think Sofia will have gone down yet. I am perfectly comfortable here, if you would like to go and deal with it? And then I would like to go downstairs again for breakfast.'

'Thank you!' I called, dashing from the room, berating myself. How could I have forgotten? Too busy lost in my girlish romantic dreams; I had better pull myself together. Put Nick to the back of my mind and focus on what needed to be done. That lasted about thirty seconds. I burst into the kitchen, and there he was, moving the mince pies from the cooling rack onto a plate. He turned as I made my rather inelegant entrance.

'Oh! You remembered! I'd forgotten all about them!'

'Morning,' he said, smiling as he wiped the cooling rack and put it back in the cupboard. 'I was down early with Steve, otherwise I would have forgotten, too. Lots of other things on my mind.'

He gazed at me as I floated across the room to him, then took my hand. He was lowering his head to mine for another kiss, when the door opened and we sprang apart guiltily.

'Good morning,' said Angela, her eyes darting between us as she no doubt correctly appraised the situation. 'Still making those mince pies?'

'They're all done,' said Nick, holding up the plate. 'Just have to put them in a window.'

'What about the number?' I gasped. 'I haven't done that, either.'

'All in hand,' said Nick, picking up a piece of paper from the table, on which he had printed out a large and lavishly decorated number three.

'You two seem to have swapped roles this morning,' observed Angela, a smile pushing at her lips as she filled the kettle. 'Nick all calm and organised and you, Laura, if you don't mind me saying, a little flustered.'

I flushed, but Nick gave an easy grin.

'Are you saying I'm normally flustered, Angela?' he said in a tone of mock outrage.

'Well, maybe more in a constant state of flux,' she replied teasingly. 'Now tell me, will this new state of tranquillity rub off on that dog of yours at all? He's in the front hall at the moment, growling at the shadows the falling snow is making.'

'I don't think Steve remembers seeing snow before,' said Nick. 'He was very surprised by it when I took him out this morning. Right, I'd better go and get this sorted before Sofia appears.'

'I'll go and help Marilise,' I said. 'She'd like to come down for breakfast again today, please, Angela.'

Soon the whole family was around the table, eating and watching the falling snow.

'Do you think there will be enough to make a snowman?' asked Sofia, who had insisted on trying one of the mince pies she found beside the bathroom window for breakfast and declared it 'awesome'.

'It looks thick,' said Astrid. 'So you might be in luck, but we have the decorating to do as well.'

She glanced at her phone for the millionth time that morning, looking anxious. I wondered what was bothering her, but it wasn't the right time to ask.

'Do you know when the delivery's coming?' asked Greg. 'I've started clearing the drive and put some salt down, so they shouldn't have any trouble getting through.'

'The trees are here already,' said India, who had been last to the table. 'I took Firefly out for a quick ride this morning and we saw them deliver them.'

'Great,' said Nick, and picked up his own phone. 'The shop texted to say the delivery will be between ten and eleven, so we'll be able to get started before lunch.'

As breakfast finished, I asked Marilise what she would like to do that morning.

'What I would love,' she said, 'is to go outside in the snow. Maybe I can watch Sofia make her snowman. Is that foolish? Am I too likely to slip?'

I frowned.

'Not foolish, no, not if we think about it carefully. You'll need sturdy, non-slip shoes and to wrap up warm, and you must promise to tell me if you start to get chilly.'

'I promise.'

'I have some shoes you can borrow,' said Angela. 'I missed Stir Up Sunday, so I'm going to get that pudding made today, with Greg's help, unless you need him?'

'I can help Laura,' said Nick. 'And I'll help Sofia, too, with that snowman. At school we used to steal one of the master's hats for ours to wear; they looked very dignified.'

Forty-five minutes later, we were togged up and helping Marilise outside. Before he had disappeared into the kitchen to help with the Christmas pudding, Greg had carried a small armchair outside.

'This is thick and padded,' he said, wiggling the feet into the snow. 'It should keep the cold out, and Angela's added a couple of hot water bottles. Right, see you in about six months,' he said gloomily. 'Making this pudding always feels like it takes that long. Cooking's not my thing, but I know Ange needs me today.'

We wished him luck and turned happily back to the snowy scene outside. The sun was filtering through the clouds now, and the garden looked magical with the sparkling snow lying in a thick blanket over everything. I made sure that Marilise was comfortable, then went to help Sofia and Nick, who were already scooping great handfuls of snow into a pile. Nick caught my eye and smiled, and a glow flooded through me, all the way to my toes. I smiled back dreamily, only leaping back into action when Sofia said, 'Come on, I'm doing all the work here.'

I glanced over at Marilise, who looked blissful, but also awarded me a quick flick of the eyebrows.

She knows, I thought, but I didn't mind. As we were packing snow up to make a body, India emerged from the house.

'Mind if I join you?' she said. 'Mum's gone to help with the Christmas pudding, but it's too nice to be inside.'

We worked hard until we had a good, fat snowman shape, almost as tall as I was.

'Okay,' said Sofia, who was almost unrecognisable from the child who had arrived a few days before. Gone was the wan expression and the averted eyes, and here was a little girl who radiated happiness and confidence, although she always had her reindeer, Reddo, with her. Right now, he was tucked into her coat, just his sweet little face poking out at the top. 'Now, our snowman needs eyes, arms, a nose, legs, a mouth, ears and clothes.'

Nick roared with laughter.

'He's going to look pretty special,' he said. 'Are you sure about the legs?'

Her forehead creased momentarily as she studied the snowy figure.

'Well, maybe we can draw those on, but everything else. Laura, India, can you go and find some sticks for his arms and stones for his mouth?'

We nodded and, with a quick check on Marilise, scurried off to hunt the items down as Sofia continued issuing instructions.

'We need to go under the trees at the front of the house,' said India. 'It won't be very snowy there, so we'll be able to find things more easily.'

'Good idea,' I said, jogging after her and wishing I was as fit as a fifteen-year-old horsewoman.

It didn't take long to find some suitable sticks and a selection of nut cases and cones for the mouth, as India said these would stay stuck in the snow better than stones. As we went to leave the wood, I hesitated.

'India, is your mum okay? She looked worried this morning and kept checking her phone – it's not like her.'

'I know,' said India, biting her lip. 'I think she was expecting Philip to be here by now, or at least have said when he was coming, but he won't.'

'I see. Okay, well, let me know if there's anything I can do. Hopefully, he'll get his act together soon.'

'Hopefully not,' snorted India, and started off back to the garden again, at what she probably thought was a stroll, but which raised my heartrate trying to keep up.

Everyone else returned at about the same time and we added our adornments to the snowman and stepped back to admire our work.

'What do you think?' Nick asked Marilise. 'Handsome fellow, isn't he?'

She studied our effort, taking in his stick arms with little gloves dangling on the ends, his carrot nose and the rather dashing dark green hat Nick had come up with.

'I think you have all done a splendid job,' she said. 'I have not seen such a fine snowman in many years. I would like some photos,' she continued, taking out her phone. 'Laura, dear, would you? I think if I take my gloves off, my poor old fingers will be too shaky for a good shot.'

'Of course!' I said, taking the phone from her. Nick and India also took photos, and we showed Marilise the results.

'So wonderful,' she said. 'I will send off for prints of some of these to put in my album. Thank you.'

She was beginning to look rather pale, so I suggested she go inside for her nap.

'Will we swim today?' she asked, as I helped her into bed.

'What about this afternoon?' I suggested. 'If you're feeling up to it. You can't miss the decorating and it's been a tiring morning already.'

She nodded and muttered something, already falling asleep. I leant closer to try to hear her words.

'Nikolai,' she murmured. 'He is such a good boy. I'm so glad.'

Before I could ask her what she meant – although I had to admit that I thought I knew – she was asleep.

She was still sleeping when the delivery arrived so, much to Sofia and India's disappointment, we couldn't get started straight away.

'There's something we can do, though,' said Nick. 'Now we have proper stands, we need to get the trees inside the house and out of their nets. Marilise won't mind us doing that without her. We'll need everyone else, though; the one for the hallway is huge.'

Personally, I was thrilled to see such a big tree; it must have been twelve feet tall. I think the largest Paulo and I had ever had was four, and that took over half the living room. He would have laughed if he could see me now, getting used to such a grand lifestyle. I could imagine him picking up his battered tool bag, off to a job, saying, 'At least your Mum and Steph would approve! And don't forget what I've taught you about wiring plugs – it's a handy skill, even if you're living like royalty.' But he would have been pleased, I think, that I was finding happiness.

This huge tree would look magnificent in the hallway, and there was plenty of space for it. The Christmas pudding was now steaming, and would be for the next eight hours, only requiring occasional attention to top the water up, so Angela and Greg joined us. The smaller tree was taken through to the living room and somehow, between the seven of us, we managed to haul the bigger tree inside and raise it up into its stand. Astrid and I were deputised to remain on the landing, clinging to the top branches while everyone else joined in with snipping and pulling off the net which was wound around the tree. Next, we looped fishing wire around the trunk in several places, which Greg tied firmly to the banisters. It was hot, scratchy work delving into the branches to push the fishing wire through, and removing the fine netting was like trying to pick off a spider's web, but when we had finished and the tree stood proudly in the hall, its branches free, it was worth all the effort.

'Oh, it's beautiful,' said Astrid, wiping her eyes unselfconsciously. She grabbed Nick's arm and squeezed him to her. 'Look what you've done, clever boy, you've made me cry, but in such a good way.'

As Nick hugged her and glanced across at me, I thought he looked misty-eyed himself and, for the first time in a long time, the emotion that caused prickling behind my own eyelids wasn't sadness, or grief, but joy.

'We need someone small for the next bit,' said Greg, brandishing a watering can.

'Ooh, me, me!' said Sofia, who had been capering about with excitement.

'You're just the person,' said Greg. 'I need you to go crawling about underneath that tree, first with a dustpan and brush for all the dropped needles and then with this watering can to fill up the stand. Are you up for it?'

'Yes!' she shrieked and, taking the things he had mentioned, disappeared underneath the tree, screaming with pleasure.

'I wish I got that much happiness out of a dustpan and brush,' said Angela, smiling fondly, and we all laughed.

'I'll go and get Marilise while all this is being done,' I said. 'She'll be so happy.'

I knew that Marilise was tired, but she was determined to come downstairs and join in as much as she could.

'Set me up with some coffee and a couple of those delicious mince pies and I'll be as right as rain,' she insisted, so that was what I did. She professed her delight with the tree and then asked that the tea chests of decorations be brought over next to her.

'If you will indulge an old woman, I would like to unpack these and give them to the rest of you to hang. My days of climbing a stepladder are, I think, over.'

Greg and Nick had already wound the lights around the tree, and they twinkled merrily as we carefully hung the exquisite decorations. Some were finely carved wood, and many were made of lace so delicate that I feared it would fall apart in my hands, but most were delicate glass in every colour imaginable, which caught and reflected the lights, making the tree look ethereal.

Sofia soon got bored with the careful work, so Astrid took

her to open some of the other boxes that had arrived, and soon they were cooing over the large reindeer and posing with them for selfies before taking them outside.

'Is Astrid all right?' asked Nick, as we both hung decorations around the back of the tree. 'She looks a bit... strained.'

I explained what India had told me.

'I'll speak to her later,' he said. 'I can't help feeling some responsibility for all this.'

I took his hand and squeezed it, gazing into his eyes and thinking how different he was from the man I had first met a few days ago. That man seemed inured to his family and their feelings, so wrapped up was he in nursing his own insecurities and sense of injustice, but now Nick seemed so caring. It crossed my mind that I still didn't know him well enough to judge which was the real him, but Marilise seemed so sure that he was 'a good boy', and my gut was telling me the same, although, if I was being honest with myself, his kissing technique could easily be throwing any of my other instincts into the shade.

'What are you two doing behind there?' came India's cheeky voice, and we jumped guiltily, then grinned at each other.

'Just making sure everything's perfect,' called back Nick and we giggled. By now, the fact that something had happened between us must have been obvious to everyone, but I didn't care.

When we emerged, Sofia and Astrid were coming in from positioning the reindeer, and Marilise's tea chests were nearly empty.

'What else did you buy?' she asked, pausing her unwrapping of the last few items.

'Half the shop,' said Nick, and opened a couple of the boxes. 'Ah, here are my candy canes,' he said, extracting them with a flourish that made India and Sofia laugh. 'More lights, and oh! Just a tiny bit of tinsel.'

He upended a large box, sending a waterfall of tinsel onto the floor.

'Oh dear,' said Astrid, with the biggest smile I had seen on her face all day. 'Your poor father will be turning in his grave. He hated tinsel.'

'Why do you think I bought so much?' asked Nick, returning her smile. 'This is for you and me to hang. Where shall we start?'

I looked around at the happy scene: Nick and Astrid with armfuls of gaudy tinsel, Angela and Greg unwinding yet more lights to twine around the banisters, Sofia giggling as she used a giant candy cane as a walking stick, India balancing on the stepladder to hang the last of the antique decorations and Marilise snapping pictures of it all on her phone. I may have only been there for a short time, but Lyonscroft was already beginning to feel like home.

SIXTEEN

The next few days passed blissfully. Everyone was upbeat, enjoying the decorations so sparkly and colourful they could probably have been seen from space and beginning to sneak wrapped presents under the tree. Sofia was enjoying school and had been quick to make friends. She hero-worshipped India, who had shown her extreme kindness, even ceasing to complain about the Christmas show they were both involved with, and which Sofia loved being in.

'I got my snowflake costume today,' she told Marilise and me one afternoon when she got home from school and we were playing cards downstairs, sitting by the window so that we could enjoy the snow without having to go outside. 'It's so pretty. Virginia's mummy made them, it's got a sort of sticky out net skirt, which is light blue, no...' she corrected herself. 'It's *turquoise*, that's what Virginia said was the right word. Anyway, it's got lots of silver sequins, and we wear a white leotard and have ribbons for our hair and around our wrists.'

She beamed at us and we both beamed back, enchanted by this delightful child, so changed from when she had first arrived at Lyonscroft.

'There's one thing,' she said, a shadow of worry crossing her face. 'Mrs Bradley said that someone needs to bring us and help us get ready before the show. She said our mummy or daddy or nanny, but I don't have any of those here.'

I glanced at Marilise, whose face was the picture of compassion. She reached out her hand and grasped Sofia's.

'But you do not need to worry about that, my cherub,' she said, with the tiniest flicker of emotion in her voice, which she quickly overcame. 'When I was a child, at the palace, my parents were often not able to be with my sister or me, and many different people would look after us. It could feel a little sad at times, but we knew our parents loved us and we remembered our royal blood; that running through our veins was the ability to be *wonderful*, no matter what, to enjoy ourselves, to bring pleasure to others, to be honest and brave. You have this same blood, you know, and you also have people here who love you and care about you. They will *all* want to accompany you to school and help you into your beautiful costume, and we will all be thrilled by your performance.'

She sat back, tired after this long speech, and I looked at Sofia, not sure how much she would have absorbed. But a smile crept onto her face, and I saw her sit up straighter than before.

'Mrs Bradley doesn't know about my royal blood,' she said. 'If she minds that it's not a mummy or daddy or nanny, then I shall tell her about it.'

'Quite right,' I said, grinning. 'But I'm sure she won't mind. Astrid will be very glad to take you, or I can?'

I cast a questioning glance at Marilise, who nodded.

'Indeed. I think that would be a very good idea, if you are happy with it, Sofia?'

The little girl looked at me shyly and nodded.

'Yes, please. You're very good at doing hair.'

. . .

I knew why Marilise had preferred me over Astrid to help Sofia. Amidst all the happiness and festive cheer, Astrid was the only person who was unhappy, although she did her best to hide it. Philip had still not put in an appearance, and I know he had been expected by now. I asked Nick about it one evening when we took Steve out for his nighttime walk, something we had taken to doing together. I looked forward to this short time together all day and, although part of me would have liked to speed things up, I could appreciate that the enforced slowness of the progression of our relationship was for the best. I still thought about Paulo every day, but the pain was softening into a glow, and I was more readily remembering the happy times and accepting that he would be glad to see me moving forward. I had not mentioned anything to my family as, if they had anything to do with it, the minute I was out of the peach satin, I would be into white tulle, and I definitely wasn't ready for that.

'Has Astrid said anything to you about Philip?' I asked, grabbing Steve's collar as his shoulder dipped in a way I had come to recognise meant he was about to roll in something smelly.

'No,' he replied. 'And I haven't wanted to ask, but she's so unhappy. Do you think there's anything we can do?'

I shook my head.

'I think the only thing is to be there for her, as and when she needs us.'

Nick stopped walking and turned towards me, taking both my gloved hands in his.

'Us,' he repeated. 'I like that.'

He bent his head and kissed me gently, then pulled away, grinning.

'Until now, "us" has always meant me and Steve – I assume you have included him?'

'Of course,' I said. 'And Steve wouldn't be left out even if I tried.'

As if in answer to this, the big dog lolloped over and pushed his head between us, demanding to be stroked.

'There are three of us in this relationship,' quipped Nick. 'But it seems to be working fine.'

A couple of mornings later, I was chatting to Marilise over breakfast in her room. It was the charity concert that evening and I wanted to check that everything was in place for Angela to help in my absence. But, predictably, Marilise didn't want to talk about logistics.

'It will all be fine,' she said, waving me away. 'Angela has looked after me for a long time, she knows what to do and can cope with the little extras.' The 'little extras' involved some new medication and changes to Marilise's evening care routine, but although I didn't like handing my responsibilities over, I knew that Angela would handle everything beautifully. 'Tell me instead about what you are going to wear this evening.'

'I have the dress I wore to the party at your neighbours, the Westmans,' I said. 'I had it cleaned, so it's ready to go.'

'I see.'

I had got to know Marilise well over the weeks we had spent together, and I could tell she had more to say.

'Don't you think it would be suitable?' I asked.

'Well, my dear, it is a very *nice* dress...' *Nice*, I thought, *being the death knell for my outfit*. 'But I think this is the perfect occasion for something a little more spectacular. After all' – she shot me a prize-winning side eye – 'you are trying to convince them, are you not, that you and Nick are a couple? They must be stunned, not underwhelmed.'

Outmanoeuvred, I laughed.

'True. But what do you suggest? I don't have time to get something now.'

'No, but I have some dresses tucked away that I think would

be suitable.' I opened my mouth to protest that we were totally different body shapes, but she pre-empted me. 'They are not all mine, some belonged to my mother and some to my sister, and I am convinced there will be something perfect. Now, when you went to the attic to look for the Christmas decorations, did you see a large armoire?' I nodded. 'Good. There is one dress in there I have in mind for you – it is dark green with exquisite beading. See if you can find that.'

I took our breakfast things down to the kitchen, then went straight up to the attic, heading for the end room where Nick and I had found the tea chests full of decorations. It felt a little spooky up there on my own, but I hummed Christmas songs under my breath for courage and felt glad that I had remembered to wear a cosy cardigan against the chill. As I had recalled, there was a large armoire with elegantly carved scrolls above the doors and large ball feet. The mirror on one of the doors was badly foxed, but I could see a hazy reflection of myself as I turned the small brass key and opened the doors to reveal at least twenty clothes bags hanging neatly on the rail. Shifting slightly so that I could use the weak light of the single bulb, I gently pushed the bags aside and unzipped the first a little. This revealed a dress in champagne silk. I longed to get it out and look at it properly, but imagined Marilise sitting downstairs, waiting impatiently for me to return for my Cinderella moment, and moved on to the next bag. In this was a pale blue dress with a floaty chiffon neckline, which I tucked in carefully as I did the zip back up. I continued along the bags, revealing beautiful fabrics in a rainbow of colours before finding one that was as Marilise had described. I wasn't sure how I felt about potentially borrowing this item which, as well as no doubt being very expensive, was far more glamorous than anything I had ever worn. I lifted it carefully off the rail before locking the doors again and heading back downstairs.

'Is this it?' I asked, showing her the top part of the dress that I had revealed.

'Ah yes, good, that is the one,' she said, sounding pleased. 'Take it out of the bag.'

Carefully, I extracted the dress. It was a deep emerald green with two layers, the first of a heavy silk and the second, top layer, of chiffon, hand beaded all over with an intricate flower pattern that glinted in the light.

'Marilise, it's spectacular,' I said. 'Are you sure you want to lend it to me?'

'Of course I am sure, I would like nothing more. And you are not to worry about it. This dress is beautiful, yes, but it is of more use having champagne being spilt down it or catching on a beau's watch as he puts his arms around you than it is sitting patiently unworn in the attic as it has already done for so many years. Try it on!'

I hesitated.

'What's wrong?'

'I'm not sure,' I said, biting my lip. 'I don't think it's really me. I'm not sure how comfortable I'd be in a dress like this.'

'You do not think you merit such a garment?' asked Marilise, her voice soft but her eyes looking at me closely.

'It's not that, exactly,' I said feebly. 'But dresses like this are made for princesses, not nurses. I don't want to look odd, like a child wearing her mother's high heels.'

'Odd?' Marilise frowned. 'Laura, it is just a dress, not a magic spell. It is for whoever wears it.' Her voice took on a stubborn tone. 'You think you will look like you do not belong in it, but I say differently. Please, try it on. If you feel awkward, or we do not think the dress works, you do not have to wear it. This is not a police state!' She grinned and swept her arm around, taking in the beautiful bedroom. 'We are just having some fun, yes?'

I laughed, feeling more relaxed.

'Yes!'

I took off my jeans and shirt and stepped carefully into the dress. As I pulled it up and slipped my arms into the elbow-length gauzy sleeves, I could tell that her expert eye had not let Marilise down; it was a perfect fit. I did up the zip as far as I could, then smoothed my hair over one shoulder and knelt down with my back to her, so that she could draw it all the way to the top. Then I stood in front of her, my residual self-consciousness pushed away by excitement. I watched her face as she looked me over, feeling relief when she broke into a smile.

'It is perfect,' she said. 'As I knew it would be. How do you feel?'

'Wonderful,' I said honestly.

She nodded briskly.

'It could have been made for you. My mother, whose dress this was, would agree, I know. Help me up.'

Quickly, I gave her my arm, and she rose to her feet and went over to her own wardrobe. After a few moments, she turned around, holding a finely knitted cream-coloured shawl, which she held out to me. It was as soft as a cloud, and I stroked it in wonder.

'This is cashmere,' said Marilise, going to sit down again. 'It will keep you warm enough to get from the car to the house.' I stammered out my thanks, which she waved away. 'I am enjoying myself far too much to be thanked. Now, shoes. What do you have with you?'

'Just the black heels you saw before.'

She clicked her tongue in annoyance.

'They are smart, and you have looked after them, so they will have to do, but I'm not happy about them with this shawl. I don't want you wearing a black one, though, not right for Christmas, not right at all.' She pondered for a moment. 'Very well, this once you can wear the black shoes with the shawl, but you must promise me that you will buy some suitable shoes as soon as possible, for the next time you wear it. It is yours now, of course, the dress and the shawl.'

I gasped.

'I couldn't accept them, thank you, but I can't.'

'Well, of course you can. Two items of clothing that fit you perfectly and are doing no one else any good. Now get changed, quickly please, I am ready for my morning nap.'

Still unsure that I should keep the dress, but not wanting to keep Marilise from her sleep, I quickly put my own clothes back on and helped her into bed. I crept from the room, even more excited now for the evening ahead.

The taxi came just before the rest of the household sat down for supper, so Nick and I had a send-off committee. I had taken extra care when doing my hair and make-up, wanting to do the beautiful dress justice. I tried to stay calm as I thought about the evening ahead and remembered how it had felt to kiss Nick. As I walked down the stairs to see the little group gathered at the bottom, a smile spread across my face, even as I felt rather shy at the unaccustomed attention. Marilise nodded in approval, although she gave a delicate wince when her eye travelled over my shoes. Nick grinned broadly and stepped forward to take my hand as I descended the final few steps.

'You look wonderful,' he said. 'That colour is stunning on you.'

Astrid seemed to be lifted from her anxious brooding and insisted on taking photographs of us together.

'I know we're making a terrible fuss,' she said to me. 'But we don't often get dressed up like this and it's such fun to enjoy it – even if I personally will be spending the evening folding socks.'

'You're making me feel like a teenager off to my first prom,' grumbled Nick.

'Indulge your stepmother,' said Astrid, smiling and reaching out to straighten his collar. 'You both look so lovely.'

'Come here,' said Nick, and pulled her into a hug, then took her phone and snapped a selfie of the two of them. 'If you insist on photos of me with beautiful women, then there's another one for your collection.'

Sofia and India were entranced by my dress, touching the beading gingerly and asking me to spin so that my skirts flew out, and Sofia conceded that it was *almost* as pretty as her snowflake costume.

The taxi ride was about twenty minutes, and Nick held my hand on his lap the whole way as he told me who I might meet at the party.

'There's Minty – Araminta – of course, who you've already met.'

'Yes, I'm looking forward to seeing her again. We've been texting a lot and she's hilarious; it's making the whole wedding thing feel more manageable.'

'Yes, she's great, but I still don't want to marry her, a fact which her parents, Colonel and Mrs Montgomery, have studiously ignored over the years. Expect them to look daggers at you tonight, but know that Minty and I are eternally grateful. I've never produced a girlfriend before, pretend or otherwise, and I'm hoping it will put the nail in the coffin of their ambitions.'

I bit my lip, unsure as to exactly what he had meant – *pretend or otherwise*. This whole idea had started as a façade to put the Montgomerys off but, given our growing closeness, it now had more than a slight ring of truth to it. But were we 'girlfriend and boyfriend'? I wasn't sure, and I wouldn't have questioned it at this stage, normally.

'Are you okay?' asked Nick.

I gave myself a little shake. The best thing to do was enjoy myself: the party, the music, the dress, the company and try not to pick it apart unnecessarily. Paulo's death had taught me well enough that *what will be, will be*, no matter how we try to control things.

'I'm great,' I said. 'And in terms of people to look out for, it's likely that my sister Steph and her chief bridesmaid Dorothea will also be there, who you already know, of course. All I can say in advance is: sorry.'

I grinned and he smiled back at me.

'Looks like we're in for an interesting evening.'

SEVENTEEN

The taxi pulled up in front of an enormous, elaborate house, with pointed arches, spires and carved finials. The neat, low hedges flanking the drive were flecked with white fairy lights and there was an enormous wreath on the dark blue front door, but otherwise no Christmas decorations. We stepped out of the car and the front door was opened to admit us. A lugubrious man in a black tailcoat and white gloves greeted us by name and led us through the house, past closed doors and console tables groaning under enormous displays of flowers, until we heard the murmur of voices. He stood in front of a door, his hand on the knob and intoned:

'Pre-concert drinks are being taken in the White Drawing Room.'

He then opened the door.

I don't mind going into parties by myself, but I have to admit that, this time, I was glad to have my arm hooked through Nick's as he strode forward confidently and thanked the – well, the butler, I suppose. I hadn't appreciated what a smart family Steph was marrying into, and I felt a pang of sympathy for her meticulousness over the wedding arrangements. There were about eighty people in the room, chattering away as they drank champagne. Everyone was dressed beautifully, the men in black tie and the women in mostly floor-length dresses in an array of gorgeous colours. I was grateful again to Marilise for the dress, which was perfect. *At least in that respect I fit in*, I thought. A statuesque woman glided over to us, a tight smile on her face. *This must be our hostess.* She held out her hand palm down to Nick, who touched it briefly, with a slight nod of his head.

'Good evening, Bridget.'

'Good evening, Nick,' she said. 'Thank you for joining us tonight.' She turned her head towards me. 'And welcome, Miss Wilde. Stephanie is here, and your dear parents, of course.' I settled for giving her a slightly sickly smile, rather than saying anything; it hadn't occurred to me that Mum and Dad might be here; stupid of me. She turned back to Nick. 'Miss Wilde and I are soon to be related, through her sister's marriage to Hugo.'

'So I've been told,' said Nick smoothly. 'I shall be attending myself, as Laura's guest.'

'Of course you will,' replied Mrs Montgomery. 'We are all looking forward to seeing you there, particularly Araminta. You must look out for her this evening.' She shot me a final look, which belied her gracious tone of voice and told me exactly what she thought of me. 'Do enjoy the concert.'

With this, she melted back into the crowd. I turned to Nick, horrified, but he was wiping tears of laughter from his eyes as he grabbed two glasses of champagne from a waiter, who had been hovering nearby, looking unsure as to whether or not he should interrupt our being greeted by Mrs Montgomery.

'Cheers!' he said. 'Let's drink to her never being my mother-in-law.'

I sipped my drink.

'I'm feeling bad about the whole thing,' I said. 'Accepting her hospitality when she so obviously doesn't want me here.'

Nick took my free hand in his and looked at me, all humour gone from his face.

'Don't,' he said fiercely. 'It's not you personally, it's anyone with me other than Minty, and Minty most definitely doesn't want to be with me. This started out as you doing me and her a favour, but you know I want you here for you, don't you?' I nodded. 'Bridget Montgomery disapproves of anything happening outside her control. That makes her amazing at supporting charities, but horrendous if you cross her.'

'I hope Steph will be all right,' I said. 'She's enjoying it all at the moment, all the fuss over the wedding, and I think she does love Hugo, but what if she falls foul of her new mother-in-law?'

'Won't happen,' said Nick confidently. 'Once Bridget has approved somebody, especially to the extent of letting her marry one of her precious sons, that person has complete immunity. Short of leaving the marriage and running off with someone else, your sister will be in the inner circle.'

'Good,' I said. I may find Steph hard work, but I wanted her to be happy. I glimpsed a waving hand out of the corner of my eye, and turned slightly, to see my parents and Dorothea advancing fast. We greeted each other and I introduced Nick to my parents, then Dorothea adopted her most ringing tones.

'I heard that you were coming, Laura. Jolly good on you, Nick, giving her a night out.'

She couldn't have reduced me to "staff" so quickly if she had tied a starched white apron round my waist. I had no quick reply, but Nick wasn't fazed by her.

'It's Laura doing me the favour, actually,' he replied calmly. He turned to my parents. 'You must be so proud of her. She's a wonderful nurse; my grandmother wouldn't be without her now.'

My parents both beamed, and I basked in their approval. It wasn't something I was used to, particularly from my mother.

'We're very proud of her,' said Dad warmly, reaching over to squeeze my hand. 'Laura is very special.'

Dorothea was looking more sour by the moment.

'Far too good for a philistine like me,' replied Nick with a self-deprecating grin. 'I know it was the music that tempted her here tonight, really.'

'Oh *no*,' gushed my mother. 'I'm sure she's *thrilled* to be here with a real prince.'

Dorothea's eyebrows nearly hit the ceiling, and I died a little inside, but Nick's smooth confidence had rubbed off. I turned to him.

'*Are* you?' I asked in incredulous and slightly offended tones. 'You told me you were an app designer.'

'Only my surname,' he said, sighing. 'A little irony, courtesy of my grandfather.'

All of this went straight over my mother's head. She laid a reassuring hand on Nick's arm.

'But you have blue blood,' she said earnestly. 'And that is what matters.'

I could see the wedding at Westminster Abbey taking shape in her mind already. She, perhaps, would arrive in a state coach; I would wear Alexander McQueen. Maybe Dorothea saw the same fantasy unfolding and was quick to snuff it out.

'I have always appreciated Giles' title,' she said grandly. 'And sharing it, of course. Being in the know is all very well, but when it's official, it does open doors.'

'Well then, let's hope it's not too long before it's yours,' said Nick gravely. 'Although his father is looking well, and so young.'

Dorothea, no doubt furious to be reminded that the title wasn't yet actually in her grasp, shot him a look of pure venom.

'Shall we go and find Steph?' she said to my parents. 'I know she wanted to talk wedding a little tonight.'

As they sailed off, I bit my lip and put a hand to my head, glancing up at Nick, who was also trying not to laugh.

'Ouch,' I said. 'Sorry about Mum.'

'It doesn't matter at all,' he said. 'She meant to be kind, unlike Dorothea.'

'Talking about my delightful sister-in-law?' came a voice, and we turned to see Minty, wearing a silk dress with a chiffon cape in the exact blue of her eyes. She hugged both of us, then drained her glass and swiftly swapped it for a full one from the tray of one of the ubiquitous waiters. 'I'm so glad to see you both, my mother has been intolerable. She keeps trying to fix me up with people now she thinks you've been taken, Nick, and no matter how much I tell her that I don't care about being at the wedding on my own, she seems to think it's some terrible indignity.'

We laughed and glanced at each other and Minty looked at us intently.

'Ooh, I think you *have* been taken!' she said. 'I'm right, aren't I?'

We grinned back at her dopily.

'You are,' said Nick, taking my hand again.

'Good,' she whispered, squeezing my arm, as the butler struck a gong which stood in a corner of the room.

'Please will guests make their way to the ballroom, where the Christmas concert is due to begin in five minutes,' he intoned.

We walked back into the hallway, and I saw that a huge pair of double doors now stood open, revealing an enormous ballroom, its walls covered in gold flocked velvet wallpaper and hung with oil paintings and large, gold-framed mirrors. A stage had been erected at one end and chairs laid out in neat rows. Minty led us to the front of the room, and we sat down as the seats filled around us. A hush fell as the musicians stepped onto the stage. A woman sat at the grand piano, which was so highly polished you could do your eyeliner in its reflection, two men sat down and picked up violins, a third man lifted a cello and another woman took up a viola while a third sat down amongst various percussion instruments. Finally, a woman dressed in a navy-blue velvet suit with diamante buttons, holding a baton, walked onto the stage and bowed as we applauded. Then she turned around, lifted her baton, and the music began.

For the next hour I was transported to Christmas heaven as the musicians played a sweeping range of pieces from carols such as 'Hark! The Herald Angels Sing' to family favourites, including 'Frosty the Snowman.' For the final piece, the conductor turned to the audience and told us it was our turn to join in. She picked out twelve people, one of them Minty, and gave them large boards with a picture of each of the presents from 'The Twelve Days of Christmas'. These they had to hold up at the right time so that the rest of us could join in. Perhaps predictably, it all fell apart around 'nine ladies dancing' and there was much laughter as the conductor untangled us and skilfully set the song going again. The atmosphere in the room couldn't have been more perfect for the time of the year as Bridget Montgomery came onto the stage, a genuine, wide smile on her face, and thanked them, then announced how much had been raised for the charity that evening. Tingling with Christmas cheer, we returned to the White Drawing Room, where round tables, each seating ten people, had been set up for dinner. A large seating chart showed us that Nick and I were at the same table, but not sitting next to each other. I had Hugo on one side, with Steph next to him, and a man called Sim Waykes on my other side. Nick was next to Minty.

'Seems kind of unfair that Steph and Hugo can sit next to each other, but we can't,' I whispered as we walked to the table. I was beginning to feel persecuted.

'To be fair to Bridget,' said Nick, 'she's following the rules. Engaged couples can sit together, but others are usually split up.

Doesn't mean to say we have to like it, though. Shall I swap the name cards?'

'No, don't do that,' I replied. 'It'll be all right.'

Hugo and Steph were already there when I sat down, and my sister greeted me with little enthusiasm. I made dull small talk with Hugo for a few minutes, before the seat on my other side was taken by a tall, debonair man with thick black hair, tanned skin and the most come-to-bed eyes I had ever seen this side of a movie screen.

'Good evening,' he said, holding out his hand, which I shook. 'I'm Sim.'

'Laura,' I replied.

'Well, Laura, I'm very happy to meet you. Very happy. Did you enjoy the concert?'

I barely noticed the first course, a delicious beetroot soup with a swirl of cream on top, being served, as Sim engaged me so totally in conversation, asking me questions about myself and making me laugh with his gently bitchy anecdotes of the Montogomery family, who he seemed to have known forever. He kept my wine glass full, complimented my dress and made thoughtful comments about the state of our National Health Service, having learnt that I was a nurse. As the second course, a rich and fragrant winter vegetable Wellington, was put in front of us, I glanced over to Nick for, much as I was enjoying Sim's company, I still would have preferred to be sitting with him. He waggled his thumb at me, a questioning look on his face, and I gave him a firm 'thumbs up', not wanting him to worry that I wasn't enjoying myself. By the time we started on the mini pavlovas with spiced stewed pears, drenched in an orange-brandy sauce and topped with whipped cream, I had not only had enough wine, but was beginning to think I'd also had enough of Sim's company, which was tipping over from the friendly to the flirtatious. As coffee was served, I took the opportunity to turn to Hugo, instead finding that he had moved and Steph had taken his place.

'Enjoying yourself, are you?' she said, raising her eyebrows pointedly in Sim's direction, although speaking too softly for him to hear. 'Please don't embarrass me here.'

I pressed down my anger and said mildly, 'We were just talking. I'd rather be sitting next to Nick, but I wasn't given the choice.'

'Well, I'm sure Bridget knows what she's doing with the *placement*,' replied Steph. 'She obviously thought that you and Sim would get on, and she was right, apparently. Anyway' – she took another sip of her wine – 'you don't want to put all your eggs in Nick's basket, do you? Very sensible.'

I knew I shouldn't take the bait, but I couldn't resist.

'What do you mean?'

'Well,' she continued, pushing her barely touched pavlova aside and picking up her coffee cup. 'He's moving back to LA after Christmas, isn't he? Everyone knows that. At least there's no danger of spoiling our plans of you being my maternity nurse.'

I gritted my teeth.

'I think they were your plans rather than ours, Steph.'

She looked at me as if I had suggested something so outlandishly funny that I must be going slightly crazy. Poor, dear, widowed, crazy sister. This was followed up by the classic tinkly laugh so beloved of her and her friends.

'Oh, Laura! You surely can't think that this...' She twirled her hand in the air as if trying to think of some suitable word for the abomination she was trying to describe. My sister is not much of a wordsmith. '...this *thing* with Nick Prince is anything more than a fling, can you?' I tried to keep my expression neutral, but she must have seen the hurt in my face, as she moved on to the next step of the routine: the concerned head tilt. 'Oh dear, you do.' She put the tips of her perfectly manicured fingers to her lips as if to hide a smile that couldn't help escaping. 'Dear Laura, Nick isn't going to give up his lifestyle for you. He's barely at Lyonscroft as it is, and everyone knows he's dying to sell it so he can cut ties even more and be completely carefree. He's the catch of the county now Giles and Hugo are taken, and he's had a parade of girlfriends, none of whom have managed to hold on to him; I can't imagine what you think it is about you that might be different.'

This final barb was said with such confidence in its truth that I could almost accept there was no malice behind it. Steph simply believed what she was saying: that there was nothing special about me. I reached for my wine glass, full again even though I had been ignoring Sim for the last five minutes and took a hefty gulp; maybe I hadn't had enough, after all. I opened my mouth to begin stumbling out some reply, some sort of defence, when a hand touched my shoulder. I looked up: Nick. How much of the conversation had he heard? The bland smile he was giving, with his eyes fixed on my sister's face, suggested to me that he had heard enough, and wasn't happy about it. He transferred his gaze to me, and the smile became warm.

'Laura, darling,' he said, sliding his hand down my arm to take my hand. 'I have a surprise waiting outside for you – if you're not too busy?'

'Definitely not,' I said, putting my napkin on the table and standing up as Steph gave me a deeply pitying look.

'Sim will be at the wedding,' she said. 'Seeing as you got on so well tonight, I'll make sure you're sitting together again.'

At the mention of his name, Sim turned, then stood up as well.

'Nick!' he said. 'I haven't seen you in years, how are things?'

The two men shook hands warmly and briefly exchanged news.

'I had no idea you were together,' he said. 'Bloody Bridget and her table settings, gets a man's hopes up. Ah well, lovely to meet you, Laura, and let's get our heads together soon over a coffee, Nick – I have a business proposal that might interest you.'

'I'd like that,' said Nick. 'I'm planning on staying around for a while, so we should be able to find a time.'

As we said goodbye, I barely dared glance at Steph, who now looked furious. Nick and I found our hostess and thanked her for the evening, then we stepped out of the front door.

'I hope you don't mind,' said Nick. 'But I haven't ordered a taxi home.'

'Are we walking?' I said rather doubtfully. The idea of a snowy, moonlit stroll with Nick was appealing, had it not been for the outfit, in which I was already feeling chilly.

'No,' he said. 'Our lift should be here any minute.'

I heard a gentle tinkling of bells and the sound of hooves before the most beautiful red sleigh, pulled by two white horses, turned into the drive and stopped in front of us.

'Your carriage, madam,' said Nick, helping me step up into the back, which was deep with cosy faux fur blankets for us to snuggle into. A word from the driver and the horses started off again.

'I thought we'd take the long way home,' said Nick, putting his arm around me. 'We probably both need to recover from the evening we've had.'

'The music was stunning,' I said. 'And so was the food, but this is the perfect ending.'

We were drawn through the quiet lanes for about half an hour before we pulled up outside Lyonscroft. We thanked the driver and patted the horses before letting ourselves into the quiet house. Nick drew me close to him, and we kissed, our faces cold.

'Would you like a nightcap?' he whispered, winding a strand of my hair around his fingers.

I shook my head.

'I'm okay.'

'Upstairs then?' he said, and I nodded, knowing what he was suggesting.

Indeed, he took my hand and led me to his room, lit softly by the moon filtering through the snow that had started falling again. There he kissed away the cruelty of Steph's comments, Bridget's disapproval and my grief for Paulo, leaving only the joy of how right it felt to be in each other's arms.

EIGHTEEN

The next morning, I woke up early, happy to see Nick sleeping next to me in the big bed. I kissed his cheek without waking him and pulled on his robe, which was hanging on the back of the door. I picked up my clothes – I had managed to place the beautiful dress carefully over the back of a chair, carried away though I had been – and peered out of the door. The passageway outside was quiet and it seemed a good time to make a dash for my own room, whilst everyone else was still asleep. Once there, I hung the dress up carefully and stepped into the shower. It was only then that, as I soaped myself, my neck felt unexpectedly bare: the necklace Paulo had given me, the necklace I always wear, wasn't there. I searched around the bottom of the shower in a panic, worried that it would be washed down the drain and lost forever, but I couldn't find it. I quickly rinsed off, dried and dressed then, grabbing Nick's robe, hurried back to his room. He was no longer in bed, but I could hear the shower running and his pleasant baritone singing *Let it snow! Let it snow! Let it snow!* I hung up the robe and turned back the rumpled duvet, instantly spotting my necklace lying on the sheet. I snatched it up gratefully and looked at it closely; the delicate chain had broken and would need to go to a jeweller to be fixed. I sat on the bed and stared out of the window, where the snow had stopped falling, but the sky was leaden. I was not normally given to flights of fancy, but the breakage of the necklace the very first night I had spent with another man after Paulo felt like some horrible kind of portent. But then the bathroom door opened and Nick came out, his evident delight to see me there sweeping away any upset.

'Good morning,' he said, bending down to give me a lingering kiss. 'I thought you'd done a dawn dash in my robe, but I'm glad to see you're both back.'

'Only for a moment,' I said, pushing the broken necklace into my pocket. 'It's time for me to go to Marilise and she's going to want to hear all about the evening. In fact, can you send me any photos you took? I have a few, but I'd love to show her as many as possible – you know how she loves them.'

More kisses nearly made me late, and I jogged down the corridor with Nick's murmured words still making me smile: 'Don't tell her *everything*, will you?'

I found Marilise on good form, and half an hour later we were eating breakfast at her table by the window and looking through the pictures from the night before.

'I was right about the dress,' she said, sounding pleased. 'You and Nick make such a lovely couple. And don't worry, I'm not going to interrogate you, but I do know that you weren't pretending. I'm glad. Now, who is this person sitting next to you? He looks very handsome, but rather slick.'

Grateful for her discretion, I talked her through the best parts of the evening: the concert, the food and the sleigh ride home, reliving it with her until it was time for her morning nap.

After our swim, which cleared the last vestiges of sleep-deprived, champagne-fuelled fuzziness from my head, Marilise and I decided to wrap some presents to put under the tree. An avid online shopper, parcels had been arriving for her throughout the past few days and, with both the girls out, it was a good opportunity.

'I'll go and make us some tea,' I said. 'And I'll find Astrid and tell her not to come in.'

I knew that Marilise had bought her a glamorous pair of tangerine-coloured satin pyjamas with turquoise piping, and it would be such a shame if she saw them and spoilt the surprise. But when I pushed the kitchen door open, all thoughts of Christmas surprises flew from my mind, for Astrid was sitting at the kitchen table, her head on her folded arms, sobbing her heart out. I ran over to her and touched her shoulder gently.

'Astrid?'

She lifted her head and quickly began rubbing the tears from her eyes, although she could not stop them spilling out. She tried to apologise, but her words were snatched away by tearing sobs and she dropped her head again. I pulled a chair up next to her, grabbed the kitchen roll from the side and pushed a piece into her hand, then I sat quietly, my arm around her, and made soothing noises. Eventually, she started to quieten, the gulps became shallower, and she raised her head again and dabbed at her eyes with the tissue. I stroked her hair away from her hot face.

'Tea?' I asked.

'Yes, yes, please,' she said, sniffing, and I stood up to put the kettle on. At the same time, I surreptitiously texted Marilise to warn her that I wouldn't be back for a little while and she should start the wrapping without me. A few minutes later, we were both clasping large mugs of tea and had made inroads into the plate of ginger snaps I thought it was necessary to also put out.

'Do you want to talk about it?' I asked.

She nodded, blotting a few more errant tears.

'It's Philip,' she said, which came as no surprise. 'He's – he's emailed to say...'

She started crying again and grasped for her phone. She tapped it briefly, then handed it to me. I read the email on the screen, which was cold and businesslike, calling off not only the wedding but the entire relationship. *With some time to reflect,* he had written, *I do not believe that it would be beneficial to either of us to continue our association. I wish you all the best for the future.* I had never met the man, but I hated him on poor Astrid's behalf.

'Wow,' I said, putting down the phone. 'Your association. Were you selling him insurance?'

She laughed at this, as I had intended.

'Not sure he was the good bet I thought he was,' she said, her voice shaky. 'How could he? How *could* he, Laura? By email. We've been together over two years, and I thought we were all right.'

'Forgive me, Astrid,' I said, 'but you deserve a hell of a lot better than all right.'

She shrugged.

'But it was so wonderful for India.'

'Well, India didn't have to be married to him,' I said stoutly. 'She'd have gone off to university or something else in a few years' time and you would have been stuck on a Texan cattle ranch with this cold fish.'

She giggled.

'He was, rather. At first, I thought he was great fun, a good old-fashioned Dallas cowboy with an oilwell or two, but' – she lowered her voice as if he could hear her – 'he was rather boring.'

'Well, there you go, then,' I said. 'You're bound to feel heartbroken; it's the shock as much as anything, but it doesn't sound like there's much to get over.'

'It was a shock,' she said. 'But I'm crying as much for India as myself. Not just the ranch and the horses,' she added quickly. 'But where are we going to go now? I'm sure that Nick's going to sell Lyonscroft and Marilise will move to London. We could go, too, of course, but what will India do with Firefly?'

The tears began to fall again.

I thought back to the conversation I'd had with Nick the day I arrived at Lyonscroft, when I had thoroughly overstepped, but he had sworn he would never sell the house from under Astrid. Had he ever spoken to her about it? Had he changed his mind? I didn't want to tell Astrid about it and get her hopes up, in case I was wrong, and I also wanted to get my own feelings in order. She seemed very sure that he was about to sell and disappear off around the world again, and where did that leave him, me and our burgeoning relationship? Maybe Steph had been right.

'Astrid,' I said gently, tearing off some more kitchen roll and handing it to her. 'I think you need to speak to Nick. I know he hates this house, but I can't imagine him pushing you all out to sell it, especially with Marilise so frail.'

Astrid gazed at me, her huge blue eyes swimming with tears.

'I shouldn't say it,' she whispered. 'But Marilise, well, she, oh dear, that is to say, she won't be around forever. I can't expect him to keep the house for me.'

'Well, I think you can,' I said. 'If it wasn't for the way the inheritance went, with Nick's father so obsessed with his son *getting* the house – the house he doesn't even want – it would be yours, anyway, as his widow. This is your home; you've lived here for, what – over thirty years?' She nodded miserably. 'India's happy here. I know she's not Nick's blood sister, but he obviously thinks of her that way. He's not going to turf you out, Astrid, I'm sure of it.'

A wan smile came to her face.

'Do you really think so?'

'I do,' I said firmly, although who was I to make such decisions about a man I had known a few weeks and she had known for almost his entire life? 'But please speak to him. You can't go on feeling worried like this.'

'I will,' she promised, scrunching the damp kitchen paper up in her hand. 'Now, what were you supposed to be doing? I'm sure I'm keeping you from something – can I help?'

'Quite the opposite!' I said. 'I came in here to make tea and instruct you not to come into the dining room. Marilise and I are wrapping presents.'

'Oh, how exciting,' she said. 'I think I might go upstairs and do the same thing, with some Christmas music on the radio.' Her face fell again. 'But what am I going to do with the gifts I bought for Philip? Do you think I should send them to him?'

'No,' I practically shouted. 'No. Why don't you give them to me, with the receipts, and I'll look into returning them?'

'You're so kind,' she said, another tear teetering on her lower lid.

'Not at all,' I said. 'And no more crying. You do plenty for other people, it's time someone helped you out a bit. Now, I'd better get that tea to Marilise before she sends out a search party.'

When I returned to the dining room, I told Marilise about Philip, but not about Astrid's fears over the house; the last thing I wanted was her worrying as well.

'I met him once, Philip,' said Marilise, carefully cutting the ends of a piece of ribbon into a 'V' shape. 'I can't say I liked him all that much. I found him brash, but I wondered if he was the sort of person I'm not used to. Astrid seemed to think he was a good idea, and who was I to question that? Maybe I should have.'

I shook my head.

'No good ever comes of interfering in other people's relationships, however well meant. I don't think Astrid is too sorry – she's more worried about India, who I think will be delighted.'

We fell into a companionable silence as we continued wrapping, but inside my head was a maelstrom. Was this new relationship, the only thing in my life which had felt right since Paulo died, going to disappear as quickly as it had come?

Later that day, when I was doing my usual paperwork, as well as making a start on returning the presents Astrid had bought for Philip, Nick came in.

'Hello,' he said, bending to kiss me. 'Sorry I haven't seen you all day, I've been snowed under with this latest app. Cup of tea?'

A few minutes later, he returned and sat down next to me.

'Such a shame about Astrid,' he said. She had told him about Philip after lunch, although I didn't know if she had also raised her concerns about the house. 'But she said she wasn't too cut up about it.'

He paused.

'Mmm,' I said. 'India told me that it's made her Christmas – she didn't like him at all.'

'It's India that Astrid is most worried about,' said Nick, frowning. 'She seems to think I'm going to kick them all out to live in London and sell Lyonscroft, like some crooked landlord.'

'Are you?' I asked as lightly as I could.

'Of course not,' he said roughly, then paused. 'Sorry. No, I'm not, although this house is ridiculous, far too big for anyone. I think that Astrid and India would be far better off somewhere smaller, still with room for the horse, of course. But it's not the time to discuss it with her. And anyway, nothing will happen until Marilise...'

'Dies,' I supplied. He nodded awkwardly.

'Quite. Anyway, I'm thinking of sticking around for a bit myself,' he said, putting his mug down and taking my hand.

I smiled.

'Good. Although maybe I'll be the one running off to LA, to avoid becoming my sister's maternity nurse.'

I had thought he would laugh, but he looked at me seriously.

'Well, why not?' he asked. 'There are worse places to live.'

'You can't mean it!' I said. 'What on earth would I do there?'

'Nursing must be pretty transferable, isn't it?' he said.

'I-I don't know.'

I wasn't ready for the unexpected turn this conversation had taken. Thankfully, Nick didn't push it.

'Well, lots for us all to think about,' he said evenly, draining his tea. 'I'd better get back to my app. See you later.'

He kissed me again and I tried to return to my jobs but found it impossible to focus. As far as I could tell, Nick hadn't altogether abandoned the idea of selling Lyonscroft and returning to LA. The house was neither here nor there to me, but I was uneasy about his suggestion that I could move my life out there as well. On the one hand, it felt thrilling: it sounded like he wanted me to be with him, and I thought that was also what I wanted, but it was far too soon to consider throwing my life in the air and moving halfway across the world together. Or was it? What was I going to leave behind? My family, who I loved but who were not that interested in me, and would be even less so once Steph started having babies? My job which was, by its nature, transitory and could be left at short notice? The thought of changing my work was something that had flitted across my mind recently, but I had not let it settle. The truth was that live-in nursing of the sort I did was not compatible with a relationship and that, of course, was why it had suited me so well. But I also could not ignore the fact that working with patients in the capacity I did comforted me, both by sustaining the link to Paulo and by helping me work out some self-inflicted penance I needed because he had died, because I had not been able to save him.

Pushing my paperwork to one side, I picked up my phone and scrolled through the photos until I found my favourite one of the two of us together. I looked at Paulo's beloved face, and was able to do so without crying or having to close the picture down quickly because it was too painful. Even this change of feeling confused me, and when I heard India and Sofia come in from school, I jumped up, pushing both work and phone to one side. I wasn't hopeful, but maybe keeping busy with something else would take my mind off my worries.

NINETEEN

Astrid, understandably, needed to talk to India so I suggested I took Sofia, who was dying to see Firefly, down to the stables and India could meet us there later. Angela said she was happy to wake Marilise from her nap, so before long Sofia and I were crunching our way over the gravel, accompanied by Steve who must have had enough of being cooped up inside while Nick worked. Sofia chattered away happily about school, the new friends she had made and the play, and I was glad to supply the occasional question but otherwise let her talk as much as she wanted. I don't know much about horses, but Firefly appeared pleased to see us and we fed him some carrots that Sofia had grabbed from the kitchen on the way, and I enjoyed the feel of his velvety, whiskery muzzle on my hand as I fed and petted him.

'Hello!'

A voice came from behind and we turned to see India, looking happier than I had seen her for days.

'All good?' I asked.

'All great,' she said, patting Firefly. 'Mum told me that you know what's happened; thanks for looking after her.'

'It was my pleasure,' I said, and quicky explained to Sofia about Philip and the broken engagement.

'That's sad,' said Sofia, concern clouding her little face.

'Not really,' said India, unbolting the stable door and leading her horse out. She tied his rope to an iron ring set into the wall, then went into a small room and emerged with three brushes. She handed one to me and one to Sofia, then grinned at what was presumably a look of complete bemusement on my face. 'Just do his neck and sides,' she said. 'Brush in the direction the hair grows and you can't go wrong.'

I wasn't so sure about that, but I undertook my task with diligence as India continued talking.

'I'm sorry that my mum's upset, but I'm not at all sorry that she's not marrying Philip,' she continued. 'I hope we don't have to leave Lyonscroft – we both love it here.'

'We should do something to cheer her up,' piped up Sofia. 'Like you did for me when I first arrived.'

'Another window of the advent calendar?' I said. 'That's a great idea. Do you think your mum would like that, India?'

'Yes, I'm sure she would. What should we give her? I've already bought her Christmas present – it's a pretty necklace, so not jewellery.'

'Maybe she'd like a reindeer like Reddo,' suggested Sofia, stroking the head of the toy, which was poking out of her coat as usual. 'He's so nice.'

I smiled.

'She may well do, but I was wondering about a Christmas plant or flower, seeing as she loves gardens so much. I'm going out this evening, so I could get it on my way, the garden centre is open late.'

'That's a good idea,' said India. 'And we can do the number to put up.'

This arranged, it was time for me to go back to Marilise before steeling myself for an evening with my family.

. . .

I picked up a beautiful arrangement of ivy and cyclamen in a basket planter before heading to my parents' house. The wedding dress designer was coming for the final fitting, and it had been deemed necessary for me to attend as well. I had hoped that it would be a three-line whip for all the bridesmaids, but Araminta had told me over text that she, at least, wasn't invited. I was sorry; it would have been nice to have her there. Instead, as I parked my car, I saw Dorothea's enormous 'compact' white SUV parked outside that she liked barging around the roads in. Why it was called 'compact' when it loomed over my modest hatchback, I wasn't sure, but it was as vulgar and overbearing as its driver. I let myself in, calling out a greeting, and Mum came bustling out of the sitting room and gave me a hug.

'Come in, Dorothea's here already and the dress lady will come at any minute.'

I followed her into the sitting room where I found Steph in an ivory satin robe with "Bride" emblazoned across the back in diamanté, looking at Dorothea, who was squeezed into the same peach satin I presumed I was supposed to wear.

'Hello,' said Steph. 'We thought we should try on the bridesmaids' dresses at the same time. Yours is upstairs on Mum and Dad's bed – go and put it on, will you?'

'I'm probably not wearing the right underwear,' I said weakly, but I should have known to save my breath.

'Well, that doesn't matter,' said Dorothea bossily. 'We need an idea of how it looks, so go on.'

Resigned, I plodded upstairs and found the dress, which I put on. I hardly dared glance at myself in the mirror. I don't have a bad figure, but the peach satin did everything it could to emphasise the bits I usually tried to disguise. It was sleeveless, with a high, collared halterneck that made me look distinctly matronly. The front was completely smooth and unadorned, leaving nowhere for a normal body to hide, and the back was scooped low, almost to the top of my bottom. Not only was I *definitely* not wearing the right underwear, but I couldn't imagine what underwear *would* be right. I nearly took it off then and there, with a promise to Steph that I would buy something else in the same fabric, but then she shouted up the stairs to me to hurry and I fell into the old habit of jumping to attention. I hobbled downstairs and displayed myself miserably to the assorted company, which now included the woman who had brought the wedding dress. She looked at me with something approaching sympathy while Steph stalked around me with a critical glare.

'Well, you were right about the underwear,' was her first comment, warming up. 'You'll need your shapewear for this dress.'

'I don't have any shapewear,' I muttered.

Steph, Dorothea, the wedding dress lady and my mother all looked at me in horror. My father poured himself another drink.

'Well, you'll have to get some,' said Steph. 'Why on earth don't you have any already?' I shrugged; I couldn't be bothered to answer. She ploughed on. 'Maybe Marnie' – she nodded at the wedding dress lady – 'will help you find something. The colour's draining you, but make-up can sort that out, and you'll have to get a spray tan a couple of days before. You can come back here for that; I'm arranging for someone to come to the house.'

There was a pause, which I belatedly realised was for me to thank her.

'I'll need to check,' I said instead. 'I'll be working then.'

'Well, you'll need to figure it out,' replied Steph, brushing aside the small fact of my job. 'Right, you'd better go and get changed, both of you – we need to get on with my dress.'

I scuttled back upstairs as quickly as I could in the tight

satin and peeled it off gratefully, pulling my clothes back on. Then I perched on the side of the bed and fired off a text to Minty:

> Have you tried your dress on yet? I look like an uncooked sausage in mine. Do you think Steph will notice if I wear a knee-length poncho on the day?

I added a few 'crying with laughter' emojis, then hastened downstairs before I could get into any more trouble.

I had to admit that the wedding dress Steph had chosen was extremely beautiful, and once I was sitting on the sofa with a drink my father had pushed into my hand – 'just a single, darling, I know you're driving, but it might help' – I started to enjoy myself. No one was looking at or criticising me, and I restricted my comments to the bland and uncontroversial, which met with approval. Steph dragged the whole thing out, even to the extent that my mother was getting twitchy, as the pasta bake she had made was slowly drying out in the oven. But eventually we bid Marnie goodbye and sat down to eat. For the first half of the meal, the conversation revolved around the wedding, then suddenly Steph asked me, 'Are you still bringing Nick as your plus one?'

I said that I was, dreading where this was going.

'He won't stay, you know,' said Dorothea stridently, helping herself to more garlic bread.

'What's this?' asked Mum, her radar twitching. 'I didn't know you were bringing someone, Laura. I thought I was just about on top of the seating plan, and now we'll have to start again.'

'I told Steph ages ago,' I said, not prepared to take the blame for the seating plan.

'But I didn't think you were *serious*,' she said, staring at me with her eyes wide open. 'I mean – Nick Prince!'

She giggled, and Dorothea guffawed.

'Well, I am,' I said, putting down my fork. 'And I don't see what's so funny about it. Even if he does go back to LA – well, maybe I'll go with him.'

Damn. I hadn't meant to say that.

There was silence at the table as everyone took this in. Steph was the first to recover.

'You can't go to LA. I thought you were going to come and help me with the baby.' Now, all eyes swivelled towards her. *What baby?* was clearly the unspoken question in everyone's mind. She looked around belligerently. 'Hugo and I are going to start trying as soon as we're married.'

'How exciting!' said Mum, her mind probably swiftly moving from table plans to cots. 'I'm going to be a grandmother, finally!' I could feel the pasta bake making its way back up again as images flashed through my mind: the miscarriages, the negative tests, Paulo. 'And how lovely that you're planning to help, Laura. You can't go to LA with this Nick, then, can you?'

It was as if the deal was done, my life stitched up into a neat parcel and handed to me.

'Do you know a lot about babies?' asked Dorothea.

I shook my head.

'But she's going to *learn*, aren't you, Laura?' trilled Steph. 'She'll do some retraining and be just in time! No need to look so glum, Laura – we'll pay you, of course.'

I pushed my chair back and stood up. I knew I had to leave before I said anything else I would regret. The hilarious idea of me moving to LA with Nick would give them enough to talk about when I had gone.

'I'd better be getting back,' I said. 'See you at the hen night.'

I made for the front door, trying to open the stiff lock with one hand while I rooted in my bag for my car keys with the other.

'Let me help.'

I turned to see Dad, his face a picture of worry and sympathy. Instead of reaching for the lock, he put his arms around me, and I fell into his comforting hug.

'I'm looking forward to seeing Nick again at the wedding,' he said quietly. 'And you do whatever it is that you need to do with your life. God knows you've had enough happen to you that you couldn't control. Steph and your mother will be fine.'

I nodded, his wool sweater scratching against my cheek, then pulled away.

'Thanks, Dad. I'd better go now, though.'

He opened the door while I found my car keys, and I gave him a wave as I drove off, feeling fractionally lighter but still with too many thoughts rushing around my head for any one person to deal with.

When I arrived back at Lyonscroft, I saw that India and Sofia had put the next number up in the window of a downstairs cloakroom, so I went there first and left the planted basket for Astrid to find in the morning. It was late, but I was feeling too twitchy to sleep, so I went to the kitchen to make some night-time tea. I could see a strip of light under the door as I approached; a rush of happiness zinged through me when it turned out to be Nick sitting at the table, eating toast and flicking through a free local magazine that had been left lying around.

'How was your evening?' he asked, closing the magazine and standing up to hug me.

I exhaled loudly.

'Pretty heavy going,' I said, filling the kettle. 'The dress I have to wear is awful, so please don't look at me for the whole day.'

He laughed.

'I'm afraid I couldn't bear that.'

'It's peach satin,' I said warningly. 'And clings in all the wrong places.'

'Ah well, there you go,' he said smugly. 'There *are* no wrong places.'

'Thank you,' I said. 'But tight peach satin could find wrong places on Kate Moss. I'm hoping for some flowers to clutch, or maybe I'll befriend one of the little ring bearers and keep them in front of me.'

'Good plan. Was it all right otherwise?'

'Well, Dorothea was there.' He pulled a sympathetic face. 'And my sister was going on at me again about her grand plan for me to retrain as a maternity nurse and help her when the baby she believes will obediently appear exactly nine months after the wedding comes along.'

'*What?*'

I went to sit down at the table next to him, my tea forgotten, and explained my sister's scheme.

'Is it what you want to do?' asked Nick.

I chewed my lip.

'If I can push aside everything I've been through and see the idea as simply as Steph does, then it's not actually terrible. It probably *is* time that I tried a different branch of nursing, and I would love working with new mums and babies. It would only mean a few weeks with Steph and painful though she can be, she *is* my sister.'

'It sounds to me as if she's asking a lot of you,' said Nick. 'You'd have to put your own life on hold for her. What if after a few weeks she decided she wanted you to stay longer? It might be hard to say no.'

I bit my lip.

'I hadn't thought about that. And it's exactly the sort of thing Steph might do.'

'I don't want you to be trapped by her.' He paused, his jaw tense and the old, closed-off look back in his eyes. 'And I'm not sure what it would mean for us either.'

'What do you mean?'

'Well, if you move in with her... You'll be so busy...'

How quickly he leapt to the conclusion that he was being pushed to one side, once again.

I took his hand and wiggled my fingers into the fist that he had clenched.

'Not too busy for us,' I reassured him. 'I'm not making any decisions, anyway, but it wouldn't mean we couldn't be together. There would be plenty of other options besides living in twenty-four hours a day with families. It's a thought.'

He nodded, then lifted my hand and kissed it.

'Of course, sorry, I'm being selfish. Now, this peach satin sounds like it will need some rapid removal after the wedding; perhaps I'd better get in some practice now...'

He kissed me properly, then, and we went upstairs to his room through the silent house, all worries for the future forgotten, for now, for the pleasures of the present.

TWENTY

After the various upsets, the next few days at Lyonscroft were idyllic. Nick and I spent every night together and got into the habit of waking early so that we could enjoy a coffee before the day started. I began to feel closer to him as we shared details of our pasts and hopes for the future. Astrid seemed not only to have thrown off the broken engagement with Philip, but to be happier than ever. As a 'thank you' to me for returning all the presents she had bought him – a job which had been time-consuming, but not difficult – she invited me to go with her to see a matinée production of 'The Nutcracker' ballet in Yeovil. It was a glorious production, and afterwards we went for an early supper at a nineteenth century pub nearby, which had a distinctly twenty-first century menu. We both decided on Dover sole, followed by an orange-infused Christmas pudding with brandy ice cream, and found plenty to chat about as we ate.

'I'm so glad you came to Lyonscroft,' said Astrid, as the coffee arrived. 'You're wonderful with Marilise and we're all so happy for you and Nick. Oops, sorry,' she added. 'I know it's sort of a secret, but it's not really – you don't have to keep being discreet.'

'I think I'd probably rather, for now,' I said. 'It's a slightly odd situation, living in the same house and me working there. Thank you for being pleased, though.'

'We are,' she said, adding sugar to her coffee. 'Nick was such a troubled little boy. Christoph – his father, that is – wasn't a kind man. I'm sure you know.' I nodded. 'He never hid the fact that his only interest in Nick was as his heir, and he packed him off to boarding school when he was tiny. I begged him to let Nick live at home, and go to school nearby, like Victoria, but he wouldn't allow it. He – he...' She took a sip of coffee. She was clearly in the mood to unburden herself. 'He had a vasectomy so that I wouldn't have a baby. He didn't tell me for ages, until I kept pushing for both of us to go and see doctors, then he told me.'

'That's terrible,' I said. 'I'm so sorry.'

'Thank you. No wonder the minute he died I rushed off and got pregnant with India.' She smiled. 'I did love her father, but it was a crazy time and I'm not sure he ever knew how I felt. Marilise was amazing when she found out about the baby. Couldn't have given two hoots about the circumstances, her son's recent widow getting knocked up by an itinerant photographer; she was glad to see me happy, finally. How she managed to have a son like Christoph I don't know. It was too late, by then, to do much for Nick – he was finishing school. I tried to make a welcoming home for him at Lyonscroft, but he's always been a nomad.'

I was seized with a sudden desire to ask about him, however painful the answer might be.

'Do you think he always will be? Am I wasting my time?'

Astrid gave me a gentle smile.

'I don't know, Laura. All I can say is that I've never known him content with someone the way he is with you. But – well –

I still wouldn't be surprised if he goes overseas again. Would you want to go with him, if he did?'

I sighed.

'We've only been together such a short time, too short a time to make decisions like that. My life is here – my work, my family. I could leave, of course I could, and maybe it would be good, for a while at least. But I don't want to throw everything up in the air for someone who ultimately doesn't want to settle down. That's not for me, and I wouldn't force it on Nick – he'd only be unhappy if wandering the world and being free is the most important thing to him.'

'It's not easy, is it?' said Astrid sympathetically. 'And I'm in a poor position to give advice. All I can say is that I have finally learnt that you are a million times better off single than with the wrong man.'

If only Nick didn't feel so right, that would be easier to take on board.

On Wednesday, Marilise and I were having our usual daily swim. She was sitting under the fountain while I floated, staring up at the ceiling, when I sensed, rather than saw, people coming into the room. I tipped myself upright lazily, expecting to see one of the family, but instead there was a tall young man, with an improbably sculpted hairstyle, wearing a sharp suit and very shiny shoes. He tapped away at a tablet, then looked up.

'Mind if I take a photo?' he asked, lifting the tablet as he did so.

'Well, yes, I do,' I said. 'Sorry, who are you?'

'It's all right, it's just for reference, it won't be the one that goes in the brochure.'

He lifted the tablet again and I saw Marilise looking worried.

'Please don't take any photos with us in them,' I said,

standing up and looking as ferocious as I could in my polka dot swimming costume. 'Who are you?'

'I'm from Lichfield and Baron,' he replied.

The estate agents?

Before I had a chance to speak, the door was pushed open, and Nick came in. When he saw me and Marilise, he looked very awkward.

'Sorry,' he said. 'I didn't realise you were still in here.' He turned to the man. 'We can come back later.'

Mr Shiny Shoes clicked his way out of the room and Nick looked at me.

'I'll catch up with you later,' he said, and was gone.

'What was all that about?' asked Marilise. 'Is Nick selling the house?'

I could hear the anxiety in her voice.

'He promised he wouldn't,' I said reassuringly, although I was far from confident. 'Should we get out? It's not long until lunch.'

I made sure Marilise was comfortable in the dining room, then went to the kitchen, where I found Angela and Astrid, talking agitatedly as a pan of potatoes, forgotten on the hob, threatened to boil over. I rushed across and turned it down.

'Oh dear,' said Angela, grabbing the handle of the pan and quickly draining it. 'We were so busy talking that we didn't notice the potatoes. I do hope the fish hasn't dried out.'

She opened the door of the Aga to inspect it, and Astrid turned to me, her eyes wide.

'Did you see that man who came to the house this morning?'

'The one from the estate agents? Yes, he tried to take photos of Marilise and me having our swim,' I replied, trying to keep my voice light.

'Well, what's going *on*?' demanded Angela, shutting the

Aga door again, apparently satisfied that her fish was okay. 'I thought Nick had given up on the idea of selling.'

They both turned to me as if I had the answer but, of course, I knew as little as they did.

'I don't know,' I said. 'Maybe Nick will say something at lunch?'

'It's no surprise,' said Astrid, twisting a tea towel between her hands. 'He's not made a secret of wanting to sell Lyonscroft, but after everything he said... Well, I suppose I should know better than anyone that you should believe what people *do* and not what they say.' There was a short silence as we all digested this truth. 'I'll be all right,' she continued, her voice brave. 'I do have my own money, and I've been building up my gardening business. I can find somewhere for India and me, but I don't know about Firefly.' The tea towel was getting tighter and tighter. 'I'll work something out. What will you do, Angela?'

'I'm sure Greg and I can find another family nearby,' she said stoically. 'Or go to London with Marilise for the time being. It's disappointing. I thought that young man was going to come through for the best, I really did. I suppose this means your new romance will be over before it's barely started,' she said, looking at me. 'Oh, I know we're not supposed to know, but we all do, and we were so happy. We thought it meant a new beginning for Nick, that he might be settled at last.'

I shrugged, feeling uncomfortable.

'I think we should wait and see what Nick says.'

'But you've got your sister, haven't you?' said Astrid. 'The maternity nursing?'

'Yes, I'm still considering that,' I replied, and quickly filled Angela in on the plan that was becoming more established all the time, even though I still hadn't made a decision about it.

'You're a sensible girl,' she said approvingly, checking the fish again, which now seemed to be cooked to her satisfaction.

'Now, let's say no more about it all and get this lunch on the table.'

Lunch was a subdued affair. No one mentioned the estate agent, and we ended up with a half-hearted conversation about what flavour stuffing goes best with Christmas dinner, which nobody seemed to care about very much. When the meal was over and I had taken Marilise up for her nap, I decided to go for a brisk walk to try and blow the cobwebs away. I was togging up in the hall when Nick came out of the sitting room.

'Going out?'

'Yes, it's beautiful outside now the sun's come out.'

'Can Steve and I join you?'

'Of course.'

A few minutes later, we were striding through the chilly fields, and I was already feeling better for the fresh air. Steve was as comical as ever, chasing after imaginary foes and bounding joyfully over to us whenever he found a stick he wanted to be thrown for him.

'Look, I'd like to explain about Tyler,' said Nick.

'Tyler?'

'The estate agent from this morning. I know it's got everyone worried.'

I made a non-committal noise and caught up another stick for Steve.

'I'd forgotten he was coming,' said Nick, sounding a little defensive. 'But when he turned up on the doorstep, it didn't seem like a bad idea at least to find out what the place was worth.'

'And take a few photos?'

'Yeah, sorry about that.'

I smiled.

'It's okay, but I don't think either Marilise or I are ready to be swimsuit cover girls at the moment.'

'I couldn't disagree more,' said Nick. 'But have it your own way.'

We walked in silence for a minute or two, then I continued addressing the elephant in the room – or in the field, as it was.

'So, you forgot he was coming?' I prompted. 'It got Astrid worried.'

'And you?' he said.

I stopped walking and looked at him in surprise.

'It's nothing to do with me if you sell the house or not. But I was concerned for the others. They're not sure where they stand.'

'And where do I stand, Laura? I can well believe you're not that bothered for yourself about Lyonscroft being sold and me going off again. Don't you mind?'

'I thought we talked about this,' I said, confused.

'I overheard you in the kitchen,' he said, kicking at a stone on the frosty ground. 'Sounds like the whole retraining idea is pretty much decided. I know you said we could still be together, but I can't see it working. Say you stay with Marilise until – until the end?' I nodded. That wasn't going to change. 'Then you retrain – what's that, a year?'

'Not that long,' I said. 'But it will depend on the course. Maybe a few months.'

'Right. Then what if Steph doesn't get pregnant straight away? You'll have committed to her, and you might find yourself waiting around for months, even years. And once you're working for her, or in any live-in job, that's not going to make seeing each other easy, even if I do stay nearby. And all of that, all of it, would be okay – I would support you in any dream or ambition – if I thought it's what you really want. But then why are you considering it? I can only think that you're putting up roadblocks that make it easier to say *ah well, it was nice, but it couldn't work out, given the circumstances.*'

'Why would I do that?' I asked, feeling a lump in my throat.

'I don't know,' he said in despair. 'But what I *do* know is that throughout my entire life people have left me, and it's happening again.'

'I'm not leaving you, I'm not,' I cried. 'But I'm so confused. I feel like I have to make some plans, and they simply can't be rushing off to live in LA, not at the moment. It's all too much, it's too soon.'

'Too soon after Paulo?' asked Nick.

'Yes – no – oh, I don't know,' I said, tears now welling up in my eyes. 'I do want to be with you, Nick, that's the only thing I am sure of. But I don't know...'

I trailed off sadly.

'You don't know if we can make it work,' said Nick in a flat voice.

'I want to,' I whispered.

He pulled me into his arms, and I wrapped mine tightly around his waist.

'We'll figure it out,' he said quietly.

I nodded and squeezed him tightly, but right now it was hard to see how that might happen.

TWENTY-ONE

We walked a little further, then I checked the time.

'I have to get back – the doctor will be here to see Marilise soon and I must make sure she's ready.'

We kissed goodbye and I hurried back to the house, glad to have something to take my mind off the situation with Nick. Was he right? Was I contemplating driving myself into something I didn't want to do, and for all the wrong reasons? I let myself into the house and shook off the thoughts. I would give them a chance later, but for now I had to attend to Marilise.

The doctor's visit took longer than I had anticipated as she needed to talk us through a change of medicine that she hoped would allow Marilise more energy.

'But you're still not to overdo it,' she said, smiling. 'No more than one party a week, and you have to make up for that with extra sleep.'

'It's not like the good old days, when one party an evening would have seemed boring,' said Marilise. 'But I will take your advice, doctor, thank you.'

I saw the doctor out, then brought Marilise downstairs. She wanted to write some Christmas cards and had left it almost too late to make the last posting day.

'I'm sure they are very mean about it,' she grumbled, picking up her pen. 'There was a time when you could post your cards on Christmas Eve and they would still get there. I suppose you have done yours already?'

'Not at all,' I said, grinning. 'I'm usually lucky if mine get there for New Year.'

'You surprise me,' said Marilise. 'So organised in work.'

'But not in life?' I asked.

'I thought you would have done them on December the first. Well, go and get them now, and keep me company. We can try to remember the names of our friends' children together.'

I ran upstairs to get the cards I had bought, still sitting unopened in a bag, and my address book. I quickly checked my phone while I was up there, to find a message from Nick:

> I've gone to see a friend in Exeter who needed
> help with some work stuff. Back tomorrow xx

Maybe that wasn't such a bad thing, I thought, as I jogged back down the stairs. We could probably both do with some space to let things percolate. But my sensible, rational thoughts couldn't quash the worry and sadness that had taken up residence in my heart.

'Here they are!' I said in an overly jolly tone to Marilise. 'I seem to be sending fewer each year, but it's still such a chore.'

We sat for nearly an hour writing our cards, then Marilise told me she would prefer supper in her room that evening. I joined her, then decided on an early night – surely a good sleep would make everything clearer?

· · ·

The next morning, I was in the kitchen preparing the breakfast tray, when Astrid came in.

'Oh, Laura, good morning. Can you check the time of the girls' Christmas show this evening? I'm terribly worried I've double-booked myself.'

I took out my phone and looked at the calendar, giving a sharp intake of breath when I saw the date.

'Are you all right?' asked Astrid. 'Have you double-booked as well?'

'No – no, it's okay,' I said. 'The show starts at seven, but I'll get there earlier and help Sofia get dressed.'

'You're an angel,' said Astrid, heading for the door again. 'See you later!'

I was glad that it had only been a flying visit, as my legs gave way and I sat down heavily on a chair. I rubbed at my tightening chest and stared at the floor. It wasn't the time that had shocked me, but the date. The anniversary of Paulo's death. And I hadn't realised. After a few minutes, despite my limbs feeling weak and shaky, I stood up again. The task of preparing breakfast had suddenly taken on a huge importance where continuing to sit there limp and helpless compounded my self-loathing. I went through the motions on autopilot, fighting the nausea that was churning in my stomach. Every year up until now I had today's date emblazoned on my mind for weeks before it arrived. Scrupulously, I had set aside time on the actual day to honour his memory, looking at photos and making a donation to the charity that had supported us in his final days. And this year I had been too distracted by all the trappings of Christmas I had sworn off as well as, of course, Nick, to bother remembering. I threw the knife I had been using into the sink and picked up the immaculate breakfast tray. *At least I could still do my job properly*. The thought brought me little comfort.

I carried the tray upstairs and went through the morning routine with Marilise, trying to be cheerful and professional, but knowing that my voice and behaviour were strained. Eventually, after fiddling fastidiously with the curtain tiebacks, I sat down and poured tea that I didn't think I would be able to drink through my constricted throat.

Marilise put her hand on my arm.

'Laura?'

I jumped.

'Oh, sorry, let me do your toast.'

'Let me do my own toast,' she said gently. 'Something has upset you; please tell me, if you can.'

I looked into her kind eyes, then dropped mine.

'I forgot,' I muttered. 'I forgot that today is the anniversary of my husband's death.' I raised my eyes again to meet hers, which were full of sympathy. 'Oh, Marilise, how could I?' My voice grew harsh with disgust at myself. 'Look at me, barely into a new relationship and so preoccupied that I forgot Paulo.'

'But this is natural,' said Marilise. 'You have not forgotten, but you were not, perhaps, dwelling as you have done in previous years. That, my dear, is something to celebrate, not berate yourself for. Life – and you – moves on, and that is the right order of things.'

How could I explain to her that 'dwelling' was what had sustained me for the past three years, that holding tightly to my feelings for Paulo and my grief at losing him had sometimes been the only way I could stop myself tumbling into an abyss of despair? Now that I had let go of that rope, would I go into freefall?

'I'm not ready to move on,' I said stubbornly. 'And not as much as Nick seems to want me to, not so quickly. He wants to leave England and roam the world, but I don't.'

I knew the words were unfair, but they brought me some sort of perverse comfort. Marilise frowned.

'Are you sure about that?'

'Yes,' I replied. 'You saw that estate agent. Nick might not be going to do anything soon, but he's getting his ducks in a row. I'm tired of trying to untangle it all. I'm making plans, too. I'm going to apply for that training today. Don't worry,' I said, seeing her anxious expression. 'It won't mean anything for us. I can do the training in the evenings, mostly, and then use it when I need to. I promise that I will stay with you for as long as you want me.'

'I worry little for myself,' said Marilise. 'Although I would be very sorry if you were to go. I worry more for you. This seems a quick decision, one that you are making through your emotions. Please give it some time – maybe you will feel different soon.'

I shook my head. The truth was that making a plan was the only way I could alleviate the turbulent feelings that were churning around inside me. When my mind turned to Nick, I felt worse; I could soothe myself with a sensible plan, even if it might not be my dream life.

'Very well, you must do what you think is right, but I hope you give Nick a chance, a real chance.'

'I am,' I said, hoping myself that I would be properly able to. I changed the subject. 'Are you looking forward to the girls' Christmas show tonight?'

She accepted this turnaround gracefully and did not bring up Nick or the maternity nurse training again that day. We had our usual swim and in the afternoon started a game of Monopoly.

'I can see why you wanted to play,' I said, regarding my thin collection of properties in comparison to her bulging portfolio. 'You're ruthless!'

'But don't give up, Laura,' she urged me. 'You can still come back, with courage and a little skill.'

'I would love to,' I said, glancing at my watch. 'But it's time I got to the school. I'm taking the girls for a snack before we have to go back and get ready for the performance. Maybe Angela could take over for me?'

'I know better than to do that,' said an amused voice from behind me. It was Angela. 'I've played Monopoly against Marilise before, and I've only just recovered. You go, Laura, and we'll see you at the school at seven.'

Sofia was excited to see me and bounced around, begging to go to a coffee shop that one of her friends had talked about. I didn't know where it was, but India did, and soon we were all sipping large hot chocolates and eating white chocolate chip cookies. We returned to the school about an hour later, when India went to find her own costume and Sofia showed me where her classroom was, down a long, oak-lined corridor, which was unlike any school I'd ever seen.

'It looks more like someone's house,' I said, as she pushed open a heavy wooden door.

'It used to be,' she said, as we entered the classroom, which had the desks and wall displays I would have expected, but also a large fireplace and marble mantelpiece behind the teacher's desk. 'It got made into a school about seventy years ago. It's *much* nicer than my usual school. Look, this is where I sit.'

I was given a guided tour of the desk's contents as the room filled up with other small, chattering girls and slightly bemused adults, and then she skipped off to some pegs at the back of the room and returned with a carrier bag.

'This is my costume. I need help doing up the ribbons and then my hair and stuff.'

She got changed as I folded the clothes she discarded, then tied up about seventeen sets of ribbons down the back of her dress, wondering what the school would do if parents or other adults weren't available to help. I hadn't met a teacher yet. I had laid out the clips and bands Astrid had given me and started brushing Sofia's hair, when a woman with a startlingly smooth and immobile face glided over to us.

'Eugenia Tytherington-Smythe,' she said by way of introduction. 'This is my daughter, Vienna.' A child with dark blonde hair and a furious expression scowled at me as I stammered a greeting. 'Are you the nanny?' continued Eugenia.

'No,' I replied. 'I'm, er, well, I...'

I tailed off, not exactly sure what to say without going into details of the family that were none of this woman's business. As a nurse I am trained to be extremely discreet. Sofia had not got the memo.

'She's Great-Granny's nurse and Uncle Nick's girlfriend,' she piped up. 'And she's very good at doing hair.'

Eugenia's expression didn't – couldn't? – change, although she darted her eyes at me sharply.

'I see. Well, please don't use *those*' – she jabbed a finger at the things laid out on the desk – 'in Sofia's hair. We have decided to keep Vienna's classic and tasteful, and the photographs and video will look all wrong if Sofia has all this. My other daughter, Camilla, has a very large speaking part, so we have professional videographers coming.'

I glanced at Sofia, who was looking worried. I know what a lovely day out she had spent with Astrid and India choosing the special hair accessories, and how much she was looking forward to wearing them.

'I'm sorry,' I said. 'The school guidelines said they could have whatever they wanted in their hair, as long as it went with the costumes, which these do.'

'I did put a message on the class WhatsApp,' said Eugenia, raising her voice slightly so that a hush fell over the room and everyone turned to listen. 'Everyone else has agreed.'

Did she think I was going to be intimidated? I had taken on scarier people than Eugenia Tytherington-Smythe in my time.

'I don't think any of us are on the WhatsApp,' I said, also

making my voice a little louder and clearer. 'Sofia chose these things specially, so that's what she will be wearing.'

I ignored the heavy silence and started brushing Sofia's hair into two high bunches. I secured them with bands that had glittery chiffon streamers, then picked up some crystal encrusted clips.

'Two of these in each side, right, darling?' I asked her, and she nodded.

'If you're putting them in, I think I will, too,' said a voice from the other side of the room. I looked over to see a woman taking a small plastic bag out of her pocket. 'I brought them just in case.' She shot me a grin, which I returned.

'I've got masses here if anyone wants to share?' said another woman, and soon there was a hubbub as the sparkly contraband was produced from handbags and pockets.

Avoiding her mother's eyes, which I feared might turn me to stone, I smiled at Vienna.

'Would you like to borrow something? We've got plenty.'

She curled her lip at me.

'No,' she said, and turned to walk back to her desk, her mother stalking after her.

'There you go,' I said to Sofia. 'You look fab.'

I dug my phone out and took a photo so she could see herself.

'I love it, Laura!' she said, starting to bounce again. 'Will you send it to Mummy?'

'I don't have her number, I'm afraid, but I'll send it to Uncle Nick and he can pass it on, okay?'

She skipped off to see her friends while I attached the photo to a message, hoping that Nick was back from Exeter and waiting in the audience:

> Sofia says please can you send this to Victoria? She is very excited! I have made an enemy of someone called Eugenia, by contravening hair accessory dictates.

A message pinged straight back.

> Sent it on, thanks. We're all here, tell S break a leg. It's easy to make an enemy of ET-S, she loathes Astrid because she wouldn't pay for India to go to Camilla's birthday party. See you soon, we're in the second row, got a seat saved for you.

Relieved, I pushed my phone back into my pocket and went to kiss Sofia goodbye and wish her luck, as a tall, smiling woman came into the room.

'Thank you, everyone, time to go and find your seats now, I'll take it from here.'

We all began gathering their belongings together, when Eugenia's loud voice cut over the noise.

'Mrs Accrington? I *do* think the girls should remove the hair adornments and everyone should have a simpler look, like Vienna. The Princes' *help* wasn't aware of my request on the WhatsApp group for a more tasteful approach.'

Mrs Accrington's experienced eyes roamed over the pair, then around the room, landing on Sofia and finally me.

'I think you all look amazing,' she said warmly. 'It's Laura, isn't it?' I nodded. 'Astrid told me you'd be here to help, thank you. Now, you'd all better go and sit down, it's nearly time to start.'

Eugenia stood rigidly by the door as the rest of us left. I wouldn't have put it past her to try to pluck the offending items from the girls' hair as they left, but I had a feeling that Mrs Accrington, friendly though she was, had methods for dealing with parents like her.

The school hall was jammed, but as soon as I came in, I saw

Astrid leap up and wave frantically at me. I climbed over legs to get to my seat between her and Nick, saying a hurried hello to everyone as the lights went down. I felt Nick's hand close over mine where it lay on my leg, setting off a turmoil of emotions that was almost unbearable. Taking a shaky breath, I forced myself to concentrate on the boy who had walked onto the stage dressed in jeans and a gold waistcoat and clutching a microphone.

'Thankyouallforcomingthiseveningwelcomeandwehopey-ouenjoytheshowhappychristmas,' he gabbled before exiting abruptly. Everyone clapped uncertainly as the lights went down then very rapidly up again, revealing a girl in a blue dress kneeling in the middle of the stage. This was safer territory, and we sat back, ready for the familiar story to unfold. Sofia made an early appearance as a snowflake fluttering around the angel Gabriel as he announced Mary's pregnancy. I was glad to see that both her smile and her hairclips were still firmly in place. The scenes followed their time-honoured pattern, and soon Mary and Joseph and the donkey – a bored-looking girl who kept pushing back her long, floppy ears until they fell off alto-gether – arrived in Bethlehem. The First Innkeeper had an extravagant eyeliner moustache that made him look like Dick Dastardly, and growled his way through his lines before sending Mary and Joseph on their way and slamming his cardboard door with as much threatening élan as he could muster, earning himself a spontaneous round of applause. The Second Innkeeper was more laconic, opening her door, glancing the weary couple up and down and saying 'Yeah?' Upon enquiring about a room, Mary and Joseph were met with a look of disgust so withering that a pantomime ripple went around the audi-ence. This energised the Second Innkeeper, who embarked upon an apparently unscripted soliloquy, which ranged in subject from the cost of living to the difficulty of getting hold of eggs that year in Bethlehem and ended with the advice that next time they wanted a room they should reserve one in advance on www.book-inn.com. By now the entire audience had perked up and was in stitches, all except Eugenia Tytherington-Smythe who was fuming and hissing loudly at Mrs Accrington to move things along before Camilla's artistic preparations were derailed.

'Oh, no,' replied the teacher, who had joined in the laughter as much as anyone. 'We do like to encourage spontaneity in our students, and this piece of improvisation is splendid.'

The Second Innkeeper was now cosily offering to see if she could make up a bed in the breakfast lounge ('I'm sure my other guests won't mind'), when she was brought back on track by Joseph, who had finally managed to stop giggling and suggested that they might need more privacy.

'No problem, ducks,' said the Second Innkeeper. 'Try up the road, he'll be full, too, but he's got a nice stable. Pop by with the littl'un, won't you?'

By now Eugenia was practically foaming at the mouth, as her daughter's prize line about the stable had been pre-empted by the Second Innkeeper, who was now cheerily waving the couple off and shouting advice about childbirth as poor Camilla opened her door and was completely upstaged, despite her stunning and historically accurate costume that her mother had bullied a seamstress friend into making. Eventually, the Second Innkeeper withdrew, and Joseph repeated his line that had already been drowned out once. Camilla replied in her very loud and monotonal voice, causing crueller audience members to giggle again, only to be quelled by a vicious look from Eugenia.

'Don't put your daughter on the stage, Mrs Worthington,' whispered Nick to me. 'As Noël Coward put it. Poor Camilla, she's far happier on the football pitch, if only her mother would allow it.'

Eventually, Mary and Joseph were admitted to the stable,

and the action moved to the nearby fields. India trooped on with her little sheep, most of whom were looking at her adoringly and one of whom was determined to do nothing more than systematically unravel every single cotton wool ball his mother had glued onto his T-shirt. By the time the big moment came for the flock, he looked more like an old English sheepdog, but, his self-imposed task complete, he smiled beatifically and belted out 'While Shepherds Watch' with as much gusto as anyone could have wished for. I clocked his mother in the row behind us, tears of laughter pouring down her face as she captured every second on her phone. Much as I loved Sofia, and being there to help her, a pang of longing for my own child shot through me so powerfully that I gasped.

'Are you all right?' whispered Nick.

I nodded, thankful that it wasn't the place for a conversation, because no, I was far from all right. The only man I had been interested in at all since Paulo, a man I knew I was falling in love with, was looking like the wrong bet, and I could hardly bear it. Ignoring my trembling hands, I focused my attention back on the show. The stars appeared again, behind the shepherds, and I took some photos of Sofia, who looked buoyantly happy.

The rest of the performance went more or less to plan and soon we were clapping as the children took their bows, the biggest cheers going to the Second Innkeeper, who proceeded to offer us all ten per cent off our next stay. Astrid went to collect Sofia and India, Angela and Greg waiting for them while Nick and I took Marilise to his car. As we walked out slowly, we were accosted by Eugenia, with her daughters in tow. Naturally, she had managed to barge through everybody to get them out before most of the parents had even made it backstage. She made a sort of awkward curtsey to Marilise, then turned to Nick.

'Nikolai,' she said throatily, drawing him into an embrace.

She shot me a spiteful look. 'What's all this I hear about you selling Lyonscroft and leaving on a jet plane yet again?'

He glanced at me, then replied, 'I'm not sure where you've heard that, Eugenia.'

'Oh, you know that news travels fast through the cognoscenti around here.' She turned her Medusa stare on me. 'Did *you* know?'

I had to admire her. Within the space of a few words, she had tried to derail me by revealing something that I didn't know, had identified me as someone she most definitely didn't consider to be amongst the 'cognoscenti' and had positioned herself in Nick's inner circle. What could I do but answer truthfully?

'I was there when the estate agent came round,' I said calmly. 'And I can't blame Nick for wanting to be part of LA's in crowd as opposed to this one. Now, if you'll excuse me, I think Marilise would like to go home.'

'I would,' said Marilise, bestowing a look of hauteur on Eugenia that the woman, for all her airs and graces, could only ever dream of matching.

'Of course, Your Highness,' she stammered, and we swept away as elegantly as we could over the icy ground.

TWENTY-TWO

When Marilise was in bed, I went downstairs, not yet ready to turn in, although I was tired after my busy day. I went into the sitting room to watch some TV in the hope that it would stop my thoughts from racing out of control. I had found a mindless but enjoyable programme about American estate agents, and was marvelling at how they managed to spend the whole day in their vertiginous shoes, when Nick came in.

'Sorry,' he said. 'I didn't mean to disturb you.'

'It's okay,' I replied, switching the programme off. 'I couldn't sleep, but I'm not invested in this. The girls did well tonight, didn't they?'

He nodded and sat down next to me.

'They were great. Look, I'm sorry about Eugenia. She shouldn't have said any of that.'

I shrugged.

'I'd already upset her over hairgate, so it doesn't matter.' I paused. 'But she had a point, didn't she? You are still planning to leave the country?'

'And you're going to do what your sister wants?'

His voice was strained, and while part of me longed to reassure him, make promises, I was also scared that there was too much risk involved in throwing away my entire life to follow this man halfway around the world. I nodded and the words came out of my mouth, although they were untrue.

'It's not just what she wants. I do, too.'

'Really?'

'Yes. I know Steph seems overpowering, but she needs me, and family comes first. How can I deny her that?'

He looked at me for a moment.

'I get it. I do. But if your life doesn't really belong to you, then I can't see where I fit in.'

'I wasn't trying to make a choice,' I said. 'I didn't think it had to be a case of one or the other, but...'

'But it clearly is,' he filled in. 'And your decision is made.'

I shook my head. This wasn't how I felt, how I wanted the conversation to go, but maybe he was right.

'I can't just leave,' I said.

'Why not?' he suddenly implored, his face full of longing. 'You've had such a bad time of it – don't you deserve to do what you want now?'

I shook my head again.

'It's too much,' I said. 'And I want the same for you, for you to do what you want. Go to LA, travel the world, be free.'

He stood up and stormed over to the window, yanking the curtains aside and gazing out into the dark garden. Part of me wished I could see his face, read his feelings, but at the same time I needed not to so that I could be firm in my decision and not swept away on a frightening and uncertain wave of emotion.

'What about the wedding?' he asked. 'Do you still want me to come?'

The truth was that I did, desperately, but I couldn't see what good would come of it. It would prolong the pain.

'No,' I whispered. 'I think I'd better go alone.'

'You see,' he said in a low voice, still not turning from the window. 'I was right. I knew you'd leave; everybody does. Anyway...' He finally turned to face me, his face tempestuous. 'I've decided not to sell the house – I couldn't do that to Astrid. But it doesn't mean I have to live in the dump.'

And, with this, he strode quickly from the room, shutting the door behind him. I sat for a moment, icy fingers wrapping themselves around my body and my heart. So that was it. I didn't cry, but I wasn't sure what I felt. There was something akin to relief, or comfort, in having straightened things out, kept myself safe, but these emotions were quickly swallowed by misery and dread. Now, I had committed to a change in my career and a future that held little joy. I would love my new niece or nephew, if and when they showed up, of that I was sure, but working for Steph might turn out to be a hair shirt too far. Need help she might, but did it have to be me? I sighed and switched the programme back on, but the golden sunshine of the Pacific coast where the estate agents strutted their stuff only served to remind me of what I could have had.

When I went upstairs an hour or so later, Astrid's door opened.

'Oh, Laura, it's you. Are you all right? It's very late.'

I nodded but couldn't stop the tears springing to my eyes.

'Come in,' she said, and pulled me into her bedroom, where she moved a pile of colourful clothes so that I could sit down on a chair next to the embers of a dying fire. She took a poker and prodded it, then put on some more wood.

'Silly, really, having a fire when there's central heating, but I do find it comforting. Would you like a nip of something?' she added, producing a small bottle of brandy. I nodded. 'There you go. Now, tell me what's up. Is it Nick?'

'Yes. We've broken up.'

'Oh, what a shame.' She looked truly distressed. 'It looked

like it was going so well, we were all so pleased. What happened?'

'He's definitely not going to sell Lyonscroft,' I said, hoping that this would allay her fears in that respect. 'But he wants to leave the country and for me to go with him, and I don't feel ready for that.'

'Don't tell me you're going to do what your sister wants?' said Astrid, looking horrified.

I nodded.

'It seems like a good idea, for now,' I said, then repeated the line that was no more convincing than it had been the first time I said it. 'She needs me, and family comes first.'

'Are you sure Nick wants to leave?' she asked. 'Quite sure?'

'Yes,' I said firmly. 'And I don't want to stop him living his life.'

'Even though you'll allow your sister to stop you living yours?'

'That's different,' I muttered.

'I wonder,' she said. 'It's not for me to tell you how to live your life any more than it is for anyone else, but you've been so kind to us all, Laura. I want to see you happy.'

I returned to my own room and mused on this as I went to bed. Maybe I wasn't able to find the happiness she hoped for, but at least I could protect myself from any more pain. There had already been more than enough of that for one lifetime.

TWENTY-THREE

The next morning, Nick had gone again, without texting me
first this time. Even Astrid didn't know where he was, he had
just said that he was 'going away for a few days'. I went through
my daily tasks with a certain numbness. I still luxuriated in the
cocoon of relief that I had successfully protected myself from
any further heartbreak, but this was being nibbled away every
day by the persistent thought that I had made a colossal mistake.
Swinging between the two was exhausting and I spent restless
nights tossing and turning but found peace during the day with
Marilise. She didn't ask me about Nick or anything else, but
instead engaged me in gentle, undemanding pursuits such as
gathering foliage for decorations, which she taught me to wind
around candles or tuck into twisted wire to make wreaths and
table displays. Sofia and India had finished school and, when
they weren't at the stables, provided excellent company. They
joined us in our simple crafting, chattering about their friends
and their hopes for Christmas presents. Astrid and Angela were
stolid friends to me. They didn't mention Nick either but
checked in on me in a more general way and every night
suggested that we sat together for a tea or hot chocolate after

Marilise had gone to bed, when we chatted about this and that, and I was deeply grateful for the company.

It was on one of these occasions that Angela said, 'You have the evening off tomorrow, don't you? Are you doing anything nice?'

I grimaced.

'It's Steph's hen party. I'm looking forward to catching up with Minty in person, but otherwise I'd gladly pass.'

'What are you going to wear?' asked Astrid.

'Well, you won't be surprised to hear that Dorothea has a dress code.'

They both groaned, half laughing.

'What is it?' asked Astrid. 'Not a costume party?'

'Absolutely not, thank goodness,' I replied. 'Although she has said there will be "traditional surprises" in that respect, whatever that means. No, we have to all dress in hot pink, not a colour I have much of in my wardrobe. I ordered something from Vinted which I'm pleased with, so keep your fingers crossed I'm not wearing a penis headband by the end of the evening.'

In truth, I hadn't thought that was Dorothea's style, and was hoping for a reasonably classy night out, but I was sorely disappointed. She had gone 'fully traditional' as she put it, and this meant a little white veil for Steph and sashes for all of us, denoting us as 'Steph's hens'. We were also presented with glittery 'Team Bride' headbands. We started at her home with pink cocktails brought by a disapproving butler, which we drank from personalised glasses, and hors d'oeuvre in shapes that we had to pretend to find funny. Dorothea, to my surprise, knocked back the cocktails rapidly, and was soon insisting on a game of 'I have never', where we were all expected to come up with outlandish scenarios, and drink if we had ever done those things. The ideas were so silly that I think we were all hoping for something like 'I have never gone to Sainsbury's', just so that we could have a drink, but it soon stopped being funny when Dorothea, a sly look in her eyes, said, 'I have never kissed a member of the Prince family.'

I glanced at Araminta, who winked at me and took a huge and very performative slug of her cocktail, then announced, 'When we were five my mother made me kiss Nick goodbye after every playdate, doubtless hoping that it would lead to marriage twenty years later. Bad luck her! My turn! I have never watched an episode of *Love Island*. Come on, 'fess up ladies!'

Her technique worked like a dream, and soon everyone was discussing the latest pairing from a show I had never watched, although I appeared to be in the minority. I raised my glass to her in a subtle toast, and she winked.

After about an hour of this, there was a knock on the door, which opened to reveal the butler, his disapproval deepening by the second.

'Your tattoo artist is here,' he said, then withdrew rapidly to admit a pretty young woman in a white coat.

'Hello, everyone,' she said. 'Not real tattoos, don't worry! But I hear you're all getting matching ones?'

A tipsy cheer greeted this news and Minty, who had managed to edge her way over to sit next to me, whispered, 'Oh God, they're going to brand us!'

She wasn't far wrong. Half an hour later, we were all sporting large round pink and black tattoos on our forearms, declaring that we were 'Steph's Set', with a cartoon picture of her in the middle. Next, we piled into a stretch limousine, where Dorothea poured us all champagne and refused to tell us where we were going. It was by now nearly nine o'clock and I hoped that wherever it was would include food. I had taken it slow on the cocktails, but my stomach was decidedly empty and beginning to roll from the unaccustomed amount of alcohol. It seemed that we weren't going anywhere specific for a while. As we cruised around, all the hens except Minty, me and a woman called Sue, who was looking slightly green, stood up and poked their heads out of the sunroof, whooping at unsuspecting passersby. Finally, we pulled up, clambering out of the car to see that we were outside a small nightclub advertising a drag queen cabaret that night. I tugged at Dorothea's sleeve as she hurried everyone out of the limousine.

'This looks great fun,' I said. 'Are we going to have supper in there?'

'Eating is cheating!' she bellowed at me and marched up to the front door to announce our arrival, as if that were necessary. I turned to Minty.

'This is going to be carnage,' I said.

'Yup. I'm moving on to whatever bar snacks they have, I'm starving.'

We went inside and were ushered to a 'VIP' area, consisting of a large, curved, red pleather bench around a couple of small tables separated from the rest of the club by a red rope, and with a great view of the stage. Dorothea ordered more champagne, but I grabbed the waiter and asked him to bring whatever food they had, even if that was just bags of peanuts. I was sitting next to Araminta on one side, and Sickly Sue on the other.

'Are you okay?' I asked her.

She gave me a slightly wobbly smile.

'I usually only drink at Christmas,' she said. 'Since having kids. I think I'll be all right, I just need something to eat.'

At that moment the waiter returned laden, bless him, with bags of Doritos. Throwing manners to the wind, I stood up and reached over to relieve him of about half his burden, quickly opened a bag and put them in front of Sue.

'These'll help,' I said. 'Do you want some water?'

She nodded, nibbling at a Dorito, and I asked the waiter to

bring several bottles, as Dorothea thrust glasses into our hands, then proceeded to fill them, slopping champagne everywhere. I knew there was no point in refusing and anyway, I didn't want to be accused of being a party pooper, so I toasted Steph, then put the glass down and gratefully took some water.

'Ladies, gentlemen, and everyone else!' came a sudden announcement over the loudspeaker. 'Please find your seats, or someone else's lap. Tonight's cabaret is about to begin!'

We all cheered, and I took advantage of the noise to open a few more packets of crisps, then the room settled down and a languid jazz trumpet started up as a beautiful drag artist strutted onto the stage. Her electric blue hair was about a foot high, and she wore a long, slinky silver dress that pooled at her feet beneath her enormous platform heels and reflected the light so dramatically that it almost looked as if it were on fire. She then went into a sultry rendition of 'Santa Baby' and I relaxed back into my seat, looking forward to the show.

The whole cabaret was spellbinding, and I loved every moment from the singing to the comedy pieces, and particularly the dancing. I was even starting to have some serious outfit envy; should I exchange my 'useful' black dress for something with a little more *va-va-voom*? Such was the fun of the show that I had also managed to push Nick to the back of my mind, giving myself a rest from the ruminations that had been disturbing me so much over the past few days. *Who knew*, I thought, as the lights went up and the applause finally faded, *that I would start enjoying Steph's hen night?* I turned to Minty and we chatted about the show. When Dorothea came round with yet more champagne, I even felt like having a sip and I held up my glass to Steph.

'Congratulations!' I said, across the table. 'Are you feeling excited about the wedding?'

She nodded and grinned and I saw the sister I had known and loved for so long break through on the face that had become disapproving and judgemental over the years. I got up and went over to hug her.

'Very touching,' drawled a mocking voice, and Dorothea sat down heavily next to me. 'If only you could have found such compassion for poor Eugenia the other night.'

For a moment I wasn't sure what she was talking about, and then I remembered the school performance and the woman with the hair accessory instructions.

'I didn't realise you knew her,' I said.

'Of course I do,' replied Dorothea. 'And she was most upset by your attitude.'

I couldn't be bothered to defend myself or try to explain.

'Well, it's all forgotten now, I'm sure,' I said neutrally.

'Not by Eugenia,' spat Dorothea. 'She has the filmed evidence of the evening, which was meant to be such a happy memory for her.'

'Well, maybe she can console herself with the thought that Sofia and Astrid have happy memories of the night,' I replied, having some more champagne.

'You've got your feet under the table at Lyonscroft, haven't you?' She sneered. 'But not for long, from what I hear.'

I felt as if someone had dropped a bag of wet sand on my stomach as the pain of recent days came back full force and the pleasantly tipsy feeling from the champagne morphed into sour sickness.

'Yes,' she went on maliciously. 'Nick continuing his glamorous international life after his little holiday at home and you only there until dear Marilise isn't. Darling Steph,' she went on. 'So generous to offer you a place with her. Giles and I are planning on starting a family soon ourselves; maybe we could find some room for you with us, for a while.'

I rose unsteadily to my feet. She mustn't, simply mustn't,

see me cry. I pushed past the table, setting the slender-stemmed glasses wobbling precariously and hurried through the tightly packed people, aiming for a door near the bar that looked as if it might lead to the loos. I opened it and slipped through, seeing more closed doors but also a small sofa at the end of the corridor. I sank onto this, drew up my knees and let out the tears. They were silent, but my whole body was shaking as I sobbed and heaved for breath. My face was buried in my knees, my arms wrapped around the top of my head, so I felt, rather than saw, someone sit down next to me. An arm went around my shoulders and patted me firmly, the touch comforting me so much that my weeping started to subside and I lifted my head. I had expected to see Araminta, or maybe even Steph, but what I had *not* expected was the beautiful and statuesque figure of the silver-clad drag queen from the performance that night. She was probably the most glamorous person I had ever seen in real life and must have cut a figure nearly eight feet tall, including her shoes and wig, but she had a look of such softness and kindness on her immaculately made-up face that I knew in my heart I could pour everything out to her.

'What's up, my love?' she said, her voice calm and soothing.

'S-sorry,' I said. 'I was looking for the loos, but I think I got lost.'

'That doesn't matter a bit. You're backstage, where the magic happens, and it looks to me like you could do with a bit of that.'

I nodded and mustered a small smile.

'You're right there. I could do with some bloody powerful magic – my life's such a mess.'

'Oh well, I know all about that,' she said, smiling. 'Messy lives are my speciality. Nothing that can't be fixed, I'm sure. Now, tell Christal everything.'

So, I spilled out the whole tale, from my happy, simple life with Paulo, then his death, to the introverted, nomadic life that had followed. I explained my family's dynamic as best I could, trying not to sound bitter or self-pitying. I told her how I had found work and then love at Lyonscroft and how Nick and I had broken up, he wracked with conviction that I had fulfilled his expectations by leaving him, me terrified of betraying Paulo and moving on from my own feelings, which had kept me safe for so long. I explained the plan my sister had come up with for my future, and how I was considering it, but knew at the same time I was committing myself to a life I didn't want.

'I've ruined everything,' I concluded. 'And I've closed so many doors that I don't know how to get out of the tiny little room I've boxed myself into.'

'You are a ninny,' said Christal, smiling at me as if I were a little girl. I gazed at her, basking in her maternal affection. 'Do you ever try being kind to yourself?'

I shook my head and sniffed.

'Not really. I always think I can do better.'

'Better than being a bloody lovely nurse and bloody brave to boot?' she asked. 'You've been through the wringer, my love, and you're still standing. Start off by being proud of that. Now, I am an expert on love, and I can tell you for sure that all is not lost with this Nick. It sounds like you both need to support each other to take a chance, be a little braver. But put him to one side for the moment. Can you do that?'

I nodded.

'Good. Because whether he's the one or not, you need to decide what you want for your life and then go and get it. Do you want to work for your sister or her horrible mate?'

'No,' I said firmly.

'Good. Do you want to be a maternity nurse at all?'

'No,' I replied.

'Good. Then don't. What do you want to do, with your career?'

I hesitated. I did have an idea, but I had barely expressed it to myself, let alone anyone else.

'Come on, I know there's something. Tell Christal.'

'What I want to do is go back to university, do an MA and become a nurse educator. I think I'd be good at that,' I blurted out.

'You wouldn't be *good* at that, my darling, you'd be bloody brilliant. Say it.'

I giggled nervously, then said, 'I'd be bloody brilliant.'

'That's right. Say that every day and get your application in. Now, do you want to meet another man?'

'Yes.'

'Do you feel ready to be with someone?'

'Yes.'

'Is that person Nick?'

A smile spread across my face.

'Yes!'

'There you go. You've done the hard bit, which is knowing what you want. Now, all you have left is the fun part – going out and getting it.'

A wave of energy swept away my worry and exhaustion.

'Because I'm bloody brilliant?'

Christal swept me into a feathery, sequinned, scented hug.

'You've got it.'

I went back to the table and, ignoring Dorothea who was now bossing people into a game of Bride Bingo that no one had any appetite for, leant over and gave Steph a huge hug.

'I've had a brilliant evening,' I said. 'And I'm so happy for you, but it's time I went home. See you on the big day.'

Minty was dancing and, when I asked her if she wanted to leave, she cocked her head at the hunk she was with and said she'd see where the evening took her.

Next, I went over to Sue, who was slumped at the end of the banquette, asleep. I touched her shoulder and when I got no response, gave her a little shake. Her eyes opened slowly and tried to focus on me.

'I'm going home now,' I said. 'I'll drop you off, too. Where do you live?'

She mumbled the name of a small town not far from where we were, so I opened my taxi app and tapped in the details. Things were going my way that night: the cab would be with us in ten minutes. I helped Sue up, got both our coats from the cloakroom and steered her out into the cold night air, hoping that it would help sober her up, rather than make her throw up. We stood, shivering, as the night life of Taunton passed us by: giggling women holding each other up and talking about how much they were looking forward to getting into pyjamas; a group of rugby players, apparently not freezing in their shorts, singing 'Oh Come, All Ye Faithful' complete with a descant that I think surprised everyone, including the six footer producing it. Before long, a silver car drew up and I checked the registration number against my app, then hopped in before anyone else could try to pinch it. Sue, thankfully, made it home without being sick and we waited until she opened her front door and gave us a feeble wave before pulling away.

It was nearly midnight when I crept through the door of Lyonscroft. I tiptoed upstairs and towards my room. There was a band of light under Marilise's door – was she still awake? Was she okay? Quickly, I ran into my room and kicked off my shoes, then hurried back and opened her door quietly. To my relief, she was sitting up in bed, tapping away at her phone.

'Hello, Laura,' she said, looking up and seeing me. 'How was your evening? Do come in and tell me all about it. I like the photos you sent.'

She patted the bed next to her, and I remembered how much she had enjoyed hearing about the Christmas concert so, tired though I was, I sat down and told her about the evening, making her laugh when I described Dorothea's party games. I skimmed over my conversation with Christal, eager to give her only the funny highlights of the night, but she wasn't to be hoodwinked.

'She sounds wise,' she said. 'What else did she say?'

Once I had explained, she folded her hands and looked at me seriously.

'I'm so glad you have clarity,' she said. 'I know I've said it before, but Nikolai is a good boy, he means only well. He spends too much time with that dog, but hey...' She gave an exaggerated shrug. 'Nobody's perfect.'

'Doesn't it make you sad?' I asked. 'The fact that Lyonscroft might be sold?'

'After I die? Not at all. I do love it, but moving on is *good*. I hope he sells, or does something else with it, makes it into a hotel or something. It's a beautiful house, but it needs new life running through its veins, and it's too big for most families these days.'

'Moving on is good,' I repeated. 'I think I'm finally coming to understand that.'

'Good,' said Marilise, pushing herself down to lying and putting her phone on the bedside table, then reaching for the light switch. 'But you and Nick would be fools not to move on together.'

TWENTY-FOUR

I woke early the next morning and, despite the alcohol and late night, felt distinctly chipper. As I showered and dressed, the previous night scrolled through my head: the hen party, kind Christal, Marilise. I had turned a corner. I still loved Paulo and I always would, but I understood now that cringing away from life, from love, couldn't bring him back, and that living my life as some sort of tribute to his memory wasn't noble and didn't prove anything. It stopped me being a whole person and worried those around me. And besides, I thought, as I turned the water off and wrapped myself in a towel, Paulo would be furious if he could see what I had done. This made me smile and, with that smile, an image of my beloved husband came to me: not an image of him ill in bed, which was what I often saw, but an image of him laughing and carefree, the way I had always wanted to remember him. It felt like a blessing and, when I went downstairs to the kitchen to start preparing mine and Marilise's breakfast and switched on the radio, the song playing was 'Sleigh Ride', which brought back that happy night with Nick. When Angela came in, I was dancing around, singing along.

'Morning!' she said, her face amused. 'Enjoy yourself last night?'

'Not entirely,' I replied. 'But things are looking up. In fact, I was wondering if it would be at all possible for me to take a little time off after Marilise's swim today. There's something I need to do.'

Angela agreed and I took breakfast upstairs with a light heart. The morning passed quickly and, after our swim, I made a quick lunch, then set out in the car to drive the forty minutes to the cosy family house where Paulo had grown up from the age of five, when they moved to England from Portugal, and his parents still lived. I had rung them that morning to check that they were free, so when I pulled up outside, they were expecting me and greeted me with the warmth and love they had shown me from the first moment we had met.

'I love your decorations,' I said, as I followed them through the small hallway and into the sitting room. They had a real Christmas tree, scenting the whole room and decorated with a riot of different baubles as well as tinsel and lights, but the focus of the room was the Presépio, or nativity scene, with a crib waiting for the baby Jesus, who would be placed there when they returned from Midnight Mass on Christmas Eve. I crouched down in front of it and let the memories and emotions emerge from my heart, so much more gently now than I had been used to. After a few moments, I cleared my throat, stood up and smiled. Paulo's mother, Azula, stepped towards me and gathered me into a hug.

'We miss him, too,' she said. 'But the memories are happy. Now come, sit down. Bernardo will bring the coffee.'

I sank into a comfortable chair and waited while the coffee was poured and the pastries offered around. I never could resist them, particularly the *massa de filhós*, a sort of flat doughnut eaten at Christmas in Portugal, and beyond delicious. I hadn't had one since the year before Paulo's illness, and the sweet, rich flavour sent my senses reeling.

'I've never tried to make these,' I said. 'But I think it's time I learnt, if you would teach me?'

I knew that each family has its own particular way of making the *massa*, and it was traditional to be shown, rather than follow written instructions.

'*Claro*,' said Azula. *Of course.* 'You know that you will always be my daughter. Now, tell me, what brings you here to see us?'

I breathed in slowly before speaking.

'I wanted to tell you that I think' – I thought of Christal and her urge to be certain – 'that I *have* met someone, a man.'

I had been unsure of how they would take this news, but the last thing I had expected was the joyful smile that spread across both of their kind faces. Putting down their cups and plates, they came over and hugged and kissed me, exclaiming in delight.

'We're so happy for you,' said Bernardo, wiping away a tear as he sat down again. '*Muito feliz.*'

'It is true,' said Azula. 'We have worried for you these past few years, you seemed stuck. We know how you loved Paulo, how much you grieve him, but we also longed for you to move forward. Tell us about this man.'

So, I told them about Nick, about how kind he was, how he wanted to help his family and make them happy but that he had been so cruelly treated by his father that he struggled to make connections – until now. I told them about Steve, which made them laugh, and about how things had gone wrong between Nick and me. I explained that everything was much clearer now and that the guilt and worry had fallen from my shoulders so that I no longer had the need to atone for the past but was ready to move forward.

'But you say that Nick has gone?' asked Azula, offering me the plate of *massa de filhós* again. I took one.

'Yes,' I replied. 'But I truly believe that we can work things out. And if we can't...' My heart dropped a little at this thought, but I continued. 'If we can't, then he will always be incredibly special to me, because he was the one who showed me how to love again. Even if I can't be with Nick, I will keep moving and be excited at what lies ahead.'

Bernardo nodded.

'You always had a wise head on those young shoulders,' he said. 'Nick would be foolish not to take the opportunity to be with you.'

'You sound like Marilise,' I said, laughing. 'You should come over one day and meet her – she's wonderful.'

We chatted for a little longer before I left to drive back to Lyonscroft, with a large box of the Christmas doughnuts to share with the Princes. I felt a tremendous sense of peace, only slightly ragged at the edges with the thought: *what if Nick has gone for good?* For despite my brave assertions to the contrary, I knew that I would be devastated.

That evening was one of the cosiest I had spent at Lyonscroft. After supper, Marilise suggested that we all go into the sitting room with more of the Linzer cookies that India and Sofia had made, and some mulled wine, or mulled apple juice.

'I don't feel like this evening should end yet,' she said. 'It is so nearly Christmas, and the anticipation is the most fun part, don't you agree? I want to teach you some games we played as children, before you young people all became endlessly distracted by Marios and Minecrafts and whatnot.'

A chorus of amused disagreement met this assertion:

'I've never played Minecraft in my life!'

'A little Candy Crush with a cup of tea doesn't mean I don't do other things!'

'Marilise, you spend more time on your phone than any of us!'

'I am old,' she said in a dignified manner. 'And have time on my hands to surf the net. Now! Let us prepare the refreshments and adjourn.'

So, with giggling and chatter we made the drinks and put the cookies on a plate, then piled into the sitting room, where Marilise, her eyes glittering with fun, addressed us.

'We will start,' she said, 'with a simple word game. Each person says a short sentence, and the next person must start their sentence with a word which rhymes with the last word of the previous sentence. Yes?'

We looked around at each other, a little bemused.

'I get it,' said Greg. 'If I say, "I like eating *cheese*" the next person might say, "*Bees* are rare in winter".'

'Exactly,' said Marilise. 'Now, we try.'

The game went slowly at first, as we all tried to think of things, then picked up speed as we all grabbed at rhyming words and the sentences became more and more ridiculous. Eventually, Astrid held up her hands.

'I'm simply wrung out!' she announced. 'Can't we try something else?'

'Very well,' said Marilise. 'The next game is called The Sculptor.'

In this game, a 'sculptor' went around everyone posing them as if they were those wooden artists' dolls. The aim of the game was to make such funny poses that the 'sculptures' laughed and were out. Angela was the first one to try. She started by positioning India as if she were riding a horse, then moved on to me. She was placing one hand behind my back and lifting up my knee, and I was trying not to giggle, when the door opened.

'Looks like some good old-fashioned fun,' said Nick.

'Where have you been?' said Astrid, going over to hug him. 'We haven't heard from you in days.'

'Come and have a drink,' said Greg.

Steve bounded into the room and straight over to me. I dropped my silly pose gratefully and fussed over him, glad to have something to do. Nick's sudden appearance had thrown me more than I might have expected. He sat down with us and Marilise suggested that we continue with a favourite game of hers from childhood, which involved more wordplay, this time thinking of adjectives in alphabetical order to create a story, and precluded any conversation. Mine and Nick's eyes met several times, and each set off an uncomfortable mix of fireworks and butterflies, which no amount of mulled wine, Linzer cookies or silly parlour games could quell.

Eventually, it was time for bed, and I offered Marilise my arm to take her up. Nick came over and leant close to me, a waft of his familiar, nutmeggy smell making me feel dizzy and confused.

'Could we talk later?' he muttered.

I paused. I wanted more than anything to talk to him, to spill out everything I had discovered, to see if we had a future together. But there was something else I wanted to do as well, something I had decided on when I was at Azula and Bernardo's home, and tonight wasn't the time or the place.

'Can we go out soon?' I asked. 'I'd like to talk.'

He nodded.

'Of course. Good night, Laura.'

I helped Marilise with her nighttime routine, then went to my own room, hoping for a peaceful night's rest so that tomorrow I might be able to show Nick that I wasn't going to do what so many others in his life had. I wasn't going to leave him, abandon him or let him down and it was time to prove it.

TWENTY-FIVE

The following morning was a busy one at Lyonscroft. It was so nearly Christmas and deliveries were arriving so often that there was barely time to deal with one before the doorbell rang again. India and Sofia kept themselves busy by baking more Linzer cookies, far more than any of us could eat. Angela had suggested that they package some up and take them to neighbours, probably to get them out of her kitchen as much as anything, and this had caught their imagination – so much so that they had also started looking up food banks and nursing homes that might be willing recipients of their efforts. Marilise had ordered piles of presents, and I helped her wrap them until I thought my fingers would bleed.

'It's probably my last Christmas,' she said. 'And I want to spoil everyone.'

In my line of work I am, of course, accustomed to patients dying, but my relationship with Marilise had become special, and the thought of losing her after such a short time of knowing her upset me, especially when, in my professional opinion, she seemed to be in particularly good health at the moment. I went downstairs on the pretext of getting more tape and stepped outside into the garden to take a few breaths.

'Are you all right?'

'Oh, hello, Astrid, I didn't see you there. Yes, I'm okay.'

'Something's upset you.'

I gave her a small smile.

'Just Marilise. She says that seeing as it's likely to be her last Christmas, she wants to get everyone lots of presents. I know she's an old lady, I know what's coming at some point, but it made me feel so sad.'

To my surprise, Astrid grinned and put an arm around my shoulders, giving me a big squeeze.

'We all know we won't have Marilise forever, but would it help if I told you that she's been saying exactly the same thing for the past ten years? She loves buying presents and has found the perfect excuse.'

I laughed.

'Thank you, that does make me feel better. And how about you? Are you all right about Philip?'

'Better than all right. I'm so much happier. I hadn't realised how much I was burying myself to be with him, and now I know that Nick won't sell Lyonscroft from under me I'm excited about the idea of buying something smaller someday, something that's just for India and me – and Firefly, of course.' She paused, then said, 'I don't want to intrude, Laura, but what about you? I know Christmas is a difficult time for you, anyway, and I can see that things haven't gone smoothly with Nick.'

'It's all right,' I said. 'I've done so much thinking, and I can remember Paulo now in a happier way. As for Nick, watch this space – if only there *was* some space, so that we could talk.'

'If it's time you need, I was going to suggest that I stay with Marilise, anyway,' she said. 'She keeps whispering to me about secrets and surprises, so I think she'd be glad if you were off for the afternoon. Go after lunch.'

I texted Nick, who had been holed up in one of the downstairs rooms all morning, working, and he texted back agreeing that this afternoon would work. I hoped that my plan would, too.

After lunch, Nick, Steve and I piled into my car, along with a flask of hot coffee and a bag of India and Sofia's cookies. As we drove the hour or so to the spot I had in mind, we mostly shared a comfortable silence, or chatted idly about Christmas and it didn't feel like long before we were pulling into the pretty village of Mells.

'There's a gorgeous walk, with a surprise at the end of it, that Paulo and I used to do,' I said. 'This is the perfect weather for it! I love sunny winter days.'

'It's something I missed in LA,' said Nick, as we started out along the bridle path. 'The locals could never understand it when I wished for a cold day, and even a really bad one, sometimes. They didn't understand the joys of snuggling up inside while freezing wind and rain lash the windows.'

I laughed.

'You can have too much of any good thing, I suppose. There have been many English winters when I've longed for sunshine, so it works both ways.'

About fifteen minutes later, a gentle sound came to our ears. I had only done this walk once since losing Paulo, too scared of the memories it would stir up, but I found now that I felt nothing but happiness and excitement.

'Is that water I can hear?' asked Nick.

'Yes,' I replied. 'That's what I've brought us here to see.'

And in a few moments, we were standing by a small, beautiful waterfall that gushed out over rocks into the river beneath.

'This is quite something,' said Nick, who had grabbed Steve and put him on the lead, not wanting a freezing cold, dripping dog to take back in the car. 'Thank you for bringing me here. Shall we sit for a while and have that coffee?'

'There's something I want to do first,' I said and, taking off my gloves, dipped my hand into my pocket to pull out my necklace, its chain still broken. 'It's time to say goodbye. I won't ever forget Paulo, or stop loving him, but I'm ready to move on.'

Nick gazed at me, a serious look on his face. Even Steve had sat down quietly, perhaps picking up on the solemn atmosphere. I stood up.

'This was a special place for us, so this is where I wanted to say goodbye properly, and finally.'

I took a step forward and hesitated, looking down at the broken necklace lying in my hand. Paulo had given it to me for my birthday, the first year we were together. I had never had a proper boyfriend before him, and definitely never been given jewellery, so when I unwrapped the small box, then opened it to find the glowing pearl inside, I had cried with joy. I remembered him wiping away my tears and saying, 'but it was supposed to make you happy!' and me throwing my arms around him sobbing, 'it does, it does!' Then we had both laughed as he helped me put it on, kissing the back of my neck as he did so. I had worn the necklace every day since, until it broke. Letting it go now, rather than having it mended and continuing to wear it, had felt right to me when I had thought of the idea, but standing on the edge of the waterfall, Nick and Steve in quiet sympathy behind me, I wasn't sure if I could do it. Then I thought about the memories I had allowed to surface in recent weeks and how wonderful it had been to feel both the happiness and the pain that they had brought, because they had made Paulo real again, a much-loved person, but one who must ultimately be let go.

Not giving myself a second longer to think about it, I raised my arm and threw the necklace into the pool where the water bubbled at the bottom of the waterfall. For a moment, I thought

I was going to cry, and then peace washed over me and, sitting down again, I spoke.

'Nick, I want to be with you. I'm not going to train as a maternity nurse.' I paused and rolled my eyes, amazed that only a few short days ago I had even been considering such a thing. 'And I'm not going to go and work for Steph – and definitely not Dorothea.'

'Thank God for that,' he said, a smile playing around his lips. 'A change of career is one thing, but you'd have had to take early retirement to get over that job.'

I laughed.

'You're right, between them they would have finished me off.'

He reached out and took my hands, cold without the gloves I hadn't put back on.

'Well, you know that I wasn't going to sell Lyonscroft, and that Astrid and India can stay there as long as they want?'

'Yes.'

'I made another decision.'

My brow creased as I looked at him.

'To go back to LA?'

He squeezed my hands more tightly.

'No. I decided that if you were going to be working for your sister nearby, then I would stick around, too. I can work from anywhere and it turns out the warmth of the Californian sunshine is nothing compared to how I feel when I'm with you. So, it's my LA house that won't have its lease renewed, and I was going to keep living at Lyonscroft.'

'But you hate that house!'

'Hated,' he corrected. 'This winter, for the first time in my life, it's felt like a family home to me. And if it meant having the chance to make things work with you, then I was happy to stay.'

'But what if...'

I trailed off, embarrassed to finish my thought.

'What if you hadn't wanted me?' he asked.

I nodded miserably. The thought that I had so nearly pushed away this kind, funny, emotional man for a life of looking after other people's babies nearly winded me.

'I don't know,' he said. 'All I was sure of was that I wouldn't give up until I was a hundred and ten per cent sure you wouldn't change your mind. I thought that by staying nearby, then the possibility would be there, without the pressure. I've never experienced the grief you did; it wasn't up to me to have an opinion on how long it should last, but I wanted to give us a chance, even if we'd just been friends.'

A wave of happiness coursed through me, and I leant forward and kissed him with such passion and relief and gratitude and joy that I never wanted to stop, and he kissed me back. It was only when Steve shoved his big, silky head between us that we broke apart, laughing.

'Oh dear,' I said, stroking his soft ears. 'Are you jealous, Steve?'

'He's delighted,' said Nick, pushing the dog back, who was trying to climb up and collapse on his shoulder. 'He hated LA; the sand got between his toes, and everyone was cross because he was so much more naturally beautiful than they were.'

'You're a lovely boy,' I said, rubbing Steve's head and getting a lick on the cheek in return. 'And much less high maintenance than Steph.'

'He'll be the perfect step-dog,' said Nick. 'As long as he doesn't keep interrupting us.'

And with that he leant forward again to continue where we had left off.

Warm though our kisses were, eventually the cold air began to inveigle its way into our clothes and shoes, and we decided, reluctantly, that it was time to go home.

'It's getting dark,' said Nick. 'But look.' He stooped down to Steve and fiddled with his collar until a bright red light came on. 'Now, he can have another run and we shouldn't lose him.'

He unclipped the lead and the big dog bounded off with his customary enthusiasm, every blade of grass seeming to hold some ineffable excitement. Nick wrapped his arm around my shoulder, and we walked the short distance back to the car slowly, despite the cold. When we were nearly there, he called for Steve, but there was no rustling in the leaves, no bark in response.

'Where has that dog got to?' he said. 'I'm sorry, I think we'd better walk back.'

We started back quietly, listening out for him, but a flash of red light caught our eye first, before his mournful whines came to our ears. Veering off the path towards the noise, we found him.

'Oh, that silly dog,' said Nick. 'Not again!'

For Steve had managed to wriggle his way inside a bush and, apparently, had no inkling of how to extract himself.

'This is where we started,' I said, crouching down and shining my phone's torch into the space. 'At least he has a nice sense of how to bookend a story. I think I can get in – can you hold my phone?'

Once again, I got down on all fours and crawled into the bush behind Steve, who greeted me with the relief and ecstasy of someone who has been trapped for months, rather than seconds.

'Come on, you,' I said and, grabbing his collar, I guided him in the right direction. Soon we were all back on terra firma, as it were, and Nick was clipping Steve's lead firmly back on.

'At least we're getting in practice for kids,' said Nick, as we started walking again. 'Surely a toddler can't be this much trouble?'

I didn't reply, but the feeling of blissful warmth that

suffused me was more than enough to chase away the coldest of evenings.

When we arrived back at Lyonscroft, we found a group of people at the foot of the driveway by the wall. I stopped the car and Nick wound down his window.

'Hello,' he said. 'That's my house up there, can I help you?'

A young woman smiled at him and said, 'Yes, we were wondering whether it would be okay to go up?' She shook a collecting tin. 'We're singing carols for charity.'

'Absolutely,' said Nick. 'Do come on up. I know my grandmother would love to hear you.'

As we parked, I couldn't help grinning.

'What's so funny?' asked Nick.

'Just thinking back to a few short weeks ago when I fear those poor carol singers would have been given short shrift,' I said.

'And all the years that my father would have done the same,' said Nick grimly. 'Looks like I was more like him than I realised.'

'But you shut Christmas out for very different reasons from your father,' I said. 'Didn't you? I mean, you were trying to grit your teeth and get through things. Why *did* he hate it so much?'

Nick shrugged.

'I've thought about it over the years. When I was a child, I was too scared of him to question anything, even to myself, and when I asked Astrid, she said that we're all different and wouldn't be drawn any further. I haven't thought about it for years, to be honest, but this year...'

He broke off, staring out of the windscreen and biting his lip. I reached across and laid my hand over his.

'This year?'

'This year, when I went away for a few days, I decided to

try and think about it all. It's hard... it's hard for me to feel any forgiveness or understanding for my father, as if by doing that I'm somehow condoning the way he behaved. But I think – maybe you will understand this better than I can – I think that his grief over losing my mother must have been so agonising that he shut down. Shut down all his feelings of misery but also of joy, as if feeling anything at all was too painful. And he made sure that everyone else did the same.'

I glanced over to the front door, which was now open, and heard the strains of 'O Little Town of Bethlehem' from the carol singers.

'I do understand that,' I said. 'I did the same thing myself. It seemed easier.'

'But you coped by caring for others,' said Nick. 'My father coped by becoming cruel. He treated me with disdain and sent me away, making it clear that my only usefulness was as his heir. He blew hot and cold with Victoria, showering her with presents one moment and telling her she was a nuisance the next. No wonder she can't bond with her own child. And as for poor Astrid, he never should have married her at all, but then he refused her a baby.' He turned to me, his face bleak in the darkness. 'I had forgotten or ignored so much, but I did some real soul searching. She was a great mother to Victoria and me, but she so wanted a baby of her own. Thank God that the minute the old bugger died, she met Art and got pregnant.'

'Shame it didn't work out with India's dad.'

'A huge shame. He was great.' Nick sighed. 'Ah well, plenty of water under every bridge. Shall we go inside?'

I nodded. It had got very cold in the car and the carol singers had moved into a four-part harmony of 'O Come, All Ye Faithful', which I wanted to hear. With Steve on a short lead, we slipped around the side of them to stand in the doorway with the rest of the family and applauded vigorously when the final strains of the music finished.

'Do come inside,' said Astrid. 'It's so cold out here, which isn't good at all for your lovely voices, and you can warm up before you go on to your next house.'

They nodded eagerly and were ushered into the sitting room by Nick, while Angela helped Marilise and wondered aloud what drinks everyone would like. There was one singer, though, who held back, a tall man in a woolly hat. I was shutting the door as Astrid hurried off to the kitchen.

'Do come in,' I said. 'No need to take off your shoes.'

'It's not that,' he said, then surprised me by suddenly calling, 'Astrid!'

She turned around and saw the man, who had been standing quietly at the back of the group. All the colour drained from her face, and she clutched at the wall as if to stop herself falling.

'*Art?*' she gasped. 'I thought you were in Argentina.'

I looked again at the man. So this was Art, India's father and Astrid's lost love. I started to edge towards the sitting room door, feeling very much like a third wheel.

'I was,' he said. 'I wanted to surprise India, but Astrid... it is you I have been longing to see for too many years.'

I could barely tear my eyes away from the scene unfolding in front of me as I groped half-heartedly for the door handle. Art stepped forward hesitantly and lifted his arms. Astrid stepped into his embrace, laying her head on his shoulder as tears streamed down her face and into his wool overcoat. Finally, I opened the door and stepped into the room.

'So, that's nine mulled wines, three hot apple juices, two coffees and a tea,' Angela was saying. 'Ah, Laura, what would you like?'

'Mulled wine, please,' I said, then lowering my voice, told her what was happening in the hallway outside. Her face was suffused with happiness and her eyes glistened.

'A Christmas miracle,' she said. 'India, love, come and help me, would you? We'll go through the garden – I'll explain on the way.'

As they left through the French windows, I went to sit with Nick and Marilise.

'What was all that about?' she asked, her sharp eyes having missed nothing.

'India's father was one of the carol singers,' I said. 'He and Astrid are catching up.'

She smiled and nodded, as if the fates had obeyed a command of hers.

'Of course,' she said. 'Things do work out as they should, you know, no matter how much time passes or how much water flows under the bridge.'

Hearing the same expression he had used in the car, I glanced up at Nick. His eyes held my gaze.

'*To every thing there is a season,*' he said softly.

Marilise grasped for our hands.

'That's right,' she said, then continued the passage. '*A time to weep, and a time to laugh; a time to mourn, and a time to dance.* And I think now is the time for laughing and dancing, is it not?'

As Astrid and Art entered the room, Angela and India with them, beaming with happiness as they handed round drinks to the assembled company, I couldn't have agreed more.

TWENTY-SIX

Steph's extravaganza would have put the royal family to shame, had they been there. I'm not entirely sure that they hadn't been invited, actually, for the coup of the century, but in the end, she had to make do with the likes of me. I had arrived, as directed, at my parents' house at practically daybreak on the morning of the wedding. Nick dropped me off, grinning.

'Will I recognise you next time I see you, or will you have had a Steph-over?'

I grimaced.

'Probably. But I'm going to go with the flow. At least Minty will be there, too; we can compare our dresses and hairdos and remind each other to behave.'

Blowing me a kiss, he drove back home; he would be at the church later but for now I was on my own.

Flinging the front door open, Steph, resplendent in a long ivory satin bathrobe, feathery mules and her hair in rollers, gawped at me.

'Was that Nick?'

'Yes.'

'Isn't that all off?'

'I don't know what or who gave you that idea, but no, of course not.'

'But Dorothea said it was. What about me?'

What about you? And why are we talking about this on your wedding day? But I knew the answers. It was, and always had been, all about Steph, and that wouldn't change.

'I'm sure you'll find someone ideal to help,' I said soothingly. 'Now, shouldn't I be getting into my dress?'

I allowed myself to be shoehorned into my horrible dress and my hair to be curled and teased and sprayed until I looked like Medusa had put her finger in an electric socket. I posed awkwardly for 'ad hoc' photos of 'the girls' getting dressed and didn't even blanch when Dorothea removed my half-empty glass of champagne saying, 'That's enough, Laura. No one likes a tiddly bridesmaid.' It was as if Nick's love had cast a protective bubble around me, inside which I could hear and see everything, but was unaffected by it.

'I'm so glad it's worked out for you and Nick,' said Minty, after she had dragged me to the bathroom, where she produced half a bottle of champagne from behind the shower curtain and poured some into a tooth mug for us to share. 'Oh god, look at my hair,' she moaned, gazing into the mirror. 'I look like my mother in the nineties.'

'I was hoping it would drop a bit as the day goes on,' I said, giggling. 'But this is the sergeant major of hairsprays; there's no way it will fall out of line until it's been washed at least twice.'

There was a sharp rap at the door.

'Hurry up in there, the cars have arrived.'

I quickly rinsed out the tooth mug and we emerged, to step into the waiting cars and be whisked off to the church.

As we walked down the aisle, I felt a swell of emotion. After all, there was my baby sister, on my father's arm, looking beautiful in her elaborate dress. I was happy for her. I glanced sideways and saw Nick, his eyes only on me, and gave him a grin Dorothea would have despaired of ('Bridesmaids should be *demure*, Laura, and resist drawing attention to themselves.') When the ceremony was over, we posed again for about a million photos before repairing to Radley Hall, Hugo's family seat, for the reception. I took longer to look at it now than I had done when we went to the concert. It was a rather forbidding – and to my mind, ugly – pile, which had been enthusiastically restored by the Victorians in the gothic revival style. There were lots of towers, pointy windows and steep roofs with grotesque gargoyle finials.

'Ghastly, isn't it?' said Minty loudly, ignoring the surprised or disapproving glances of several wedding guests. 'God knows what the Victorians were thinking; there was a perfectly serviceable Jacobean house there before, until my ancestors decided to mess it up. I think it's even worse inside – you're quite sure that Dracula's going to pop out any second and sink his teeth into you, if he could find his way past all the soft furnishings. No wonder Dorothea feels at home there.'

Giggling, we walked in through the looming porch into the large, ornate hallway where we were each given a glass of champagne and were soon joined by Nick as well as a steady flow of Minty's friends and family. By the time we were ushered through to dinner, held in the ballroom, which had been set up with about twenty round tables, my feet were killing me, and I kicked off my tight, high-heeled shoes. I was, of course, seated at the top table, with Nick elsewhere in the room. Given the cost and the elaborate nature of the wedding, I had fully expected a modern, fancy parade of tiny portions decorated with jus of this and foam of that, with a shaving of the other, so I was surprised to be presented with a traditional, rather flavourless, British menu, which started with leek and potato soup.

'My mother insisted on our cook masterminding the whole

thing,' muttered Minty, who had swapped around the name cards so that we could sit together. 'She trained about a million years ago and has never changed a thing, so don't expect any garlic or colours other than brown and orange.'

'I'm surprised Steph was okay with it,' I said, breaking off a piece of the rather tough bread. 'I would have thought she'd wanted something more frou-frou.'

'She probably did,' said Minty. 'But can you imagine challenging Dorothea and my mother? This is how weddings at Radley have always been done; anything else would be considered distinctly beneath them. At least the wine's good, and there's plenty of it. Probably had to develop that tradition to wash down the awful food.'

Four courses later, with my gigantic portion of sticky toffee pudding and custard barely dented, came the speeches. Dad did brilliantly and brought a tear to my eye, and Hugo managed an adoring few words about Steph, which she looked pleased with, and a barely audible thanks to the bridesmaids. Next, we were ushered into yet another huge room for coffee and, when we returned to the ballroom, all the tables had been cleared and rearranged around the sides of the room while a band had set up at one end. Hugo and Steph took to the floor, guests forming a circle around them as the strains of 'Everything I Do' by Bryan Adams started up. All the bridesmaids had been instructed to participate in the first dance, swaying awkwardly in a line to watch the bride and groom. As soon as they were joined by Dorothea and Giles, then others, Nick came over to me and held out his hand. I took it gladly and, as his arms slid around me, felt happier and more relaxed than I had all day. I just had to hope the hairspray wouldn't asphyxiate him.

'Are your duties over?' he asked.

'Just about. I'm required again in about three hours to jump around excitedly for the bouquet throwing – but definitely *not* catch it, because Jen-Jen's going to do that—'

Nick burst out laughing.

'It's already decided who's going to catch the bouquet?'

'Oh yes,' I said solemnly. 'But we all have to fight over it like desperados, otherwise it won't *look right*. Then I have to be there to wave them off on their honeymoon. Only then am I allowed to go home. I'm not sure I can stay awake that long, to be honest.'

'I'll keep you going,' said Nick, pulling me onto the dance floor. 'And our reward at the end can be a twelve-hour sleep followed by a huge breakfast and an invigorating walk with Steve.'

I danced happily in his arms, thinking how perfect that sounded.

EPILOGUE

'Come in,' said Fallon Knight, smiling as she opened the front door to Nick and me. 'Everything's ready.'

We walked into the hallway of Lyonscroft, glad to be out of the freezing October evening. It had been transformed into the atrium of a jazz age nightclub, draped with black and gold, towering palms in huge pots set around and a smiling hat check girl with an immaculately smooth bob waiting to take coats.

'Your guests will be offered champagne or a cocktail here, then they'll go through to the main space,' she said, opening the door to show the living room transformed. The furniture had been removed and a temporary dance floor laid. There was a small stage at one end, where a band would play, and some little tables dotted about. Golden fringes hung all around the walls, and lamps with red, tasselled shades lent the room a sultry glow.

'The dining room is a sort of break-out area,' continued Fallon, leading us there. 'People can come here to rest and chat, and it also has the memorial to Marilise.'

'It looks incredible,' said Nick, his voice catching as we gazed at the room. There were low sofas, tables and a small bar and, on the wall, a screen which was showing photos and videos from Marilise's life, from the childhood photos in the snow I remembered her showing us not long after I first arrived at Lyonscroft, to video clips from last Christmas when we had prepared our final advent window for her, where she found a ticket for a horse-drawn sleigh ride exactly like the one Nick and I had taken on the night of the concert. Tears filled my eyes as I remembered how much joy it had brought her, how tenderly Nick had helped her get in, how she said it had given her the best Christmas of her life.

'Are you okay?' Nick whispered now, taking my hand.

I nodded. I was. The grief I had felt at Marilise's parting was different from that I had experienced over Paulo; no less important, no less profound, but softer somehow, lacking the hard edges of pain it had taken me so long to smooth.

'I'll leave you both to get ready,' said Fallon, stepping away. 'I'll be here all evening, as will Sam.'

She left, and Nick and I sat down on one of the sofas and watched the pictures scroll.

'I'm so glad she saw us married,' he said, as a photo of our wedding, held just over six months after we first met, came onto the screen. Funnily, it hadn't felt at all rushed, but the most logical, almost inevitable, thing to do, mostly for us but also because we had so wanted Marilise to be there. We only invited a handful of people: our families and some close friends, including Paulo's parents Azula and Bernardo, who couldn't have been happier for us. India and Sofia were lovely bridesmaids in summer dresses they had each chosen themselves. I had worn another of Marilise's dresses from the attic, this one a pale pink silk A-line with a sweetheart neckline. It came complete with a huge petticoat to help it stand out and had a tulle overlay, embroidered with flowers. It belonged in the

Victoria and Albert Museum rather than on me, but Marilise insisted, and it felt truly special. The photo we had chosen for the display was of us sitting either side of Marilise on a bench in the garden of Lyonscroft. It was a glorious June day with the roses in full bloom, and we had been caught by the photographer as, clutching glasses of champagne, we all collapsed with laughter because Minty had dressed Steve up as a pageboy and sent him trotting over, looking pleased as punch with his cute sailor collar and a pair of sunglasses. Both were shaken off almost immediately, but he did look funny. For me, it was the perfect wedding: simple, happy and heartfelt. My mother and sister saw things rather differently, trying to persuade me into ivory, if not white – 'I know it's your second marriage, but it's perfectly *fine* for a widow' – as well as a hen night and vast guest list. I rebuffed them politely at every turn and, in the end, even they enjoyed the day.

When all the photos had scrolled through, we went upstairs to get ready. Marilise had often encouraged me to wear her old clothes, so it seemed fitting that today I slipped on an elegant, floor-length black dress made from heavy, flowing silk crepe with embroidered lace sleeves. I added some delicate gold jewellery that Nick had given me and styled my hair in a simple chignon. As we came out of our room and walked along the landing, Astrid and Art stepped out of another door.

'Oh, look at the two of you!' exclaimed Astrid. 'Such a beautiful couple.'

'We could say the same ourselves,' said Nick, smiling.

It was true. Since Art had appeared amongst the carol singers, he and Astrid had hardly spent a moment apart, making up for the years they had lost. India was thrilled to have her parents together, and the three of them were making plans to move out of Lyonscroft into a place of their own.

The four of us walked downstairs together. Art and I left Astrid and Nick in the hallway to greet the guests and went into the living room, where a tall, blonde woman in a dark grey tailored suit sat at one of the tables with a little girl, listening to the band.

'Sofia!' I said, holding out my arms for a hug as she spotted me and ran over. 'I didn't realise you had arrived. Oh, it's lovely to see you!'

'This is my mummy,' she said, gesturing shyly towards the woman, who stood up slowly and glided over.

'Victoria,' she said, holding out a slim, cool hand for me to shake.

'How nice to meet you at last,' I said. 'I'm so glad you were able to come today.'

'We were very sorry to miss the wedding,' she said with a slight trace of an American accent. 'But I wanted to remember Marilise, and I'm pleased to meet you. Sofia has obviously become very fond of you.'

'And I of her,' I said warmly. 'You have a fantastic daughter.'

She smiled faintly and touched Sofia's hair.

'I do.'

'And thank you,' I said. 'For agreeing to the plans for Lyonscroft.'

She inclined her head graciously.

'It was good of Nick and Marilise to consult me – they didn't have to. And I think it's a very good idea.'

From then on, the guests poured in, all with colourful memories of Marilise that they wanted to share. Fallon had suggested setting up a memories book for people to write in or add photos to, and soon a small group had formed of friends wanting to add their stories.

'Marilise would have loved this,' said Araminta, as we sat for a moment, our feet tired from dancing.

'Wouldn't she?' I said. 'She helped plan it, you know. She wanted to be sure that everyone would have a good time and that she would be remembered properly.'

'As if anyone could ever forget her!'

'I never could,' I said fiercely. 'I just wish I had known her for longer. She was so inspiring.'

'That's true,' said Minty. 'And actually, she's inspired me.'

'How?'

'I've been stuck in a rut here, complaining about my family trying to matchmake me, living in that huge house that doesn't want me there anymore, especially now both my brothers are married and an heir on the way.'

'Dorothea still hasn't forgiven me for refusing to become her maternity nurse,' I said with a giggle. 'When she found out she was pregnant, she came to me and asked me to reconsider. She doesn't even like me, so I'm not sure why she was so determined.'

'She doesn't like not getting her own way,' said Minty.

'That's true. So, what are you planning?'

'I'm leaving,' she said. 'Soon. I've got a job in New York writing for the social pages of an American magazine – apparently, they like my 'British wit', and I have the right contacts to get invited to the sort of parties they want to feature.'

'That's brilliant,' I said. 'It sounds huge fun, but I will miss you.'

'Don't worry, I'll be back all the time – and maybe you and Nick will visit?'

'Definitely,' I said, giving her a hug. 'Oh look, there he is now, he's going to do a speech.'

Nick stood on the stage and waited while everyone was ushered into the room, then he took the microphone from the band leader.

'Good evening, everyone. I want to thank you for coming tonight to celebrate Marilise. She was a remarkable woman, and I consider myself incredibly lucky for having known her and benefited from her wisdom – and the odd telling-off!' A ripple of laughter went through the audience. 'Her voice still resonates so strongly in my head that it is hard to believe that she is gone. I suppose that when you have such vivid memories of someone, when they are still changing your life, they are not gone at all. Marilise left many legacies of one sort or another: her Christmas traditions, her encouragement to follow your heart, her determination that things should work out, her sheer joy for life. But there is one more legacy that I want to share with you all tonight, one that she and I discussed at length before her death and which Astrid, of course, and also Victoria, were a part of.' He smiled at his sister, who was looking more relaxed than she had before, and gave him a warm smile in return. 'Between us, we decided that – inspired by my beautiful wife, Laura, and her amazing nursing work – we wanted to transform Lyonscroft into accommodation for nurses who work at our local hospital. It will be a mix of both long and short term; some will live here for several years, calling it home, others may need it only for a night or two. Some of the rooms will be set up as studies, so that student nurses can stay, and a small part of the house will remain private, so that we Princes can always call it home. We felt that this was a fitting way to transform Lyonscroft and make it a joyous place. Marilise's only stipulation was that it should always, always be extravagantly decorated at Christmastime, and I will make it my personal duty to see that happens. Thank you.'

There was a thunderous round of applause as Nick stepped down from the stage and came over to me, taking me in his arms. We hugged and kissed as we both wiped tears away and he pulled me onto the dancefloor as the band started playing again.

'Looks like people approve,' he said.

'Of course they do,' I replied. 'It's the best possible thing.'

I had been overcome when they had told me their idea: a way to keep the house in the family, help others and put a final end to the unhappy memories that had suffused its walls.

'And you don't mind not being lady of the manor?' he asked teasingly.

'Well, I was looking forward to having Dorothea over for tea and exchanging tips on keeping one's staff in line, but I'll survive. And I'm sure the Californian sunshine will smooth away any residual pain.'

For we had decided to go there for a while, for a change, and to see where the wind blew us next.

When the evening ended and we had waved off the last guest, Fallon and her team swung into action, restoring the house to its usual appearance with remarkable speed. As they did so, I disappeared for a while, preparing my final surprise of the evening. When Nick and I were the only people left, I took his hand.

'Come outside for a moment,' I said, and we stepped into the chilly night. I led him a few steps away from the house, then we turned to look at it. A downstairs window was illuminated, with a large sheet of paper in it, painted with a number one.

'What's that?' he said. 'It's not advent yet.'

'Should we go and see?' I asked.

We went back inside to a small study, where I had decorated the window with fairy lights and placed a box on the sill.

'Open it,' I said.

Nick removed the lid and looked inside at the little knitted booties I had placed there. A huge smile spread across his face.

'A baby?' he said, and I nodded.

Then he took me in his arms and squeezed me tightly

before kissing me with so much love and passion I thought I might faint.

'You've made me so happy,' he said. 'I never dreamt such happiness was possible.'

Kissing him back, I thought: *I never dreamt it was possible twice.*

A LETTER FROM THE AUTHOR

Dear reader,

Thank you so much for reading *Christmas with the Princes*. I hope you enjoyed Laura's journey from lonely widow to loved-up lady of the manor. If you want to join other readers in hearing all about my new releases and bonus content, you can sign up here for emails from Storm:

www.stormpublishing.co/hannah-langdon

Or for my monthly newsletter here:

www.hannahlangdon.co.uk

If you enjoyed this book and could spare a few moments to leave a review that would be hugely appreciated. Even a short review can make all the difference in encouraging a reader to discover my books for the first time. Thank you so much!

For my third book in the *Manor House Christmas* collection, deciding on a setting was easy! I just had to decide which era my house would be from this time, and thoroughly enjoyed trawling through estate agent websites for million pound plus inspiration. My heroine, Laura, was a different matter. She was in my head, demanding her story be told, but death and Christmas didn't feel like natural bedmates for a romantic novel; not only was she a widow, but she specialised in palliative care, and I also knew that wonderful Marilise would die before the end of the story. So far, so festive! But as well as trepidation, I felt a strong urge to push forward. Bereavement is part of all our lives, and Christmas can be a particularly difficult time; I wanted to honour that. Nick and his ridiculous red setter, Steve, were initially easier to tackle, but I knew he had to be worthy of Laura for better reasons than his big inheritance. I loved spending Christmas with the Princes – I hope you found them as real as I did.

Thanks again for being part of this amazing journey with me and I hope you'll stay in touch – I have so many more stories and ideas to entertain you with!

Hannah Langdon

 instagram.com/hannahlangdonwrites
 facebook.com/hannahlangdonwrites

ACKNOWLEDGEMENTS

I emerge from the initial process of writing a book having been sequestered with my characters for months. I know them, I love (or hate!) them, and I feel a certain maternal protectiveness towards each one and to their stories. To hand this newborn bundle over to other people to critique is always nerve-wracking and done with a certain reluctance, so I couldn't be more grateful to the team at Storm for their amazing handling of each book. My editor, Kathryn Taussig, has incomparable skill and tact. Her comments, suggestions and changes *always* make the book much better than it was and simultaneously give me confidence and help me improve as an author. Rose Cooper has once again created a beautiful cover that oozes with Christmas joy. I love it, thank you. And thank you to everyone at Storm who helps get the book to the finish line, including Alexandra Begley, Naomi Knox, Amanda Raybould and Catherine Lenderi.

Thank you, as always, to my mum, who champions every one of my books and encourages all her friends to read them! She also keeps an eye on early reviews for me and tells me about the nice ones, when I'm not brave enough to look myself.

John and Rose always deserve my thanks for their support and love. The world of the romantic novelist is something of a mystery to both of them, but they know how much it means to me. Special thanks to Rose for naming Nick's dog; the minute she suggested 'Steve', I knew it was perfect!

Finally, thanks go to my sister, Sarah, to whom this book is dedicated. She has supported and encouraged me right from the start, but, crucially, gives very generously of her time by reading my first drafts and offering comments and corrections. I think *I'm* thorough, but no grammatical or spelling error escapes her eagle eye, or fact goes unchecked. Thank you – I really appreciate it.